W9-BNQ-242

Some Danger Involved

A Novel

Will Thomas

A Touchstone Book
Published by Simon & Schuster
New York London Toronto Sydney

TOUCHSTONE
Rockefeller Center
1230 Avenue of the Americas
New York, NY 10020

This book is a work of fiction. Names, characters, places, and incidents either are products of the author's imagination or are used fictitiously. Any resemblance to actual events or locales or persons, living or dead, is entirely coincidental.

For information regarding special discounts for bulk purchases, please contact Simon & Schuster Special Sales:
1-800-456-6798 or business@simonandschuster.com

Designed by Melissa Isriprashad

Manufactured in the United States of America

10 9 8 7 6 5 4 3 2 1

Library of Congress Cataloging-in-Publication Data

Thomas, Will, date.
Some danger involved / Will Thomas.
p. cm.
"A Touchstone book."
1. Private investigators—England—London—Fiction.
2. Great Britain—History—Victoria, 1837–1901—Fiction.
3. London (England)—Fiction. I.Title.

PS3620.H644S66 2004
813'.6—dc22 2003071158

ISBN 0-7432-5618-2

To Julia

You are all fair, my love, and there is no spot in you.

—Song of Solomon 4:7

Some Danger Involved

Prologue

IF SOMEONE HAD TOLD ME, THOSE MANY years ago, that I would spend the bulk of my life as assistant and eventual partner to one of the most eminent detectives in London, I would have thought him a raving lunatic. It was my intention from an early age to aspire to a quiet life of letters, an Oxford donship, if possible, with the occasional slim volume privately printed every couple of years. The last thing I expected was to live with permanently barked knuckles, bruises and contusions over most of my body, and the compulsion to scan every room I entered for the exits. Life doesn't always turn out as we plan. Perhaps for some of us that is a good thing.

I find myself at a loss when trying to describe my employer, Cyrus Barker, to someone who has never met him. He is, in turns, wise and stubborn, thoughtful and oblivious, gentle and terrifyingly lethal. I have seen him agonize over the pruning of a Pen-jing tree and grapple a man to the ground, both in the same day. For all that, I can state without hesitation that he is one of the most noble men I have ever known. He is also the most exasperating fellow in the world to work for, but he is a detective, not a saint.

Barker took me in off the streets in March of 1884 in circumstances I will relate presently. He clothed me, fed me, and provided a roof over my head. More importantly, he taught me skills that were only his to teach. So, while at first I thought myself ill-used, and thoroughly unequal to the duties Barker had asked of me, eventually I found the work stimulating and rewarding, with some reservations. Actually, with several reservations, but some things cannot be helped.

I'm going to relate the first case that Barker and I worked on together, the one that changed my life completely and that began what I've come to think of as my second education, in the School of the World. It took me into the very bowels of London and introduced me to people and places I would never have met otherwise. It also very nearly killed me. If I could change any aspect of work as an enquiry agent, it would be the danger, but then, Barker warned me on that very first day, right there in the advertisement.

1

ASSISTANT to prominent enquiry agent. Typing and shorthand required. Some danger involved in performance of duties. Salary commensurate with ability. 7 Craig's Court.

SO RAN THE ADVERTISEMENT IN THE "SITUations vacant" column of *The Times* for the fourth day straight. On the first day, a Monday, I had arrived early, but not early enough. A long queue of hopeful clerks was already spilling out into Whitehall Street. So many applicants were ahead of me, and so eminently more suitable did some of them appear, that after a quarter hour's turn I abandoned my place and went in search of more realistic prospects. The Tuesday advertisement was, I assumed, mere thoroughness on the part of the employer; at a shilling a line, he could afford to advertise for two days, though the position might be filled on the first. On Wednesday, I was intrigued, but my attention was drawn to a situation in Hammersmith for which I believed I might be better suited, one that didn't offer "some danger involved in performance of duties." But when the request appeared the fourth day, I exclaimed over the newspaper in the Reading Room of the British Museum and vowed to try my luck again. Like young Arthur standing before the Sword in the Stone, I assumed I couldn't fail worse than anyone else.

I set down my pasteboard suitcase on the pavement at the end of the queue and looked at the line of applicants. They seemed identical to the gentlemen from the first day. I am sure that many of them were better qualified than I, but none was as desperate. The cheap suitcase at my feet contained all that I owned in the world, all that was left that could not be pawned. That morning, I had abandoned the garret I occupied, several days in arrears of my rent, with but threepence to my name, which I squandered on a tin cup full of chalky coffee and one of the thick slices of bread and butter they call "doorsteps," at a stall in Covent Garden. This was to be my final day of hunting for a situation. If I was not gainfully employed by seven o'clock that evening, I planned to take one last look from atop Waterloo Bridge at the premier city in Christendom, then snuff this guttering candle with a long jump into the Thames. Truth be told, I almost wished for the release, for my shattered faith still clung to the belief that I might be reunited with my wife, dead now almost a year. It was a trade I would only too gladly make.

Although I did stand in line, pushing my suitcase forward every minute or two, my hopes were not sanguine. There is a look which comes into a prospective employer's eye when he glances through your references and comes across the words "Oxford Prison." It's not a happy look, but an interesting one: first the eyes pop open with astonishment; then the brows knit together in a solid scowl; finally one brow raises sardonically, as if wondering how you have the brass to go on breathing after such a disaster. There may be further ocular calisthenics, but I was usually out the door by that time, one step ahead of the boot. At first I had agonized over these dismissals, but lately I'd just grown bored with them. One can only go through so much eye popping before it begins to pall.

There was a high brick wall beside us, and unlike the other applicants, I took the opportunity to shelter myself from the cold March wind. Somewhere on the other side, I heard a sound, the soft, rhythmic slap of rubber on brick. Someone was practicing tennis, or a child was playing ball. I thought it bitterly ironic that not five feet away someone was enjoying his life, while I was so close to forfeiting my own. I was beyond the stage of anger, however, and merely prodded my suitcase forward another few inches, with the toe of my boot. As I reached the steps of the building, I noticed a dustbin off to the side. I felt it was an omen and tossed the suitcase into it. What need had I now for a few threadbare collars and some moldy books of poetry?

Finally, I squeezed my thin frame through the door, into a kind of waiting room. Inside, the applicants were seated in a row, across from a bored-looking fellow behind a desk, his face buried in the *Police Gazette.* He took my name and asked me to be seated, as if the request were a complaint. I had never been in the offices of a "prominent enquiry agent" before, but the room looked much like several antechambers of bureaucrats and barristers that I had visited in the area, during my long search for work. When I entered I felt a tension in the room beyond the mere suspense of waiting for an interview.

"This is a rum one, no mistake," an older applicant said to me in a low voice, as soon as I sat down in a newly vacated chair.

"Rum?" I asked. "How so?"

"His nibs here announces each candidate, who goes in through that yellow door there. Then they come out madder than a wet hornet. Some come out right away, some in five minutes, some ten, but each one acts like he's been horsewhipped. This fellow must be a regular tartar. It's no wonder he can't find someone to fill the post. If you can't stomach the interview, however will you get on with the situation itself?"

It was just as my neighbor had foretold. Each applicant went through the yellow door behind the desk with the fatalism of French noblemen going to the guillotine. Some were ejected immediately, indignant at being dismissed with a cursory glance. Others returned after a few minutes, with a scowl on their faces, and after a longer wait, one fellow stormed through the office amid a volley of curses and slammed the outer door, making us all jump. When it was my neighbor's turn, he tipped me a sly wink and sauntered in. After a few minutes he returned, favored us all with a bow, placed his silk hat atop his head, and walked out with a droll smile on his face.

"Llewelyn," the bored man behind the desk announced, consulting his list. It was my turn in the lion's den. I wiped my hands on my trousers, swallowed, and walked through the door.

The chamber I entered was well furnished and dominated by a large desk and chair. Bookshelves lined most of the walls, but the heavy tomes shared the space with vases, statues, and objets d'art, most of them oriental in style. As I came in, the tall chair swiveled around to face me, and its occupant stood and pointed to a place on the Persian carpet in front of the desk. I moved to the spot and stood.

My prospective employer came from behind the desk, without bothering to offer his hand, and began to walk in a slow, clockwise circle around me, as one does when considering a horse. The light streaming in from the bow window behind me served to illuminate any patches, repairs, or weaknesses in my apparel and boots. He came about in front of me, having completed his circuit, and I was prepared for my immediate dismissal. Instead, still silent, he began a second revolution, counterclockwise this time. I had a different sensation now, as if we were two boxers in a prize ring. I would not have been surprised if he had shied a blow at my head.

"You're a black little fellow," he said at last, in a deep, raspy voice. "Welsh, I take it?"

It was true, but I took offense anyway. I am not tall (the fellow was a head taller than I), and I do have the black hair and swarthy skin of my once great race, the true Celts of Britain, but I didn't care for the way he phrased it. I could see only too easily what had put so many of my competitors in a lather. I was desperate, however, and inured to hardship, and so I merely nodded.

He held out a hand, palm upward, and I gave him my entire history laid bare in print. I waited for the eye popping. Here it goes, I thought. I shall be out in the dustbin with my suitcase in ten seconds.

"Thomas Llewelyn. Read at Magdalen College, Oxford, in Classics, and at Oxford Castle, picking oakum," the man rumbled. Or was that a chuckle?

He walked around behind the desk again and, turning his chair away from me, he sat. That was it. I was dismissed. At least his eyes hadn't popped, or perhaps they had. I couldn't see them. I gathered the papers, which he had tossed on the desk, thinking the Thames must be cold this time of year.

"Describe me, Mr. Llewelyn." This came from the depths of the chair.

"Sir?"

"I'm still speaking English, am I not? I haven't switched to Mandarin or Javanese, have I? I said, 'Describe me!' "

I marshaled my thoughts. "Yes, sir. You are about forty years of age, I believe, stand six foot two inches tall, and weigh about fifteen stone. You have a large mustache which extends down to your jawline and are wearing a pair of round, smoky spectacles with sidepieces. There is a scar dividing your right eyebrow. Your hair is black and combed to one side, the right side, I believe. Your face is pitted and seamed by what I assume was smallpox."

"Boils. Do not theorize. Continue."

"You are dressed in a dark gray morning coat, as I recall. Your trousers are striped in shades of gray, and your black pumps are highly polished. Oh, and your accent is Scottish, but it is not very thick. Lowland, perhaps."

I thought I had acquitted myself rather well, but the man turned his chair back to me without expression or remark. He reached into a desk drawer and slid a small notebook and pencil toward me.

"Take a letter, Mr. Llewelyn:

Cyrus Barker
7 Craig's Court
Whitehall, London
13 March 1884

Mr. Wilhelm Koehler
The Albany

Dear Mr. Koehler:

Have received your letter of the eleventh. My client has met with me regarding the conditions therein. I have encouraged him to publish the document in your possession, which he has reconstructed with my aid, and it shall appear in this evening's edition of the Standard. *Any further attempts at blackmail shall be similarly declined. Should you feel it necessary to meet with my client in person, please be advised that he is now accompanied by Mr. James 'Bully Boy' Briggs, and that your face would no longer be your entrée into society's drawing rooms after such an encounter.*

Your humble servant,
Cyrus Barker, etc."

Mr. Barker reached down behind the desk, and came up with a small typewriting machine in his hands, and placed it on the blotter. It was a Hammond and just new. He pulled back his large leather chair and offered me a seat in front of the machine. Typing and shorthand required, indeed.

"Paper?" I asked, as I sat down on the edge of the chair.

"First drawer left."

I put a piece of paper into the machine and began to type the letter he had dictated. I am not fast, but I am competent and careful. I made no mistakes. As I was typing his name at the bottom, Barker took an envelope from the drawer and placed it beside the machine. I pulled the freshly typed letter from the roller, returned the machine to its former place on the floor, and reached for the inkstand. He was testing my penmanship as well as getting some business done, not a bad trick with dozens of applicants. I set down the addresses in my best hand, then pulled open the middle drawer and retrieved a stamp, which, I admit it was luck, happened to be there. I licked the stamp and affixed it, then waited for my next instruction. Barker's brows disappeared in a frown beneath the disks, then he opened another drawer and removed a small sponge, which sat in a shallow dish of water there. He sealed the envelope and placed it on the right-hand corner of the desk. I noted that it was exactly half an inch from the front edge and the same distance from the side. Coupled with his scrupulously neat appearance, his fastidiousness made me think that he would make someone a most exacting employer.

Again, Barker made no comment but turned and opened a door on the opposite side of the chamber from the entrance, beckoning for me to follow. We walked down a rather featureless corridor of yellow doors until we came to the end. Barker opened the last and led me into a small, bare outdoor courtyard, surrounded by brick walls and covered in ancient paving stones. The icy March wind toyed with the dead leaves in the corners of the little square. He directed me to a bare wall, while he himself walked in the opposite direction, to where an open wicker basket stood against the brick. As I neared the wall, I recognized it as the other side of the one I had sheltered against while waiting to get in. I ducked just in time, as the first ball struck the wall an inch from my head.

He hadn't given me any instructions, but I assumed the object of Barker's little game was not to be struck by the ball. The basket was full of them, small, black spheres of hard India rubber, and I was determined not only that would I not be struck, but also that none would get by me. Barker proved himself a wicked hurler. I had been a competent goaltender on the football team in my village in Wales, and I caught or batted away every ball that came in my direction. Barker went through the entire basket. As I slapped what I assumed was the last one back at him, I saw one more missile coming my way. I was reaching for it when I realized it was not a ball at all. By the telltale glint of silver, it was a knife heading straight for my breast. I barely dodged out of the way as it flew past and struck the wall with a loud smack. It, too, was made of India rubber, cunningly painted.

We stood and looked at each other. I was breathing heavily, creating clouds of vapor in the cold spring air. Barker did not appear to be taxed in any way by his exertions and stood immobile, contemplating me. For a moment, I thought of repeating the words of the angry applicant who had slammed the door, with a few choice ones of my own thrown in. I mastered myself, however, and said, "I presume you shall inform me when the situation is filled. Good morning, sir." Then, with as much dignity as my five-foot-four-inch frame could muster, I bowed and marched from the courtyard.

I stalked through the empty corridor, past the blind doors, through Barker's chambers, and into the waiting room. All the applicants stared at me apprehensively. I opened the outer door and was considering a hearty slam that would rattle the door frame, when I heard a voice over my shoulder. Barker's voice.

"The situation is filled. You gentlemen may go. Jenkins, mind the office until I return." With a nudge in the small of my back, he pushed me forward, out onto the step.

"You look like you could do with some lunch," he said, conversationally.

"I have the position?" I asked, astounded.

"Never any doubt." He leaned out over the balustrade and retrieved my case from the dustbin. "Don't forget your belongings. Come, we'll take a hansom cab."

2

WE DID INDEED TAKE A HANSOM CAB. IT was my first. It was awkward climbing the small steps and twisting around the leather doors, into the seats. It was even more so sharing such intimate quarters with a perfect stranger. Barker sat just inches away, facing forward, and did not speak once during the entire journey. He might have been a wax figure from Madame Tussaud's for all his animation. We crossed Waterloo Bridge and rode for miles. Stamford Street was followed by Southwark; Saint Thomas turned into Druid Street. There were dozens of public houses and restaurants along the way, but we passed them all. Tower Bridge took us back across the Thames again, and then we were in the East End. The cab glided through a maze of shabby streets until I became hopelessly lost. Were we in Whitechapel? Stepney? Bethnal Green? Finally, the cab turned toward an alleyway so narrow that the horse shied, and the cab would have scraped axles on both sides. It was a villainous alley, with ancient stone arches overhead and litter at our feet, but Barker alighted and headed down it, as if it were his home. Perhaps it was. Maybe all his money went into the upkeep of his office, and he lived in some hovel alongside the sailors and asiatics of Limehouse. Barker came to an unmarked, peeling door at the end and opened it, ushering me in with the nod of his head.

It was black as pitch inside. I heard metallic scraping in the darkness, then a match sputtered into life. My new employer lit a naphtha lamp and held it high. We stood in a confined space, with concrete walls on both sides. Barker pointed down a flight of long steps into Stygian blackness. He was playing Virgil to my Dante. *Abandon hope, all ye who enter here.* Very well, I motioned, lead on.

I followed him down the dark stone steps, our footfalls echoing and multiplying until the sound filled my ears. There was a pressure in my ears as well, and I reasoned that we might be under the Thames. After a couple of dozen steps we found ourselves in a long stone corridor, just barely wide enough for two men to walk abreast. Twenty-five or thirty paces later we reached another staircase and began to ascend, not soon enough for me. The light winked out, there was a scraping of the lamp on concrete, and a door opened before my eyes.

We entered a long, low-ceilinged room full of people eating and talking. The room was dark and smoky, and full of a strange aroma. My stomach recognized food when it was close; it constricted to the size of a cricket ball. I won't go into how little I had eaten over the past few weeks, or what I had lived upon, except to say that I was now in no way particular. Whatever they were serving, I would gladly eat.

A shadowy figure shuffled forward and led us to a table, lit by a flickering penny candle. I squinted and tried to see my neighbors, then wished I hadn't. The first had a bristling beard and a disreputable hat on his head. The second looked like he'd arrived straight from the steppes of Mongolia, and the third was a stage version of an anarchist from a Russian play. I glanced at my employer. With the scar on his brow and his fierce mustache, he seemed as sinister as his fellows.

"What are we—" I began, but Barker raised a hand. A man

stepped into the nimbus of light cast by our candle and looked intently at us. He was Chinese, but far from the normal everyday Chinaman one sees in the area. He was shaved bald on top, had a long rope of hair in a plait hanging down his chest, and his earlobes were an insignificant distance from his shoulders thanks to the heavy steel rings in them. He wore a splattered apron over an undershirt and trousers, and rope soled shoes. His arms were a riot of tattoos, and his stomach preceded him to the table. He reminded me of statues of Buddha I had seen in photographs or stereopticons, save that he wasn't jolly or serene. This was a Buddha that would as soon have your liver out as look at you.

The man spoke to us in Chinese, and you can imagine my surprise when Barker replied in kind. My new employer rattled off Mandarin as if it were his native tongue. The Chinaman nodded once and left.

"That was Ho, the owner," Barker said. "I ordered for both of us, presuming you've never been in an Asian restaurant before. Don't overeat; in your condition it will only make you ill. Understand also that one of the terms of your employment is that you do not gain back your former weight. I want you thin as a lath and wiry as a terrier. It is your best chance of survival."

My stomach was trying to tie itself into knots by now. The pain was so intense I could barely sit in the chair. In a few moments, an Asian waiter appeared and slapped down two bowls of a colorless broth, with all the grace of a Spitalfields barmaid. I waited for a spoon, but none was forthcoming. Barker raised the porcelain bowl to his mouth and strained the soup through his big mustache. I hazarded a sip. It was not bad, not bad at all, really. There were spices and vegetables and some sort of noodles at the bottom. Definitely edible, even without a spoon.

The bowl was whisked away, and a plate of small sweetbreads put in its place. Barker reached forward and speared a piece between two thin sticks of wood. Chopsticks. I'd seen them before in pictures of China.

"So, how do you use these things?" I asked. Barker showed me. It takes some knack. No one exactly stood and applauded my performance, but I managed to get a few pieces of fried pork in my mouth before the plate disappeared and the next arrived. It was a good thing, too, for I was just about to set my chopsticks down on my plate.

"By the heavens, man!" Barker cried, making me jump. "Never set your chopsticks across your plate like that. It announces that you are finished with your meal. We'd have had to pack up and leave before the main course. It is a definite insult to the cook, and believe me, it is not wise to insult Mr. Ho."

"Yes, sir!"

The main course proved to be steamed duck in a white wine sauce. If the soup was subtle and the sweetbreads delicious, the duck cemented my opinion that the Chinaman was a genius in the kitchen.

Barker hoisted a watch at the end of a long chain from the well that was his pocket and consulted it. His hand went down, decisively, and placed his chopsticks across a corner of his plate. Then he removed a sealskin pouch from his coat pocket. I watched him with some interest. At this point, there was nothing I could discount that he would do. If he suddenly pulled a wavy sword from under the table, lit it afire from the penny candle, and swallowed it down to the hilt, I would probably just nod my head and say, "That Barker, anything to put you off guard." As it was, he reached into the pouch and pulled out a pipe, one of those white meerschaums, with a stem made of amber. It was carved in his own image, from the bowler hat to the spectacles and mustache, and still further to an effigy of the pipe itself, stuck in the little pugnacious jaw. The white mineral had taken on a rich ivory hue from much smoking, and with loving care, Barker charged it with tobacco from the pouch, tamped it down with a meaty thumb, then topped it off with a few more strands before striking a vesta on the rough table in front of us. He ran the flame in circles around the inside of the bowl and blew out the match, before tucking the stem of the pipe between his strong, square teeth.

"This place is unique," he stated. "Ho does not advertise, but the place is always full. There are unspoken rules here. Don't ask what is in the food, and don't repeat what you hear within these walls. This is neutral ground. An Irish Fenian may plan to assassinate a member of the House of Lords tomorrow, but today, they are seated at the same table here, enjoying a meal. Isn't there a child's game that has a safe spot where no one may be tagged or captured? That is Ho's."

"Remarkable. And the only way in is through that passage?"

"Yes. I don't know what its original purpose was. Smuggling, perhaps, or a Catholic bolt hole during the reign of Henry the Eighth."

Barker puffed for a moment, silently, then heaved a sigh of contentment. We, most of us, have these safe places in our lives, where we can go and eat food that is meant not to impress but merely to satisfy. Seeing my employer contentedly leaning back in his chair, with a pipe going and his boot against the base of the table, showed me beyond any word that this was such a place to him.

"The interviewing of candidates for assistant has taken more time than I had hoped," he said eventually. "I have an investigation or two that had to be set aside during the hiring process. I must now make up for lost time. I shall not return to my home until late. Here," he said, retrieving a folded sheet of paper from his pocket, "is a list of places for you to visit this afternoon. Now, listen carefully. You must follow the same procedure in each case. Locate each building, circle it, and enter through the back entrance, if there is one. Once inside, ask to speak to the manager. Tell them Barker sent you. Then, do as they ask. Is that clear?"

"Yes, sir," I responded. "Barker sent me."

"Do you have any questions?"

"Only about a thousand, sir."

"Wonderful," he said, giving a wintry smile. "It will give us something to discuss over breakfast. Now we have work to do. I've given Ho instructions to let you eat but to toss you into the river if you're still here in ten minutes." He stood up to leave. "Ah, I almost forgot. There is a stack of books on the desk by your bed—"

"My bed, sir?"

"Yes. Didn't I make myself plain? Lodgings and meals are included in the terms of employment. I cannot have my assistant sleeping in doorways or park commons. It is not a sound advertisement for my agency. Now the books; begin studying them tonight. We'll discuss them in the morning. I'm off, then." And he was.

I sat there for a moment or two, trying to gather it all in. Was this all legitimate, or was Barker some sort of eccentric? Was he really a "prominent enquiry agent," or was this a hoax, and if so, to what end? I couldn't even credit that the room I was seated in could exist in the middle of London. In Shanghai, perhaps, or in a penny thriller, but not in good old, matronly London. Here I sat, eating God only knows what, in the employ of a complete cipher, who spoke Chinese and whose every statement seemed to spring from a disturbed mind. Perhaps, I considered, I should bolt. After all, with a full belly, I had now come out ahead. It was possible I could still find normal employment. And yet . . .

A roof over my head, three meals a day, a position with a regular salary: these were not things to throw over lightly.

Who knew, perhaps this was routine for an enquiry agent's assistant on his first day. I could always resign later, if the work didn't suit me. I should stick it out and give the fellow a chance.

The burly Chinaman suddenly appeared at my elbow. His mood had not improved since we arrived. He was sharpening a wicked-looking cleaver against a whetstone in his hand.

"You go now."

I retreated down the long tunnel, the naphtha lamp throwing weird shadows on the walls. When I was mid-distance between the two staircases, I stopped and listened. As I suspected, I heard the water coursing above the smooth ceiling overhead. I was under the Thames. I'd heard rumors that there were all sorts of tunnels, passageways, abandoned underground lines and caverns under the old town, but this was the first time I had ever been inside one.

For the second time that day I came out of a dim passageway into bright light. As I extinguished the lamp, it occurred to me that Barker had not advanced me the money for a hansom cab, and that obviously I couldn't pay for the fare myself. How was I to fulfill the instructions he had given me? This was not a propitious start.

As I came out of the alleyway, still reflecting on what to do, a cab appeared almost out of nowhere and clattered to a stop in front of me. I raised a hand to shield my eyes from the sun overhead.

"I'm sorry, I have no money to pay you!" I called, over the jingling of the harness and the nickering of the horse.

"Perhaps not," the cabman answered back, "but I bet you know some magic words that'll make this magic carpet fly."

"Barker sent me?"

"A regular Ali Baba, you are," the man observed, motioning for me to get in. I'd barely found my seat before we were off like a shot.

The trap over my head opened up and I got a view of a square face with a long red beard shining in the sun. The man's arm was thrust through.

"List!" he demanded, and I handed it up to him. He grasped my outstretched hand and gave it a brisk shake before letting go. "Racket's the name. John Racket. Or it'll do for one. This here's Juno, best cab horse in Whitechapel."

"Thomas Llewelyn," I called over my head.

"Thought I smelt coal!"

"Are you Barker's personal cabman?" I asked.

"Don't I wish! No, us dogs go for whatever scraps old 'Push-Comes-To-Shove' throws our way. Best tipper in London, he is."

The first address was in Holborn on a street which had reached its heyday during the Prince Regent's reign and had been declining ever since. Racket stopped the cab a half block away from the address, and I sauntered by casually. It was a tailor's shop: K and R Krause, Fine Gentlemen's Apparel and Alterations. Of course, I needed a new suit if I was to be Barker's assistant. It seemed silly to play the spy in front of a simple tailor shop, but I obeyed orders and passed down an alleyway, then backtracked in the next street. I judged the approximate door which might belong to the back of the shop and opened it. An elderly man looked up from his cutting table, then nodded when I gave him the words. In a few moments, he had measured me thoroughly and seen me out the door again. I had no idea what sort of clothing I had been measured for and only hoped that the establishment had standing instructions from my employer. I climbed into the cab and was borne away again.

The next few stops began to fall into a predictable pattern. First there was a cobbler, who mourned the state of my old shoes and measured my feet, but did not discuss cut or color. Next was a barber, who cut my hair without asking how I wanted it. A haberdasher provided me with a black bowler hat, and I was measured for new collars at a shop in Saville Row.

I was reduced to running errands after that. First there was a tobacconist in Oxford Street who gave me a pound of Barker's tobacco, which they blended for him specially on the premises, then I picked up a caddy of tea at an import firm in Mincing Lane, the City. According to the proprietor, a talkative Greek fellow, Cyrus Barker was a regular customer, with a strong addiction to what he called 'green gunpowder tea.' The leaves, he informed me, were not minced, but rolled into tiny pellets.

At last I reached the final place on the list, Barker's private residence. By now it was near six and growing dark, and I was exhausted. The house was on a quiet street in Newington. From what I could see in the gathering gloom, it was a three-story brick house from Regency times that looked well tended but not ostentatious. Mr. Racket, showing some familiarity with the premises, drove me around to the back and set me down in an alleyway by a round wooden gate. Tapping his tall hat with his whip, he rattled off into the night. With Barker's parcels in hand, I lifted the latch of the gate and stepped into a garden.

It was a beautiful garden even in March, an oasis in the middle of the city. A small stream bisected the courtyard, perhaps pumped from some hidden spring by a miniature windmill that turned in the breeze. Like Barker's office, the garden showed an oriental influence, with a little jewel of a bridge, and moss covered boulders, like islands, in a sea of white pebbles. The garden was awash in plants of all sorts, some budding, some still dormant, but very satisfying in arrangement as a whole. There was an anonymous outbuilding or two, and as I followed the meandering path of stepping stones, I came across what looked like an herb garden or kitchen garden by the house. I was glancing at a dark clump of brush near the end of the path, when the bush suddenly surged forward and, before I could move, attached itself to my ankle. I felt teeth break the skin, and yelled out in pain and surprise. The back door of the house opened directly in front of me, flooding the garden with light, and before I could say anything, a man stepped forward, raised a sawed-down shotgun, and set both barrels on the bridge of my nose, like a pair of spectacles. Needless to say, the peace and tranquility that had begun to set in as I wandered through the garden was doused, as if with a bucket of cold water. What also deserted me was my employer's name. Right out of my head, when I needed it most.

3

IT IS DIFFICULT TO CONCENTRATE WHILE staring down the barrel of a shotgun, and even more so when an unknown creature is shredding your trousers at the ankle. If only I could remember those three little words. The more I grasped for them mentally, the farther away they receded. The man in front of me was growing more stern with each passing moment, and the animal more manic. Just then the creature broke off his assault and began to bark at me furiously. Barker! That's it!

"Barker sent me!" I squeaked, hoping the charm would work one last time. It did. The man put down the gun and motioned me in, as if this happened daily.

"Ah, Assistant. Why didn't you speak up? Come in. Harm, let the man be."

The creature stepped back and peered up at me. It was a dog, a very small dog, with the fiercest and most grotesque features I had ever seen, a creature out of an oriental nightmare. Its fur was coal black and its face looked as if it had been smashed in with a shovel. It had a mouth full of assorted cutlery and protruding eyes in danger of falling out at any moment. The little thing suddenly began emitting the most unearthly screeches, incredible sounds for so small an animal. I jumped, which angered it, and the thing froze onto my other ankle. The man turned and snatched the dog from my pant leg and lifted it so that it hung suspended by its collar, wheezing for breath, with its tongue lolling out and its eyes rolling in their sockets.

"I said, let him be, Harm," the man warned, and tossed the creature into the outer darkness before closing the door. I heard the little fellow yapping and scratching at the door in a moment, so I assumed that he was all right.

"The dog suffers from too much dignity. It's necessary to bring him down a peg or two from time to time. Now let me get a look at you."

The two of us regarded each other for a moment. I'm afraid I came out the lesser of the two specimens by a good margin. The man before me was perhaps the handsomest man I had ever seen. He was Michelangelo's David in a Saville Row suit. The only thing out of place was a small cap at the back of his curling black hair. With a start, I realized that the fellow was a Jew.

"I don't know how he picks you fellows," he said, shaking his head. "I'll give you the benefit of the doubt for now. I'm Jacob Maccabee. Everyone calls me Mac."

"Thomas Llewelyn."

"Set the parcels down on that table there. I'll show you to your room," he said, leading me up some stairs. The stairwell was carpeted and the hallways varnished to a high gloss. Everything was understated but of good quality, and in excellent repair.

"Have you dined yet?" he asked. "No, of course you haven't. I'll see about getting you something to eat from the larder. This is your room."

He opened a door into a comfortable, though spartanly furnished chamber. The walls were plaster, there was a marble grate, and the floor was as polished as the hallway. There was a heavy wooden bed, black with age, and an equally ancient wardrobe in a corner. The only other furniture was a desk and chair, the former having seen much use, with ink spots, bottle rings, and scars from a century or more of masculine hands. If there was a word I could use to describe the room, it would be "companionable."

While the young Jewish man went downstairs to get my dinner, I sat on the edge of the bed and felt rather dull. A lot had happened to me since the morning. The events of the day had fair worn me out.

The door opened soundlessly and Mr. Maccabee entered with a tray. It contained a meat pie, bread and cheese, a dish of olives, and a glass of red wine. I thanked him profusely. It thawed his chilly manner a little.

"What is your position here, Mr. Maccabee?"

"Mac, please, sir. That's a difficult question. It changes from day to day. Factotum, butler, bodyguard, housekeeper, valet. Take your pick. At present, I'm also secretary, accountant, and messenger, but those are your duties. Did the Guv'nor give any indication of when he might return?"

"Mr. Barker? He said he'd been neglecting some cases while filling my post and would speak to me at breakfast."

"That sounds like the Guv. I believe there's a spare nightshirt in the wardrobe, and some other clothing that might fit you. How are your ankles? I make an excellent liniment."

"No, thank you. I'm fine."

"I'll bid you good evening, then, sir."

I like to read with my meals when I am alone, and I recalled Barker's order to study the books in my room. I picked them off the desk and read the spines. The first was called *Methods of Observation and Ratiocination,* followed by *Implied Logic in Everyday Life, Understanding the Asiatic Mind,* and *Folk Tales of Old Edo.* It was an instructional cramming course. I settled on the Japanese tales, which seemed the least dry reading of the lot, and perused them while eating my meal at the desk. A Welshman is always glad to add to his private store of tales.

Having finished my meal, I crossed to the bed, wincing at the pain in my ankles. At that point I noticed that the window near the bed was ajar an inch or two, and since there was no fire in the grate, I got up to shut it. It was bolted open, another of my employer's eccentricities. I changed into the nightshirt and read in bed for an hour or two, until the events of the day overtook me, and my lids grew heavy. I closed the book and turned down the gas jet over my bed. The night before I had shared a garret with five other unfortunates, waiting for them all to settle down before I packed my bag and stole out. Now I had a room all to myself, with a comfortable bed and a butler bringing me meals on a tray. A man's life can change completely in one day.

In the middle of the night I was awakened by something binding my lower limbs, and there was a strange sound in the room. I sat up and looked about, attempting to straighten my bedclothes. Something was there by my feet. It was my assailant of the previous evening, Harm. He'd stolen into my bedroom and curled up at the foot of the bed. The sound, I realized, was his snoring. I shrugged philosophically. I supposed if I had a nose so mashed against my face that my eyes protruded, I'd snore as well. I pulled the covers higher, the black bundle of fur coming with them, and went back to sleep.

I woke up stiff and sore the next morning, with the beginnings of a cold. I cursed the open window and reflected on the irony that I had escaped a frigid garret room only to catch my death because of an employer's whim. The sun was up, but low in the sky. I judged it to be about eight o'clock.

Somehow, through all the bustle of the first day, my battered old pasteboard suitcase had found its way to my room. I shaved and combed my hair with the aid of a pitcher and bowl on the nightstand. The suit I picked out of the wardrobe wasn't an exact fit, but it was better than my own. I made my bed, wondering what had happened to my predecessor that he didn't need his entire wardrobe anymore, and straightened the room before going out into the hall. I hesitated, not certain what to do next.

"Llewelyn? That you, lad?" Barker's voice came from overhead. He must have ears like a cat.

"Aye, sir!"

"Come up here, then. There's a good fellow."

I climbed a narrow and steep staircase to the upper story. The entire top floor was one single long room going up to the roof peak, with a pair of gables on each side. The walls were a deep cardinal red. The room was dominated by a large canopied bed at the far end, with heavy curtains of the style made popular at the turn of the last century. Low bookshelves lined the walls, and every foot of the slanting wall space was hung with weapons: swords, scimitars, blowguns, harquebuses, spears. It was a fantastic collection, if a bit bloodthirsty.

A blaze was burning in the attic grate, and two chairs were set before it. Cyrus Barker was in one of the chairs. Though he wore a dressing gown of gray silk, his wing-tipped collar was crisp and his tie securely knotted and pinned. With one hand he was scratching Harm behind the ears, and in the other, he held a dainty cup and saucer containing a pallid liquid which could only be green tea. Of course, he wore those strange spectacles. I wondered if he slept in them.

"Have you settled in?"

"Yes, sir," I responded. "But, about that window . . ."

"A house rule you must humor, I'm afraid. Most of the deaths in this country are due to shutting up the patient in a room full of his own noxious fumes and microbes. Fresh air was meant to flow freely about our bodies at night. To shut oneself up in overheated rooms stultifies the brain and lowers one's natural ability to fight infection. I never catch cold, Mr. Llewelyn."

"I believe I've caught one."

"Your body is not accustomed to fresh south London air. Give it time. Soon you'll be as a steam boiler glowing red in the chilly night. Now come, have some of this delicious tea."

I watched my employer's large hands pour tea from a tiny pot into a cup and saucer. We were grown men playing "tea party." The tea was passable, I suppose. I wondered what he'd say if he knew there was a coffee drinker under his roof.

"How were your errands? Did you find everything?"

"Fine, yes, sir. No problems at all."

"And did you study the books I placed on your table?"

"I spent the evening reading the Japanese tales. Fascinating they were, too."

"Excellent," he pronounced, standing and exchanging his dressing gown for a frock coat. "I'm going to the office. I want you to spend the day studying the rest of the books. We'll discuss them thoroughly after dinner." He tucked the dog under his arm like a book and preceded me down the staircase.

My day was spent in hard study. It reminded me of my time at university. Mac brought me several cups of green tea, no doubt at the insistence of my employer. I thought there was a sardonic gleam in the young butler's eye. Lunch proved to be a rather tasteless stew and a hard roll. Later, dinner was even worse, a Scottish feast of mutton, mashed turnips, and potatoes. Not that I was grumbling, but I would have preferred a plate of jellied eel over this lot. Barker didn't seem to notice. It was my own fault for hiring myself out to a Scotsman.

My employer called me up to his eyrie after supper. He was standing in one of the gables, looking out over his garden.

"Fog's coming up," he noted. "Are you prepared for our little chat?"

"I am, sir."

Oral examinations were the dread of most students during my university days. One needed to be thoroughly grounded in the subject and able to think on one's feet. Luckily for me, Barker questioned in a straightforward and logical way. I found myself answering almost conversationally. He expounded after some of my answers, and it was evident that he was well informed on all of the subjects in the books. Far from the torture I expected, I found I was almost enjoying myself. The gentleman in his own home was far removed from the tyrant in his chambers at 7 Craig's Court.

"That's enough, then," he said, finally. "You've proven to me that you now have a rudimentary grounding in the subjects I desired."

"May I ask a question?" I hazarded. "I understand the need for logic and ratiocination, but why all the oriental studies?"

"The Foreign Office considers me an authority on the subject and frequently calls me in for casework and interpreting. I'm something of an orientalist, though my knowledge was acquired firsthand, rather than out of books."

"Firsthand, sir? You've lived in the East, then?"

"I was raised there. Foochow, Shanghai, Canton, Kyoto, Manila. All over, really. That's enough now, lad. Get some rest. Be ready for your first day tomorrow."

I wanted to question him further, but I had been dismissed.

The next thing I knew, Barker was bellowing my name. It was not an ideal way to start one's first day of employment.

"Sir!" I answered, sitting up in bed.

"It is time you were about, lad. It's nearly seven." The voice was over my head, vibrating down from his garret.

Mac had failed to wake me. "Where is Mr. Maccabee?"

"It is the Shabbat," he answered. "Mac's day off."

I rubbed a hand over my face vigorously, then just to show it who was in charge, I climbed out of bed and threw some cold water on it. I put on one of my predecessor's suits and prepared myself for my first day at work. I wanted to make a good impression.

Barker was all hustle and bustle as he came down the stairs, dressed in a spotless double-breasted black morning coat. He inspected my suit critically, then led me out to the curb. Raising his stick, he brought the first cab to our feet.

Barker's residence was just off the circle known as Elephant and Castle. The street was named for the well-known public house, which, if you believe the guidebooks, was corrupted from *L'enfant de Castille,* after a Spanish noble's child that stayed in London some time in the city's obscure past. If one were to look at a map of London, one would note that the E and C is a kind of hub around which lie the spokes of major thoroughfares, leading to all the famous bridges of the city: Lambeth, Westminster, Waterloo, Blackfriars, Southwark, London, and the Tower. All of them could be reached from Barker's residence in a matter of minutes. It was this fortunate placement, I think, that made Barker choose a home on the unfashionable Lambeth side of London.

It was Waterloo we were crossing this time, before turning south. I was to work in Whitehall, one of the most famous streets in the world. Rattling down Whitehall Street in the hansom, I could look directly ahead and see the Parliament clock tower containing the bell called Big Ben. Over my shoulder were Trafalgar Square and Nelson's Column, and down the street was the prime minister's residence, and the Home and Foreign Offices. Everywhere you turned there was a monument, a statue, a famous landmark.

Craig's Court is a quiet little cul-de-sac backing up against Great Scotland Yard and the police headquarters that have appropriated the name. Despite its abbreviated length, Craig's Court has a reputation, for it is where most of the enquiry agents in town keep their offices.

Inside the agency, the antechamber, the scene of such trepidation two days ago, now seemed dull and vacant. The clerk was still there, buried behind another *Police Gazette.* Barker continued on, but I stopped to introduce myself.

" 'Lo. You're the new assistant. Welsh fella."

"Yes, Llewelyn."

Jenkins didn't improve on second glance. He was in his early thirties, sprawled in his chair as loose-limbed as a marionette, and was so nearsighted he almost used his chin for a paperweight while copying down my name.

"You just had to have a long name," he complained. "Last one was named Quong. Nice and short."

"What happened to him?" I asked. Jenkins raised a hand and formed his fingers into a gun. He brought his index finger to a spot between his eyes and squeezed the trigger. My predecessor was dead. That was what I had been afraid of.

"Here," he said, pulling himself up, as if an inspiration had hit him. "Jones is a Welsh name, init? That's not long."

"Are you proposing I change my name to Jones so you'll have less work to do?"

He shrugged his bony shoulders. "Just a thought. Have you got a cigarette?"

"I fear not."

"I need a cigarette. Tell Mr. B. I shall return directly."

He left. It was a wonder Barker got any work done, taking on charity cases like us. I went into the inner chambers.

If I was fearful of being shot at on that first day, I needn't have worried. I spent part of the morning taking shorthand notes for my employer and the rest typing them up. Aside from the odd hint of blackmail or other crimes in the letters he dictated, I might just as well have been working in a bank or a government office. The only excitement of the morning was trying to make sense of Barker's notes. His personal handwriting was almost indecipherable.

There is no need to wonder what time it is in Craig's Court when Big Ben peals noon. We had a ploughman's lunch at a pub around the corner, called the Rising Sun. I've never been able to abide pickled onions, but Barker polished off a plateful with his lunch, washing them down with abstemious sips of his stout. I ate fresh bread and cheese and drank a half-pint of bitters, all of which was excellent.

"What shall be our itinerary for the rest of the day, sir?" I asked. I hoped I had the rest of Saturday free, but with Barker as an employer, it was not good to presume.

"I'm going out of town this afternoon. You may have the rest of the day off. It is a beautiful day, and I suggest you don't waste it. Why not walk home, and get to know the area better?"

"Certainly, sir. I will."

"I'm off, then. Tell Mac I shall be late again." And he was gone. He moved fast for a big man.

So that was that. An invigorating walk across half of London. Of course, it began pouring rain halfway across Waterloo. I had no umbrella, having pawned it months before, but I did have a stout bowler and heavy woolen Ulster coat that had once belonged to my *late* predecessor. It had no bullet holes, I noticed. I pulled up the collar and tugged down my hat and settled into a regular, plodding pace. Being poor and Welsh, I'd learned to walk in hilly country. These flat streets were nothing to me. I walked steadily down Waterloo Road, watching the rain cascade in a stream from the brim of my hat. I passed commercial and residential districts, by small parks and churches. It was not the worst way to spend a Saturday afternoon. London is a beautiful city, and never more so than when it rains. The streets gleam, the buildings all take on a dappled color, and the lights from butcher shops, tobacconists, and tea shops cast a cozy shade of ochre upon the pavement.

Mac regarded me severely as I sloshed into the back passage, and Harm was displeased that I was dripping on the linoleum. He nipped at my heels (the dog, that is, not Mac, though he looked like he might have considered it), but it was a halfhearted and perfunctory attempt. Mac finally spoke.

"Out for a walk, I see."

"Very observant. You should be a detective," I replied. "Mr. Barker thought I should get to know the area better."

"I don't believe he meant that you should swim the Thames," he said acidly. "Give me your wet things. I've laid a fire. Actually, your timing is perfect. Your wardrobe has just arrived from Krause Brothers, and I believe your new boots are here as well."

"Excuse me. Did you say 'wardrobe'?"

The next morning, the rain had stopped, but a fog had rolled in thick and heavy. Luckily, it was a white fog and showed every intention of dissipating by noon, rather than the yellow kind, the London "particular," full of coal smoke and the effluvium of every factory in the old town. That kind can float about the area for days, choking out the lives of the aged and consumptive.

I didn't let the weather bother me, however, for I had a new wardrobe. Not one, but half a dozen suits in various cuts and fabric, and all tailored to fit like a kid glove. Needless to say, I spent the night alternating between trying on the various articles and thanking my employer for his generosity. It was more and better clothing than I had ever had in my entire life. Gruffly, Barker muttered something about not wanting the agency to look less than professional, but I believe he was pleased. At least I passed muster.

So that morning, I was fully dressed and beginning a new stack of books that had suddenly appeared on my desk overnight, when the Guv appeared at my door.

"I see you're already into the new books. Good work, lad."

He came in and wandered about, doing those things one does when one is uncomfortable, such as inspecting the wardrobe for dust or distress, and whistling quietly off-key.

"Is there something you wish, sir?" I asked.

"Well, here's the thing. I am in the habit of attending the Metropolitan Tabernacle, Charles Haddon Spurgeon's church, which is right across the street. I was wondering whether you might like to join me."

I closed my book. "Certainly, I'll go."

He smiled. That is to say, his black mustache changed shape, like a bow whose string had been relaxed.

"Thank you," he said formally. "We leave within the quarter hour."

The church was, indeed, almost across the street. I had noted it in my walk, but it hadn't registered in my mind that it was a church. To my Methodist eyes, the building more closely resembled a bank or museum.

Inside, the building was immense, seating thousands and including a gallery. The latter had a long, gleaming brass rail encircling the room, and in one corner, it bulged out into a small balcony, not unlike a stage. As the first hymn began, I learned something else about my employer. His singing is no better than his penmanship.

The famous preacher got up to speak. I was impressed by his passion and energy. Spurgeon almost bounded about the stage. He lifted us to the very gates of Heaven, then swooped down and dragged us along the coals of Hell until our coattails were singed and brimstone was in our nostrils.

Coming out of the tabernacle and down the steps, I had to admit I'd had a good time. I'd even felt spiritually uplifted. Now, like most of the attendees, I was looking forward to a nice Sunday supper, a little reading, and perhaps a Sabbath nap. Alas, such was not to be.

A four-wheeler stood at our door across the street. In front of it a figure waited impatiently for us to arrive. It was a tall, thin man in a long coat and wide-brimmed hat. His face was pale and hawkish and he had a long black beard. From his temples hung the long side curls of the traditional Jew. I felt a sudden sense of foreboding.

Barker walked up to him, and they murmured for a moment in what I suppose was Yiddish. The Guv read over a note the man handed him.

"I fear we shall miss lunch," he told me after a moment. We climbed into the vehicle and were off.

4

I'VE ALWAYS BEEN INTERESTED IN ARCHItecture and the way that buildings resemble their function. Churches point toward Heaven, banks reflect prosperity, and constabularies give us a sense of security. Even gin palaces attempt to show the supposed gaiety and good times to be had inside their doors. But what of morgues? You will never find a plainer building. They are boxes of bricks tucked away out of sight, discreet and anonymous. They are warehouses for bodies, communal coffins. Most are a single long hall, with rooms on both sides, an entrance at one end, and an attempt at a portico at the other, but which more closely resembles a goods dockyard. And why not? It is usually in the morgue that, officially, a person ceases to be a person and becomes merely a piece of property.

There was a guard at the front entrance with a logbook he required everyone to sign. I thought it was absurd, so much security around dead bodies, but then I remembered the old tales of resurrectionists, of Burke and Hare, and wondered if medical students were still desperate for cadavers. Had Barker not chosen me, for whatever reason, I might have been pulled from the river nearby like some unfortunate from *Our Mutual*

Friend and lying here even now, awaiting some fledgling surgeon's scalpel.

There were pallid-looking men in shirtsleeves and gutta-percha aprons moving from room to room, stains on the floor, and the reek of decay, carbolic, and formaldehyde. I didn't want to be here. This was a part of the work I hadn't considered. I wanted to go back to my little room, my bed, my books, but I couldn't. Barker was depending on me, and I needed to prove myself.

As we walked down the hall, a man came out of the far room and began putting on his gloves. He was tall and thin, and his hair was carefully brushed to cover a balding patch. What he lacked on top, he made up for below. His gingery side-whiskers hung thick and heavy and ran into his mustache, giving him the look of an amiable walrus. Ignoring the sepulchral hush, Barker bawled out the name "Terry!" and the man turned our way.

"Hello, Cyrus. Come for the Jew? Never seen anything like it in all my days. They say you see everything in police work, but this takes it. It's a sick world, no mistake. How's business?"

"Fine, thank you. Busy as ever. This is my new assistant, Thomas Llewelyn. Thomas, this is Inspector Terence Poole of the Criminal Investigation Department. Is the evidence still here?"

"We'll be taking it back to 'A' Division soon, but I think you've got time for a quick gander."

"Do you have a name yet?" my employer asked.

"Yes. Louis Pokrzywa, a Polish Jew. That's P-O-K-R-Z-Y-W-A, but they pronounce it *Po-SHEE-va*. Leave it to the Eastern Europeans to come up with a name like that."

"Who identified the body?"

"A member of the Board of Deputies, Rabbi Mocatta. The deceased had no relations in this country, though he'd been here for several years. A teacher at the Jews' Free School by day and a rabbinical scholar in the evenings. A very earnest young man, according to the rabbi."

"Will there be a postmortem?"

"That's the question the Jews and the coroner are trying to decide. The rabbi wants him in the ground tomorrow, but Vandeleur wants to open him up today. Nearly had us a fistfight in here a while ago."

"May we view the body?"

"Help yourself. He's in there. I'll get P. C. Morrow to bring you the board and rope after he's had his cuppa. He caught a bad case of rubber legs a few minutes ago."

Barker walked into the room the inspector had just quitted, and I joined him. Inside were several long tables containing still forms under sheets. In the middle of the room, and connected with one wall, was a larger, stationary table with troughs along all sides for the draining of bodily fluids. The atmosphere in here was more pungent. Large carboys of chemicals were set in two corners to fight the powerful stench of decay.

There was a body on the large table, its sheet rumpled from recent examinations. Without preamble, Barker seized the sheet and pulled it back. The corpse was that of a man a few years older than myself. His skin was ashen, almost grayish, and I noticed there were several bruises about his face and chest, which showed that he had suffered some ill-usage before his death. The skin around both eyes was dark and swollen, and his nose looked broken. Death appeared to be due to a nasty cut in the left side, just under the breastbone. In life, the poor fellow had worn his hair a little long for British custom, and though he sported a beard and mustache, if he had the traditional curls of Jewish tradition, they were tucked behind his ears. He reminded me of someone, but I couldn't remember who just then.

Barker didn't touch the body, but instead ran the tip of his walking stick under the shoulder and arm, then raised the wrist with it. The arm was stiff, and I assumed rigor mortis had set in. Then I saw what Barker was trying to show me. I saw it, and the ground careened out from under me. I hit the floor hard, my cheek taking most of the blow. Barker was there instantly, helping me up.

"He's been . . ."

"Aye, lad. Take it easy."

"He's been crucified!"

The next I knew, I was in another room, drinking strong tea from a tin cup next to Constable Morrow. His color was just beginning to return, but I was still quite pale. My cheek had begun to swell. I would have a nice welt by which to remember my visit.

I don't know what I had been expecting under that sheet, but I knew it was not an El Greco painting of Christ's passion come to life. Or death, rather. Those ashen limbs and that battered face would haunt me forever. My old Methodist preacher back in Wales was always fond of pouring on the agonies of the crucifixion, especially during Easter week, but his thousand words did not do justice to the picture I saw in the other room.

I could have sat there all day in that dark, quiet room, drinking muddy tea and trying to get over what I'd just seen, but I told myself I didn't have the luxury. I had already disgraced myself in front of my employer, and it was probable that he needed me to take notes. I took a final pull from the tin cup, wishing it contained something stronger than tea, and pushed myself up. My limbs were not quite as rubbery as before. I nodded to the constable and left the room. Barker was pacing in the corridor.

"Ah, lad. Good to see you up and about. How was your tea?"

"Not as good as the green tea we have at home, sir," I lied through my teeth. "But it's done the trick. I apologize for collapsing like that. I didn't expect—"

Barker waved his hand in dismissal. "Who would? Don't count it against yourself. I already knew what to expect, but you didn't. Let's go back in." He rubbed his hands together, impatient to get back to work.

Barker whisked the entire sheet off this time, and I noticed a few more details. The body was still clad in drawers, modern rather than first-century, and the feet had not been pierced. Logistically, I suppose it would have been impossible to transport and set up a man on an entire cross, so the killers had settled upon a representation. The nails piercing the hands would not have supported the body, and abrasions on the forearms showed that they had been tied to the cross with stout rope.

From where I stood at the foot of the table, I looked at the victim, with his fine Semitic features, the long hair and beard. I suppose I had blacked out from the sudden shock of finding Christ on a postmortem table in Tower Road. Now I saw the man, Louis Pokrzywa. *Poor blighter,* I thought. *Whatever did you do to deserve this?*

"He really did look like Christ," I remarked. "Or at least, as I pictured him."

"Close enough, if it matters, lad," Barker sniffed. "But Isaiah fifty-three two states, 'He hath no form nor comeliness; and when we shall see him, there is no beauty that we should desire him.'"

Just then a man came bustling into the room, and Barker continued his examination. He had a hawk nose, steel gray eyes, and white hair combed severely back and falling straight to his shoulders, like a music impresario. He wore a smock displaying every type of bodily fluid and gore a human corpse can produce, with a respectable collar and tie peeping out the top.

"Hello, Barker," he said. "Are you almost done here?"

"Yes, Dr. Vandeleur," my employer responded. "I am. Did you get your postmortem?"

"No, blast the luck. I would have loved to test the strain on the musculature of the arms and rib cage. One doesn't get the opportunity to examine a crucified body every day. A paper in front of the British Medical Association would have made me famous. But there's no question about the cause of death. It was that knife wound, straight up into the heart."

"So he was not alive when he was crucified?"

"No, but he was for the drubbing they gave him. I'd say he must have received ten blows at least, some to the face, some to the rib cage. Either an entire party went at him, or one fellow who was hopping mad."

"Any other marks?" Barker prompted.

"Scratches, splinters, and creosote smears on his back, where he was hoisted up the telegraph pole."

"Telegraph pole?" I wondered aloud.

"Yes, they found him this morning in Petticoat Lane, hoisted up a pole right in the middle of the Jewish quarter of the City. That took brass," Vandeleur said.

"And brains," Barker added. "They must have moved swiftly in the fog last night and set him up before the first vendors came with their barrows. Now the Sunday market is at its busiest, wearing away any clues they left. Llewelyn, would you please find Constable Morrow, and bring the beam and rope?"

"Yes, sir."

There were two benches in the hallway, the first occupied by three biblical patriarchs who could only be the rabbi and his assistants waiting to claim the body, and the other by P. C. Morrow, looking somewhat improved. He had a long coil of rope over his shoulder and a length of wood across his knees. I motioned for him to bring them in. I noticed he followed me reluctantly.

Barker plucked the stout board out of the constable's hands the moment he saw it. It was a rough-hewn piece of wood, about five feet long, and gray with age. My employer turned it over. The entire length of the back had been written on in chalk. The legend read "The Anti-Semite League. Psalm 22:14."

Barker quoted it from memory. " 'I am poured out like water, and all my bones are out of joint; my heart is like wax; it is melted in the midst of my bowels.' "

"Not a bad description," Vandeleur said. "His bones would have been out of joint while he was suspended, and the thrust of the knife up under the sternum into the lower left ventricle would have produced a watery discharge with the blood."

"A Bible-quoting group of killers. I don't like it," Barker rumbled, his chin buried in his coat. "Murder and faith make nasty bedfellows. Hand me the rope there, Constable."

My employer took the rope and counted the yards by measuring it between his outstretched hands. Then he examined the cut at both ends, the texture, and even the smell of the rope.

"Llewelyn, your notebook, if you please. This is common hemp, over an inch in diameter, and a little short of ten yards long. To what was the other end affixed, Constable?"

"A nearby gas lamp, sir," Morrow spoke up.

"What sort of knot?"

"Bowline, I understand."

"And was the rope tying Mr. Pokrzywa's body to the cross the same sort of rope as this?"

"Yes, sir. It's still in the other room. Shall I trot it out?"

"Aye, please do. This rope smells of animals. It may have come from one of the tanneries in Leadenhall Street, or a knacker's yard, or possibly a ship that transports livestock. Thank you, Constable. Yes, it is the same rope. Not as much blood on it as you would expect. He didn't bleed much from the hand wounds, since he was already dead. Thank you, Dr. Vandeleur, for your patience."

I was relieved we were finally leaving. The strong odors were making me light-headed again. We almost made it out the door when we were stopped on both sides, me by the supercilious guard, who demanded we sign out, and Barker by the rabbi. I filled out the time of our departure, while Barker conversed in low tones with Mocatta, a salt-and-pepper-bearded scholar of perhaps fifty. There were nods all around, the guard included, and we finally left, stepping out into blessed fresh air again.

I took in several lungfuls. Granted, we were near the river and a block or two from the fish market, but compared to inside, we might have been standing on the cliffs of Dover. Barker, as usual, appeared unaffected.

We entered the four-wheeler again and headed north into Aldgate, the Jewish quarter. Every square foot of pavement space contained a sign in English and in Hebrew, a stall of some sort, or an individual—man, woman, or child—engaged in personal commerce. Match sellers, book dealers, clothing merchants, men selling jewelry from a suitcase, women hawking handmade silhouettes in paper. All this on a Sunday, when church-going Christians in London daren't even ride the "Sabbath Breaker" to Brighton, for fear of breaking the Third Commandment.

Though it was a ghetto in name, Aldgate was not quite what I expected. One side of the quarter backed up onto the worst streets of Whitechapel, but we were just a few minutes' walk from Threadneedle Street and the Bank of England. Even as we drove, the streets began to improve, and within a few moments we were stopping in front of a prosperous-looking residence in Saint Swithen Lane.

A footman in powdered wig and breeches met us at the door. I noticed, just before we entered, that Barker set his walking stick against the wall, outside of the building. A small silver box attached to the doorframe glinted in the pale sunlight. It was my first glimpse of a mezuzah.

Inside, the hall was richly furnished in a somber and conservative style. Frosted globe lamps gleamed against mahogany paneling, and a rich Persian rug carpeted the floor. The footman led us down an opulent hallway lined with cases displaying relics of old Judaica. Silver menorahs, terra-cotta oil lamps, faded silk prayer shawls, ancient Hebrew coins and alms boxes caught my eye as I walked by. I wished I could have stayed a moment and inspected the small cards that told their histories, but Barker and the footman were pulling away, and I hurried to catch up.

We entered a room lit by two fires, so warm that it felt like a Turkish bath. An elderly man sat in a chair facing us, both hands resting on a cane between his feet. He wore a coat that may have fit him at one time, but which now threatened to engulf his frail frame, and a collar so high it looked like his head was resting on a marble pedestal. As I neared, his face seemed even older, his skin like parchment, but the eyes under the bushy brows glowed like coals. As we came up to him, he favored us with a gentle smile. I didn't have to ask if it was this man's note which had summoned us to Aldgate. Barker stopped and bowed low.

"Sir Moses," he murmured.

5

OF COURSE, I HAD READ OF SIR MOSES MON-tefiore. Who hadn't? He was the unofficial ambassador of his people to the world, unofficial only because the Jews had no country of their own. Among his titles were knight, baronet, sheriff of London, deputy lieutenant for Kent, magistrate for Middlesex and the Cinque Ports, and president of the Board of Deputies. Since the 1840s he had been crisscrossing Europe, getting Jews out of scrapes in Russia, Romania, Italy, and countless other countries. Now, it seemed, he was finding trouble closer to home.

"Mr. Barker," he began, "pray be seated. You, too, young fellow. Thank you for coming on such short notice, and forgive an old man for calling you away from your observation of the Sabbath. Your devotion does you credit. This is, I believe, the second time we have availed ourselves of your services, is it not?"

"It is," Barker said, sitting relaxed but upright in his chair. "We have just returned from the City Morgue, where we have been examining poor Mr. Pokrzywa."

The old man stiffened. "You have not . . ."

"Touched the body? No, sir, or I would not have entered

this residence. The stick I used to examine the corpse is out on the curb."

Sir Moses relaxed. "You know your Jewish customs, Mr. Barker. So, was he literally crucified? I have not viewed the body."

My employer tented his fingers in front of him. "He was tied and nailed to a board that was hung from a telegraph pole."

"Barbaric. A Gentile custom, despite our unwarranted title as 'Christ-killers.' Stoning is the only form of execution permitted to the Jews."

"Perhaps," my employer said, "but Gentiles haven't used crucifixion as a means of execution for over a thousand years. This form of killing is an anachronism, and as such, anyone with enough motivation could have done it to prove a point, regardless of their race or religion."

"Do you consider yourself a Christian apologist, Mr. Barker?" Montefiore asked, looking at him through shrewd eyes. "If so, you have much to answer for."

Barker gave a rare smile. "I am but a humble Baptist, Sir Moses, and have enough to apologize for among my own people. I find that, like the Jews, we tend to divide the world between ourselves and everybody else."

The old man tipped his head back and laughed. "You argue well. You should have been a Torah scholar."

"I read Torah as well as the next man, Sir Moses. But come, I believe we're dancing around the main issue. Are you engaging me to find the killer of Louis Pokrzywa?"

The elderly man knit his brow. "There is more to it than that. Perhaps much more. In Germany the Anti-Semitic Party has been gobbling up parliamentary seats. There have been major pogroms in Kiev, Odessa, and several other Russian towns. Jews in Poland are starving or fleeing because of government sanctions in the Pale. And all of the refugees are coming here by the thousands, by the tens of thousands! We Jews take care of our own, but this is not a mere exodus, it is a deluge. Feeding and housing them all would beggar even a Rothschild. Hundreds are arriving in London by steamer every day. They are good people, though green to the ways of England. They don't speak English and have nothing but the clothes on their back. They want a place to live and employment, but they are taking work and housing from the English workers and from other immigrant groups, such as the Irish and Italians. They don't know any better."

Barker moved forward to the edge of his seat. "You think things will get out of hand? You fear a pogrom here in England?"

"I do, and I forbid it!" Sir Moses cried, punctuating his remark with a thump of his cane. "I will not have a pogrom on my watch. I have not fought against anti-Semitism so long only to see my people evicted from my own country. We have come this far and shall go no further. Our backs are to the sea, gentlemen . . . and I do not believe the Almighty shall part the Atlantic Ocean all the way to the New World."

The two men sat silent for a moment, and I pondered how history repeats itself. Here again a Moses was leading his people in the wilderness, making plans and trusting in his God to defend them. The old man thumped the arm of the chair and I saw, just for a second, the power and vitality he once possessed.

Barker shifted in his seat. "A single dead Jew does not make a pogrom. Surely there is more that you have not told me."

The old fellow nodded, swinging the silk tassel on the small velvet cap he wore. "I must have my finger on the pulse of my people at all times. Anglo-Jewry has always been an uneasy alliance. I'm seeing warning signals everywhere. Last week a rabbi heard a speaker in Hyde Park denouncing the Jews, and when he tried to intervene, he was beaten. There is a successful production of *Merchant of Venice* at the Pavilion Theater with the most deplorable portrayal of Shylock it has ever been my misfortune to see. Several shopkeepers have had their windows shattered by bricks this month, and a number of workers have been assaulted by ruffians. The new arrivals are fanning the flames. They are so alien-looking they frighten the East End Gentiles. Truth be told, they frighten even us! To the average Londoner, however, one Jew is like another. One of the businesses that was damaged has been a family-owned establishment for almost two hundred years. If a pogrom should occur, I do not believe our attackers will stop to ask how long each family has lived in this country."

"Do you believe there is a connection between the murder of Mr. Pokrzywa and these other events?" Barker asked.

Sir Moses shrugged his bowed shoulders. "Perhaps. Who can say? That's what I want you to discover."

Barker paused. No doubt he was debating all the factors in the case. Finally, he nodded once, decisively.

"Very well, then. My agency accepts your case. For now, as a working hypothesis, I shall assume that the murder was part of an attempt to harm the Jewish community as a whole. But I will not force it. Should I discover that Pokrzywa's death had no connection to those other events, to which endeavor would you have me concentrate my energies?"

"I will trust your judgment on that."

"Then I shall endeavor to earn your trust. I'll need a list of pertinent names and addresses, as well as a letter of introduction from you, to verify that I am working for the board until I get my own sources working on this."

Montefiore reached into his pocket and handed his card and a folded sheet of paper to my employer. Barker thrust them into his own pocket unread, and stood.

"We haven't discussed your fee," Sir Moses stated. "I presume you'll require some money for expenses."

Barker frowned, and I noticed he moved his shoulder. I

sensed that he was uncomfortable discussing money. "I cannot state a fee because I don't know yet what is entailed in the work. We will discuss it when the case is complete. For now, my customary retainer is five pounds sterling."

The old patriarch pulled a thick gold clip of notes from his pocket. He removed one from among them and proffered it. Barker did not move.

"Please hand it to my assistant."

Montefiore smiled at the little eccentricity and gave it to me instead. "You know," he said, "in my younger days I would have hunted down this killer myself, but since I have reached the century mark, I must rely upon you young fellows. *Mazel tov,* gentlemen. May the Father of Abraham, Isaac, and Jacob bless your efforts."

The footman led us back to the entrance. I was almost out the door when Barker stopped us and turned his head. There was a comfortable-looking drawing room to our left, with two large easy chairs flanking a crackling fire.

"Good day, my lord," Barker called out. There was a rustling of newspaper and a *harumph* from the chair. We retrieved our hats and coats and left.

"Who was that?" I asked.

"Lord Rothschild, of course. This is one of his pieds-à-terre, down the street from his bank. Sir Moses is his uncle, and since he has reached one hundred years of age, the baron takes close care of him."

"So he is really a hundred years old?"

"He is. Not exactly Methuselah, but they are a remarkably long-lived race."

Barker picked up his stick, which was still leaning against the wall. I had to amend my first impression of the area; if one could leave such a fine stick at the curb and find it safely there a quarter hour later, it was safer than most streets in London. The stick had a shiny brass head, and the shaft was of polished maple. It couldn't be bought for less than three quid. Perhaps the fact that it leaned against a Rothschild property gave it some special protection.

"Petticoat Lane is but a few blocks from here. Let me show you about Aldgate and tell you some of its history. I have no doubt," Barker said, setting a brisk pace, "that a few Jews accompanied the Romans when they were building Londinium in the first century, but there was no organized community until William the Conqueror brought merchants and artisans here from Europe a millennium later. They set up shop in Aldgate, in the street known as Old Jewry. By law, money lending was forbidden to Christians, so the Jews were able to offer high interest loans and grew rich—rich enough to form the backbone of the royal treasury, when needed. Still, they were not immune to persecution. Conditions quickly began to deteriorate for the Jews, and the government taxed and persecuted them systematically. Finally, in 1290, Edward the First expelled all Jews from the kingdom. They were exiled for three hundred fifty years. Watch your step here, Thomas."

"Thank you, sir. That's terrible, what happened to the Jews."

"Yes, England has much to answer for. During those missing three and a half centuries, Marlowe wrote *The Jew of Malta* and Shakespeare his *Merchant of Venice.* The first is vitriolic, but then Marlowe always was a waspish fellow. Shakespeare's play is, on the other hand, brilliant. Have you ever seen it staged?"

"No, sir," I gasped, "but I've read the play."

"Step lively, lad. You're lagging. Where was I? Oh, yes, three hundred fifty years. Of all people, it was the Puritan, Oliver Cromwell, who restored the Jews to England in 1656, at the request of Rabbi Israel, a man not unlike our own Sir Moses. The first synagogue, Bevis Marks, opened in 1701. It was a Sephardic synagogue, Spanish and Portuguese, but the

German and Dutch Ashkenazim followed almost immediately. Since then they've been emancipated and have prospered for the most part. The Jewish leaders, led by Sir Moses, formed the Board of Deputies in 1863 to protect all Jews. Which brings us to the present and, not coincidentally, to the Lane. Good heavens, lad, are you all right?"

"Fine, sir," I said, putting my hands on my knees. "Just a bit winded."

"First a cold, and now this? We need to get you in better shape, put you on beef tea until we can build you up. Welcome to Petticoat Lane, Thomas."

We'd turned east at Lombard from Saint Swithen, and come down Fenchurch Street into Aldgate High Street, crossing half of the City's royal mile. We now stood not a stone's throw from Whitechapel, facing Middlesex Street, the Lane's more prosaic name. This was the heart of the Jewish ghetto, where the east end of the City gave way to a strip of land known as Spitalfields. On the map, the street changes names several times, but it is all the Lane on Sunday, including the various alleyways and gated courts that back into it.

The scene before us was like a football skirmish. It was as if half of London had been compressed into one street. People stood elbow to elbow like sardines in a tin, and any space underneath was packed full of children. Makeshift booths were set up, with every inch of space filled with used clothing. Handkerchiefs, ties, and hosiery were tacked to the rickety wooden supports and fluttered in the chill March breeze. The articles for which the street earned its sobriquet hung on low-slung clotheslines overhead. Portable racks of shirts and overcoats lined both sides of the street, and the more permanent merchants had signs in Hebrew and English together. Shoes dangled by their laces from upper-story windows, and hawkers called down to the crowd to use the stair. In front of a shop, which proudly boasted that it had been in this location since

1705, sat a fellow fresh off the boat from Moravia or somewhere, selling his few pitiful possessions from a handkerchief on the street.

"Good heavens!" I cried. "How ever do we get in?"

"It's quite simple," my companion said, insinuating his elbow between two men standing back to back. "We push."

The din was appalling. Every hawker in London was here, yelling "Who'll buy?" "Better as new!" and "Hi! Hi!" Sailors walked arm in arm with handsome-looking young Jewesses, children with white pinafores and red cheeks scuttled about like mice, and East End matrons in their long shawls sailed through the crowd with the grace and dignity of clipper ships. Here a man offered gold and watches in the same singsong voice in which he had offered prayers to his God the day before, and there an old crone sold vestas and warmed herself from a pail full of coal embers. One could buy any article of clothing here, from a gypsy's silk scarf to a guardsman's bearskin busby. Perhaps it was my imagination, but I think every vendor in the street noticed my new clothing.

"Oy, there! Give you a good price on that there suit!"

"Pardon, young fella! I'll 'schange that suit and give you the difference!"

"Very dapper young gentleman, we have here! I can get you a more comf-table-like pair o' boots cheap!"

"Just ignore them, lad," Barker ordered, pulling me through the crowd.

"Why aren't they bothering you?" I asked. "You're dressed as well as I."

"They know better."

I looked at the faces of the crowd. Most looked like average Londoners, and a few like music-hall versions of Jews, but now and then I saw true Semitic faces: Russian Jews with babushka scarves or fur-trimmed hats, old men who would have looked at home in bazaars in Damascus or Casablanca, and bright-eyed children with black curls and earrings, looking as if they'd just fallen off a gypsy caravan.

"Mind your wallet," Barker continued. "This is a knucker's paradise."

I tapped my back pocket. My wallet had no money save the five-pound note of Barker's, but it contained a few things important to me, so I held on to it. I hadn't heard the word "knucker" since prison. Where had Barker picked up the word?

"What are we looking for?" I shouted over the noise.

"The telegraph pole they hung him on!" Barker growled back, pointing to the wires overhead.

"How do we know which one it is?"

"Poole will have stationed a peeler underneath, to keep people from climbing it! Evidence, you know!"

We pushed on, and I do mean pushed. It was like being a drone in a beehive, everyone speaking at once, everyone slowly working toward his or her own destination. Barker seemed to have little problem moving through the crowd, but someone plucked at my sleeve every moment or two.

"Aha!" he said, after a few minutes. "I spy a blue helmet in the crowd about a hundred yards ahead."

A merchant more determined than the rest had attached himself to my sleeve and was telling me in rapturous terms all about the goods and services he had to offer a fine gentleman like myself. It was flattering to be addressed in such terms, considering I was less than a week away from being a homeless idler, but Barker was pulling away again. So, with one hand I separated him from my arm, then planted the other full in his bearded face and pushed. He gave up and sent me on my way with several curses in Hebrew, before latching on to another fellow almost immediately.

Finally, we reached the center of the Lane, where a burly constable guarded an ordinary-looking telegraph pole. The coroner, Vandeleur, must have been right in his assumption that Pokrzywa had been killed somewhere else. There was almost no blood to be found, just a few rusty stains on the pavement by the pole. It was no secret among the Jews what had happened here, and they vented their displeasure at the terrible event and the presence of the law by spitting on the pavement, though none would dare spit near the constable. He looked like he could tear your head off and use it for rugby drills, were he so inclined. He also looked so inclined.

"I'm Barker," my employer told the constable. "Inspector Poole sent me to view the scene of the crime."

"Yes, sir," the constable responded, tugging at the brim of his helmet.

"Has anything been disturbed?"

"Nothing really to disturb, sir. There's no soil here to leave impressions of feet and such. Just cobbles and paving stones."

"Was any blood found in the Lane beyond these few spots?"

"Only at the entrance to the High Street, sir, and that was probably from the Leadenhall meat market."

"Was there any indication of a wheeled cart having been used? A dogcart or barrow?"

"Well, sir, the fog had deposited a heavy mist on the road, and there were already a coupla' dozen barrows here when we arrived, so it's hard to say."

"So, nothing. These fellows covered their tracks well." He stepped back and surveyed the telegraph pole, making a slow circle around it.

"Were the street empty, I'd climb this thing, or have you do it, Thomas. But we'd attract too much of an audience, I suppose." He contented himself with circling the pole, like a lion that had trapped a pygmy in a tree. He pointed upward.

"You see that roughening up there near the top? That's where they threw the rope over to hoist him up. I'll hazard there's a groove worn there. And look, here's the gas lamp to which they tied the other end of the rope."

"Ghastly way to die," I muttered.

Barker held up a finger. "Remember, lad, he died from a stab wound and was already dead when he was brought here. Not that it was any less painful."

He walked around the pole a final time, looking at the surrounding pavement. It was free of any soil which might leave tracks.

"Nothing. Clever rascals. Come, lad, let's continue our tour of Aldgate."

We left the crowds. Barker turned down a street called Harrow and moved swiftly through a number of short streets and odd turnings. It was obvious he knew the area very well. We turned up in Duke's Place, a respectable-looking street of the middle class. We hadn't gone a block when my employer suddenly nudged me into a side lane or court. The alley had a stone archway with large finials shaped like pinecones.

"What is it?" I asked. Barker pointed to a doorway behind me. There was a white stone entranceway engraved with Hebrew lettering, set into a brick wall, with delicate iron tendrils reaching out to bracket a lamp in front of the door.

"It is Bevis Marks, the Spanish and Portuguese synagogue."

"What's it doing in this alley?"

"One of the demands of the Church of England in 1700 was that the synagogue not attempt to attract converts with an ostentatious entrance."

"So, what are we doing here?"

"We're interviewing our first witness, the fellow who got into that spot of trouble in Hyde Park. According to Sir Moses' little note, he is the *shammes* or caretaker of the building. Let's go in."

We entered through the discreet doors. Inside was a lobby lit by a huge chandelier. The place seemed deserted. It was afternoon. Barker raised an eyebrow my way, with an almost conspiratorial look, and led me forward to the door of the sanctuary. We dared to peek in. The interior was dim, even with more chandeliers casting a warm glow. Ancient high-backed pews took up the middle aisles, and there was a gallery with latticework, where I assumed the women were to sit. There were marble pillars, and a large ark on the east side for the sacred scrolls. For all that, it didn't have the alien feeling I expected.

"Architecturally, it's not much different from the Tabernacle this morning," I said to Barker.

"That's because the builder was a Quaker. Jews were prohibited from building for themselves."

"May I help you gentlemen?"

We both jumped. Barker let go of the door, which swung shut with a biblical finality. Our discoverer was even less foreign than the sanctuary. Instead of a solemn-faced Ezekiel, or a devout Moses, he was a red-haired, jovial Pickwick of a fellow in spectacles and starched white tie. Young, and tending toward portliness, he could have posed for a John Bull advertisement for ale or cigars.

"I'm looking for Michael Da Silva," Barker said.

"Look no further, then, for I am he. How may I be of service?"

Barker rummaged around in his coat, and for a moment, I saw him through Da Silva's eyes. Were I caretaker of this edifice, I'd look twice at this tall, dark-spectacled stranger. He finally produced the carte de visite Sir Moses had given him and explained in a few words his purpose in coming.

"Are you here because of the murder in Petticoat Lane?" the *shammes* asked. "Was he actually crucified? We heard the wildest reports at service this morning. Yes, before you ask, we do have service on Sunday morning, just not Shabbat service."

"We are investigating the murder for the Board of

Deputies. They are also concerned about a possible increase in anti-Semitism in town. May we speak privately?"

"Certainly. Let us step into my office."

I would more likely have called it a broom closet. Space must be at a premium in the old synagogue, or perhaps people were smaller in 1700. As we squeezed in and sat among the chairs and desk and filing cabinets, I had a closer look at our witness. There was little to suggest his Semite blood at all, save the small gold Star of David suspended from his neck. His sleek stoutness, his ruddy hair, and his entire costume bespoke the well-fed country parson.

"Mr. Da Silva," Barker rumbled in that foggy voice of his, "could you tell us about the incident in Hyde Park last week?"

"Oh, that!" the caretaker said, as if he'd suddenly found which cubbyhole to put us in. "'Straordinary thing. We weren't but a few hundred yards from Sir Moses' old residence in Park Lane. I was coming back from a Jewish women's organization luncheon, the Daughters of Judah, where they had asked me to speak about my work. Bevis Marks is the oldest surviving synagogue in England, gentlemen, and we pride ourselves on the fact that almost everything in the building is close to two hundred years old, including the chairs you are sitting in right now."

"You were coming back . . . ," Barker prompted him.

"Yes, I was. They feed you well at these luncheons. To be truthful, I would have liked to retire to my office and close my eyes for about twenty minutes. I wasn't even really listening to the fellow ranting in the Speaker's Corner, until I heard that unfortunate word."

We looked at the caretaker for a moment, before Barker finally asked, "What word would that be, Mr. Da Silva?"

"Well, I will not say it. Bad enough that it should be forever in my ears. I do not wish it to pass through my lips." The man's yellow sleekness began to mottle red, as if one had adjusted a valve at his collar and admitted some steam.

"What exactly was he saying, beyond the unfortunate word?" Barker continued.

"He claimed we were responsible for a lot of good men being out of work. He called us bloodsuckers, charging usury on loans, and living off people who could ill afford it. He said London would be knee-deep in Eastern Europe refuse if something wasn't done. He hinted at unnatural rituals . . . I assume he was talking about the old blood libel. He just went on and on. It was the worst amalgam of old superstition, prejudice, and blistering invective I've heard in years. Pure vitriol."

"What did he look like?"

"Fortyish. Average height and build. He had a red birthmark on his chin. Middle class at best. He had a strong voice, rough, but it carried. I'll bet they could hear it on Serpentine Lake and Rotten Row."

"Had he attracted much of an audience?"

"He had, indeed. When I arrived, there must have been close to three dozen men listening, and a few in the periphery, I'd say."

"How would you describe his audience? Were they upper-class or lower? Young or old?"

Da Silva looked to the right, and I saw he was concentrating.

"Lower-class idlers, mostly, in the area as a lark. A few may have been drunk. No women or children. All sorts of ages."

"And how were they responding to the message?"

"There were a few 'hear-hear's' and 'that's right's' while I was listening. That's why I spoke up. I couldn't let this fellow sway the crowd."

"What exactly did you say?"

Mr. Da Silva ran a hand over his face, leaving a whitish print across his mottled features where his hand had passed. "I have little idea now . . . Something like 'Dash it, you're getting it all wrong.' I tried to argue with him point by point, but he wouldn't argue. He just called me an idiot and a Jew-lover. The crowd was getting surly, and one of them seized my jacket. That's when they saw the Magen David hanging around my neck. One took hold of my collar and cuffed me in the head. The next I knew, I was lying in the grass, being kicked in the ribs and shoulders. Can you believe it? In Hyde Park! In broad daylight!"

"How did you get free?" Barker asked.

"I heard a police whistle, and two constables came running from different directions. The listeners all scattered, including the speaker who'd started it all. The constables were not exactly solicitous when they found out I was a rabbi, but they realized an outrage had occurred. They took my statement and told me they would look into the matter. If you ask me, that statement is in a rubbish bin in Hyde Park right now."

"Perhaps," Barker conceded. "Most constables are conscientious, but a case like this could involve more than they're willing to pursue. Did they escort you back to Bevis Marks or take you to a police station?"

"Neither. They simply let me go. I took an afternoon train back to Aldgate, stopped off at a wine house in Cornhill to steady my nerves with a glass of sherry, and came back here. Everyone was upset, of course, and the Chief Rabbi insisted that I go to a physician. My head was all right despite the clout. The doctor says I am thickheaded! But I may have cracked a rib."

"Did you happen to notice if you were followed?"

The caretaker turned pale all of a sudden and clutched his ruddy curls. "No. I didn't look. Do you think I may have been followed? My word. I'm glad I didn't go home. Wait, I did go home later! Do you think some of those fellows may have waited around and followed me?"

"Calm yourself, Mr. Da Silva. I doubt you were followed. But this is not the safest time to be a Jew in London. I would be more circumspect in the future, were I you. Thank you for your time."

We took our leave of the synagogue. Outside in the lane, Barker took a deep breath, exhaled, and delivered his opinion.

"The Sephardim have been here so long they think like the English middle class. You'll never catch an Ashkenazi so oblivious to danger."

As we were standing there, an old man passed between us and walked into the synagogue. Barker suddenly opened a note in his hand, perused it, and thrust it into his waistcoat pocket. He consulted his watch.

"I know we have yet to break our fast, but it is tea time. I don't believe it shall spoil our dinner if we stop for a small bite."

I was near wilting. "I thought you'd never ask."

6

RACKET'S CAB WAS WAITING FOR US AS WE came into Duke's Place. It was uncanny the way he and his "magic carpet" turned up at a moment's notice. His beautiful chestnut mare, Juno, stood comfortably in her shafts, her mane and tail glossy from brushing. John Racket was now taking the brush to his wheels. Many hansoms still had metal wheels, and a passenger could have an unforgettable ride when the cab went over cobblestones, but forward-thinking cabmen like Racket had installed rubber tires. They allowed a passenger to glide along the city streets, as if he were in a gondola in Venice. The cabman turned as we approached, scampered up onto his perch, and set the mechanism that opened the doors in the front for us.

"You again, Mr. Racket?" Barker asked, looking up at him over the reins.

"Aye, sir," Racket replied. "Wife's on holiday. Thought I'd make an extra bob or two."

"Brick Lane, then," Barker bellowed as we took our seats, and in a moment, Juno was clopping down the street with us in tow. We were back in Aldgate Street in a moment.

As we came up on Petticoat Lane to the left, I leaned forward. It was close to five now, and the once tumultuous street was nearly deserted. A few forlorn merchants stood staring at nothing, the hawkers had left off their cries, and the stalls were being dismantled for another week.

Barker sat silently across from me, his thoughts turned toward the new case, no doubt. It was my first moment to myself all day, and I took the time to reflect as we rode. So this was what a private enquiry agent's life was like: the sudden start of an investigation; the visits to morgues and conversations with the police; the formal summonses to clients and the hiring process; the questioning of witnesses; the endless walks and cab rides; the skipping of meals. As far as situations went, it was satisfactory. I wasn't locked up in chambers all day, and there were frequent changes in scenery. I could do without the gruesome bits, but presumably I'd grow accustomed to that. It was even rather thrilling. There was something daring about being an enquiry agent, or at any rate, an enquiry agent's assistant.

Racket brought us up in front of another foreign restaurant. I would have complained, were it not for the fact that the "good British fare" I'd been experiencing at Barker's residence over the past few days would have choked a pariah dog.

It was an outdoor café this time, called the Bucharest. We were seated at a table not far from the curb. Having not eaten all day, I was ravenous. Nothing save the coffee looked familiar on the menu, but it was in English at least. As my eyes bounced between the moussaka and the goulash, my employer seemed distracted, though I knew he hadn't had so much as a cup of his precious green tea all day.

Barker actually spoke English to the waiter this time and ordered coffee. The silken tassels which peeked out from under the waiters' waistcoats told me they were Romanian Jews. I remembered the note the old man at Bevis Marks had given Barker. This was to be a rendezvous, obviously.

"Should we dine, or is the cook expecting us at home?" I asked.

"We shall eat presently," Barker responded, still holding his cards close. "Have a bialy to tide you over."

A bialy turned out to be a flat, yeasty roll, whose center was filled with onions and poppy seeds. The Jewish community often had them for breakfast, and while they weren't bad, I'd need a strong cup of coffee before facing one over the breakfast table. The coffee arrived in little glass cups with metal handles.

"Bialy!" an unfamiliar voice called in my ear, and a fellow out of a Tolstoy novel sat down beside us, helping himself to the rolls and my coffee. A long beard spilled down his coat front, and his greasy hair splayed out in all directions from beneath a disreputable fur cap. He wore a long and ancient green coat with an almost military stamp to it, and his boots had seen better decades. Barker shook his hand and made the introductions.

"Rebbe, this is Thomas Llewelyn, my assistant. Thomas, Reb Moishe Shlomo, Mr. Pokrzywa's rabbi."

The rabbi held out a none-too-clean hand and pumped mine vigorously.

"Who should want to hurt poor Louis?" he asked. "Such a waste, a waste of good life, I have never seen. A more promising Talmud scholar you couldn't find in all of London. I held great hopes for that boy."

"Tell us more about him," Barker prompted. "We need to know what he was like."

"He was born in Smyela, south of Kiev, and came here six years ago. His parents were killed in the pogrom there, and he fled the country with just what he could carry. He came overland on foot to Amsterdam, and then took the ferry to London because he heard a young fellow can get ahead here. He applied himself diligently. Had you met him, you would not have noticed the slightest trace of an accent. You'd have thought he'd been brought up in Whitechapel."

"Did he have any close friends or a sweetheart?"

"Oh, he was well liked by everyone in the community. His special friends were the boys of his *chevra* and the other teachers at the Free School. As to sweethearts, he could take his pick. He was not an ugly fellow, and his earnestness was very charming. He had so many mothers throwing daughters at him, the air was thick with them. But Louis was a good Jew. He would choose no bride until he finished his studies and became a rabbi. Now some poor girl has lost herself a fine husband, and Zion a future leader."

"Can you think of any way in which he could have brought danger upon himself?"

The rabbi bawled for more coffee and turned over the matter in his shaggy head.

"He had . . . what do you call it? A warm heart? A soft heart! He wanted to solve everyone's problems. He gave away too much of his meager salary to the *schnorrers.* He could never keep a winter coat. He worried about the Jewish women in Whitechapel, that poverty might cause them to lose their virtue. He went about doing good works and listening to everybody's problems. He overtaxed himself, always trying to squeeze two days into one."

"It is a hard life as a rabbinical student, I'm sure."

"Oy, you have no idea! Such a life I wouldn't wish on a dog. The Board of Deputies has scheduled the funeral for the morning. The Jews' Free School cannot have so disreputable an old scholar as myself to perform the service, but I shall be there just the same, to see my boy is put into the ground properly. Of course, both of you shall come. I insist upon it."

"Had Louis seemed in any way secretive in the past few weeks?"

"The *chevra* boys would know better than I, but he did cancel a lunch I was to have with him last week."

"What is a *chevra,* if I may ask?" I put in.

"It is a burial society," the rabbi said. "They collect money for your funeral while you are alive."

"But it is more than that," Barker added. "The members of your *chevra* are your brothers and closest friends. It is a fraternal organization."

The waiter brought a new cup of coffee. It was strong and sweet in the Turkish manner. I rather liked the relaxed atmosphere of the outdoor café, as you sipped and let the world parade before you. Barker watched a drab woman in a shawl walk by.

"I know that very few Jewesses are harlots, but how many do you suppose there are?" he said.

The rabbi shrugged his shoulders. "Who knows? A dozen or more at least, perhaps."

"Could any of them have had a ponce, a man who looked after them and to whom they paid the money? Someone who might be angry if Louis urged a girl to quit?"

"Not in Whitechapel," the rabbi said, smiling at the idea. "This is not the West End. Rachel's sisters make little more than a few pints of ale and a roll per night. No one is willing to enter into any partnership with the women here. There is no money in it."

"And there is no chance that Louis . . ." He left the sentence dangling.

"Nyet! Louis would not make use of a prostitute. Apart from it being forbidden to him, he feared, as all young Jewish men fear, the diseases. Any weakness or lapse on their part could be ultimately fatal."

Barker gave up on the coffee after a few sips and began patting his pockets. His pipe helped him think. He was back to smoking the one with his own image, which I had come to think of as his traveling pipe. Reb Shlomo stopped chewing his roll to stare at the miniature version of the original. He tipped me a wink, as if to say, "Your boss is some fellow!" Barker took no notice, being deep in thought. I liked the smell of the tobacco I had brought him on my first day. According to the tobacconist, it was a "mostly aromatic blend, with a hint of sweetness and a mere touch of latakia for balance." That was the kind of nonsense one hears when pipesmen get together. They are as bad as vintners.

"Would you say," Barker asked the rabbi, as he twirled the vesta around the bowl, "that Louis Pokrzywa spoke to strangers every day, that he went out of his way to be helpful to people?"

"Yes, of course."

"Did he speak to Jew and Gentile?"

"He did."

"Married and single Jewesses?"

"Yes."

"Ashkenazi and Sephardi?"

"I sense you are hinting at something, Mr. Barker."

"Louis was a good-looking fellow, Rabbi. Women fall in love, it is their nature. Some women have boyfriends, or even husbands. Some are very needy and attractive. Rabbinical students are often naive and romantic. Do you see what I'm getting at?"

"Of course I do, Mr. Barker, I'm not an idiot. But I think you are mistaken."

Barker pushed his sealskin pouch toward the rabbi, almost as a peace offering. *"Shmek tabac?"*

The rabbi shrugged, pulled an old and disreputable briar from his pocket, and charged it from the pouch. He borrowed a match as well. Our coffees were replenished and we were ready for another round of questions.

"Did Louis do any proselytizing?"

"Not consciously. He was a zealot, and his enthusiasm was infectious, but I don't think he was specifically out to convert Christians."

"What about the so-called Messianic Jews?"

"Oh, they are fair game. There are Jews, and then there are Jews, you know. Some will welcome Messianics into their homes as brothers, and others will cut them dead in the street, figuratively speaking, of course. I think Louis believed that a Jew who turned Christian was still following most of the tenets of his faith, but he also enjoyed a good argument, and the splitting of hairs."

"Have you noticed evidence of anti-Semitism in London lately?" Barker spoke plainly.

"I was knocked down this morning, if that is what you mean. They were a band of youths, perhaps in their early twenties, in cloth caps. By the time of day, I'd say they were out of work."

"English?"

"English, Irish, Scottish. You all look the same."

Barker and I both smiled at the remark. I bet the rabbi could have listed twenty differences between a Latvian and an Estonian Jew.

"Do you have an address at which you can be reached, should we need to speak to you again?"

"I have what your police call 'no fixed abode,' but ask around. I can always be found. Now, gentlemen, I would like to pray over you and your search."

Reb Shlomo stood, raised his hands palms up, and began speaking a Hebrew prayer in a loud voice. People stared at us as they walked by not three feet from our table, and I was a little embarrassed. He finally finished his blessing and turned to Barker.

"Good hunting," he said, then clapped a hand on my back. "Stay alive, Little Brother. And keep away from trapdoors."

He stuffed the last roll between his fierce teeth and launched himself into the passing crowd. Barker picked up a menu and began to look it over, while I sat there puzzling.

Trapdoors? What did he mean by trapdoors? I thought the fellow a little touched in the head.

"The rabbi seemed a bit primitive for a scholar like Pokrzywa, from what I've seen," I remarked. "I would think a fellow like Da Silva would be more to his liking."

"The Ashkenazim have always prized their little country rabbis. The more dirty and superstitious they are, the better they like them, even the sophisticated Jews from the cities. You will often find an educated Moskovite bending a knee to the latest near-illiterate holy man. Sometimes the more outrageously they act, the better they are liked. Not that I include Shlomo in that category. He seems rather wise. Shall we tuck in then, lad?"

After a satisfactory dinner of moussaka, Barker announced that we'd done enough for the day. Racket, who had been lurking about, picked us up for the long ride south. Once we were settled in our seats, Barker made a rare comment.

"The hansom cab," he said, "presents you with drama, of a sort. The cab is like a proscenium arch, and the town of London the stage. It's fascinating, if you know where to look. I can't tell you how many pedestrians I've seen on the street who are wanted men, or how often I've witnessed a crime committed in broad daylight. I've seen dozens of watches and wallets stolen, and confidence men plying their trade. Several times I could have stepped from the cab and collared someone Scotland Yard would very much like to see."

"Why didn't you?" I asked.

He shrugged. "Often I was on an investigation of my own, and Scotland Yard isn't exactly gracious when a private agent nabs a suspect for them. It makes it look like they're not earning their shilling."

Once home, Barker sent the cabman to his well-deserved rest with a handful of silver. We retired to our rooms, but I was restless. Barker had sent up a new stack of books. They were all

Jewish titles: *Zionism and the Jewish Question; The Chosen People; Anti-Semitism in Medieval Europe;* and *Yiddish Folklore.* The latter, of course, interested me the most, but I was not in a reading mood. I was just about to chuck it across the bed and stare at the ceiling, when there was a knock at the door.

"Come in!"

My employer stuck his large head into the room. "Reading already, are you? Good lad. I won't interrupt you, then."

"No, no! Please do!"

"I was just wondering if you'd like to try a little shooting practice."

I sat up. That's what I needed, something to stir my blood. So far I'd felt like a counterfeit detective, driving about, watching Barker ask questions, reading out of books. Perhaps the scent of gunpowder in my nostrils would convince me of what I was to become.

"I've never shot a gun before," I admitted. "Is there a firing range in the area?"

"I have one set up in the cellar. Come along."

On the ground floor, in that long hall which ran a straight line from the front door to the back, there was a blank-looking door which led down a set of steep steps. The cellar was a single large room, with a section set off as a kind of lumber room. The walls and floor were lined with thick padding, which might have given the room a sinister appearance, if it weren't for the Indian clubs, medicine ball, and other accoutrements of physical culture. On the far wall was a circular paper target. I looked about but didn't see any pistols. Instead, Barker picked up an Ulster coat from the stair and held it out for me to put on.

"This was a little late in arriving, being specially made for me. The Krause brothers did the tailor work, while another friend of mine made the . . . modifications. Reach into the right pocket. What do you feel?"

"The butt of a pistol . . . and something else. Stiff leather?"

"Correct. The holster is built into the pocket. Look at the lining along the right, inside. What do you see?"

"A buttonhole. What's a buttonhole doing here?"

"Your patience, a moment longer. Put your hands in both pockets and face the target. Good. Now spread your feet, shoulder width. Step forward with your right foot. Raise your right arm, still with your hand in your pocket, firmly grasping the pistol, and pull your left arm behind you, shifting the entire coat."

I did as he said, moving the entire overcoat behind me as I stepped forward, and an amazing thing happened. The barrel of the pistol pushed out through the buttonhole.

"Fire!" he yelled in my ear, and I squeezed the trigger almost involuntarily. The shot went low, about a foot below the target. It was intensely loud in the small chamber.

"Really, Thomas," he said in mock disapproval. "Shooting a fellow in the vitals. Not very sporting. It takes too long for him to die, and it's a painful and ignoble death."

"Sorry, sir. The coat is rather heavy."

"It is. There is lead padding in the chest and back. I won't guarantee that it will stop a bullet, but it may at least slow it down. There are four more shots in your revolver, which, by the way, is a Webley Irish constable issue, with the site filed down. Let us see if you can hit the target this time."

I placed all four of them on the target, but only one within an inch of the bull's-eye. I thought the coat ingenious but not, as Barker would say, "sporting." A fellow might already be shot before he realized you had a gun.

"Better," my employer said. "There are a half dozen ways to aim and shoot, but the best is still to point as if one were pointing a finger. Too much thinking slows one down. Here is a box of rounds. There's cotton here for your ears' sake. Open that window to the garden when you're done or the whole house shall smell of powder. Keep practicing a few times a week, and you'll be as good as I."

"And how good is that?" I wondered aloud.

He stopped on the step and looked back over his shoulder. His hands moved up under his arms. He whirled, pulling two revolvers from out of nowhere. Bullets spat in unison not inches from my face. Emptied, the pistols were thrust back under his arms, where I heard them strike leather. Then his hands moved down to his pockets. His coat moved, the barrel appeared through the little eyelet in his coat, and a half dozen shots went off like firecrackers. Then he shifted the coat around and fired from the left side. The room reeked of gunpowder. Barker nodded good evening and left. If he said anything, I couldn't hear it. I couldn't hear anything.

Need I even mention that the bullets were clustered round the bull's-eye like four-and-twenty blackbirds? As I looked at the neat ring of holes, I remembered that, in prison argot, "barker" was the word used for a pistol. I thought he rather deserved the name.

7

THE NEXT MORNING, MONDAY, I WAS AWAKened to the sound of men working in the garden. Barker's bass rumble could be heard, offset by the tenor chatter of Chinese workmen. I seemed fated to be surrounded by Orientals these days. I got up and dressed and was on the ground floor, nearly to the end of the hall, when I was stopped in my tracks. The heavenly aroma of fresh coffee was in the air, pungent and earthy, the last thing I expected in Barker's house. My olfactory sense led me to a door on the left and through it. I found myself in the kitchen.

It wasn't a remarkable room; everything was functional rather than decorative. All the tools of a well-stocked kitchen were there, as well as vegetables in baskets, onions and garlic in strands, and herbs drying in bundles suspended from the ceiling. What was missing was the sturdy, middle-aged matron who reigned over kitchens the length and breadth of the land. In her place was a fleshy, bearish-looking man with a coffee cup in his hand and a sour look on his face, glaring out at the workers through a bay window in the back. He was unkempt, his nose was the hue and shape of a turnip, and he smoked a cigarette in imminent danger of burning his lips.

"Who in hell are you?" he snarled, in heavily accented English.

"I'm the new assistant," I answered. "Who in hell are you?"

"I am the cook." He was French, I decided. "'Allo, Assistant."

"Hello, Cook. Is that coffee I smell?"

"That depends. Do you like coffee?"

"I'd decimate an entire native village for a good cup about now," I said.

The man crossed to a silver pot by the stove and poured coffee into a stout mug. "Spoken like a man. *Noir* or *au lait,* monsieur?"

"Noir, s'il vous plaît," I answered in my best schoolboy French.

"Come over by the window and sit," he said, pointing to a small table with two chairs. "I am Etienne Dummolard."

"Thomas Llewelyn," I replied, grasping his offered hand, as broad as a flipper, and sitting down.

"So tell me, Monsieur Llewelyn (it came out 'le Vellan'), how do you like my cooking so far?"

I hesitated to be honest but took the chance anyway. "It must be difficult to keep all these spices from accidentally falling into the food."

The cook smiled and tossed the last of the cigarette onto the flagstone floor. "Very droll, monsieur. It is unfortunate that you have arrived in the middle of a disagreement between your employer and myself. I contend that he has no taste buds. I could cook one of his books for him and he would eat it without comment. I wished to discover just how bad my cooking could become before he would complain, for scientific purposes, you understand. Nothing so far. My Scottish feast was a work of art, wouldn't you say? Not so much as a grain of salt in the entire meal. A Frenchman would have shot me dead on the spot."

"You can cook, then?"

"I am a chef, trained in Paris, monsieur. I own the best French restaurant in Soho, La Toison d'Or. Would you care for an omelet?" He went to the stove, lit another cigarette on the hob, and took down a saucepan.

"Yes, please! So, why work for a man with no ability to appreciate your cooking?" I asked.

"*Mon capitaine* and I, we have a long history together. I could not desert him now. It was he who financed my restaurant. I work here in the mornings, and in my own kitchens during the afternoons and evenings. I leave the evening meals for Monsieur Mac to . . . what is? Heat up? Heat over?"

"Why do you call him *capitaine*?" I asked, watching my employer in his shirtsleeves working in the garden.

"Because that is what he was, a ship's captain aboard the *Osprey,* a steamer trading along the South China Sea. I was his galley cook. He was a good captain, though not above cracking the occasional skull or two."

I leaned forward, conspiratorially, and asked, "What happened to his eyes?"

The Frenchman put a knowing finger aside his purple-veined nose. "Not my secret to tell, *mon ami.* Here is your omelet."

He set down a plate containing a perfect semicircle of eggs. Cheese and mushrooms spilled from the center. It was golden, fragrant, and beautiful. I took a bite.

"My word, that's incredible," I said.

"I hope you don't mind a little cigarette ash in your eggs. You didn't complain about it in the stew yesterday. More coffee? You don't know how refreshing it is to see someone in this house who enjoys my cooking. Mac won't touch anything that isn't blessed by his rabbi, and the last fellow was a damnable Chinaman who picked at my food as if I'd put a rat in it. I almost did, just to spite him."

"I hear the fellow died," I said, pressing for information.

"*Oui,* but not from my cooking. As your police say here, he caught the 'lead flu.' It's good to have you here, Monsieur Llewelyn. I believe I shall declare the contest at an end and return this house to proper cuisine, but only for your sake, not for *mon capitaine.* Unless you think I should try some haggis. I've never stuffed a sheep's stomach before."

"No haggis, please. I suppose I had better go out and see if Mr. Barker needs me. Thank you for the wonderful coffee and the omelet. *Au revoir.*"

"Really, monsieur, whoever taught you French has a grudge against my country."

I was shaking my head at Barker's choices in help as I stepped out of doors. Chinese gardeners. Jewish butlers. Lazy clerks. Temperamental French cooks, and last but not least, downtrodden Welsh assistants. I stepped out into a regular flurry of Chinamen. Barker was easy to spot, being the only one of us over five and a half feet in height. Harm sunk his teeth into my boot in jovial greeting, and I dragged him across the white pebbles to his owner.

"Morning, sir! What are our plans for today?"

Barker put down his rake and wiped his forehead with a handkerchief. "We are attending Mr. Pokrzywa's funeral in about an hour."

"His funeral? So soon?"

"Not soon. In fact, it is late. The Jews do not embalm their dead, you see, and the body must be in the ground within twenty-four hours, if possible. They believe the body should be treated reverently and allowed to decay according to nature's timetable."

"I've never been to a Jewish funeral. Are Gentiles allowed?"

"We are, provided we observe their rituals. I'll explain everything as we go along, but you must pay close attention. Though they may be intent on the ceremony, there will be many eyes upon us. You must act with respect and sincerity. If you do, it shall cement our relationship with the community. If you fail, we might as well send a note to Sir Moses declining the case."

"I'll not fail, sir," I promised.

"Good lad. It is a beautiful service, with deep meaning behind every action, different in some ways from our own funerals. In fact, you'll hardly believe that such a service goes on in London every day."

"You say different, sir. In what ways is it different?" I asked, hoping to prepare myself.

"What?" Barker asked. "You want me to give away the surprise and miss the chance to watch you squirm? Not hardly. You'll get on. Or you won't."

While the workmen showed signs of leaving for the day, we went inside. Barker went upstairs to change, while I chose a more somber waistcoat and tie. When we stepped outside, Racket and his cab were just pulling up to the curb. The warm sun lit up Racket's red beard, which fairly glowed against his dark clothes. We clambered up into the vehicle and made our way east, skirting the Thames.

I had passed the old Jewish cemetery a time or two in the past, on the way to an interview, but I had never stopped to peer inside. Aside from the Hebrew lettering on the gravestones, the main difference between this and any Christian cemetery was the lack of memorials and mausoleums. There was little to distinguish one family from another, just rows of similar-looking markers.

Beside the cemetery there was a prayer hall, not much different from a chapel. The entire ceremony would be graveside, and not, as I had supposed, in a synagogue. At the door, a man corresponding to an usher presented us each with four items: a skullcap, a hair clip, a black ribbon, and a small pin. As if he did such things every day (and who can tell about Barker, perhaps he did), my employer turned me about and attached the skullcap to the back of my head with the hair clip. Then he pinned the ribbon to my lapel. It was strange to see him in a skullcap, but he wore it with dignity.

Inside, we sat close to the back, but the room was small enough that I had a good view of the coffin. It was an unadorned pine box of simple workmanship, and I knew the body inside it was swathed in a shroud, just as the one to whom he bore an uncanny resemblance had been swathed nineteen hundred years before.

"That's a very plain coffin," I remarked to Barker *sotto voce.* "I thought he'd been paying money every month to his *chevra*-whatever."

"They believe in simple burials. I assure you that Sir Moses, and even Lord Rothschild for all his millions, will have a similar burial."

"There are no flowers," I whispered.

"No," Barker answered. "They are not part of a Jewish funeral. There will also be no music. Now listen, lad, when I give you the nudge, I want you to seize the ribbon on your lapel, and rip it."

"You want me to what?"

Just then a rabbi got up to speak. It might have helped me had he spoken in English, but the entire ceremony was in Hebrew. To me, whenever someone speaks in another language, it always seems to drone on and on. The rabbi pontificated through his long, curling beard, and after a quarter hour or so, I was beginning to stifle a yawn. Just then Barker cracked me in the ribs, his little "nudge." I gave a loud cough and ripped my ribbon. Simultaneously, the entire assembly tore their own ribbons, and even their clothing, and gave a brief cry of grief. This, as it turned out, was the *kriah,* the first formal act of mourning.

"Rather large crowd," I whispered to my employer. "I thought he had no family."

"The fact that he had no family is why the crowd is so large," Barker explained patiently. "It means that the entire community becomes his family. Also, the Jews have great respect for the teachers of their children."

The rabbi motioned to the pallbearers, who shouldered their brother's remains. We followed them out to the gravesite. The coffin was let down into the ground with due gravity, and the rabbi spoke a brief eulogy. A Methodist minister would have been just warming up, only beginning to hint coyly about the perils of going to the grave and eternal damnation without the sin-cleansing blood of Jesus Christ.

At this point, the rabbi seized a shovel and, turning it around, used the back of it to push dirt onto the coffin. The sound of the clods of earth rattling atop the lid made some mourners flinch. He passed the shovel to the next person, who followed his example, then passed it on to the next, and so on. The mourners were filling up the grave themselves. Eventually, the shovel reached us. Barker used the backwards shovel to throw in some earth, and so did I. I liked it, the doing of it, I mean. It made me feel a part of it all, that I had done something.

The rabbi ended the brief service with a prayer. We mourners formed two lines, and the rabbi led the pallbearers, the dignitaries of the school, and Pokrzywa's closest friends between us. Among them was Reb Shlomo, who patted my hand as he passed.

It was while the mourners were filing out that I saw a young Jewish woman coming down the line. She was dressed all in jet and wore a veil of mourning, but even her somber habit could not conceal her comely appearance. I was just looking down the row when she glanced at me. I felt those eyes on me for a moment, and it was as if unspoken questions passed between us: *Who are you? Why are you here?* Then the moment passed, as she looked down demurely again. An older woman came up beside her and took her arm, and then they were lost from my sight. She was the first young woman to look at me since my wife had died a year before.

Outside the cemetery, the usher was there to collect my cap and hair clip. In exchange he gave us each a beeswax candle to pray for Pokrzywa's soul and sent us on our way. We didn't see Racket's cab, so we walked along the street with the mourners.

"Why did we fill in the grave ourselves?" I asked Barker.

"It was for the benefit of the bereaved," he answered. "The sound of the dirt striking the coffin lid is proof that the deceased will never return, so that real grief can begin, and eventually acceptance."

"Why the back of the shovel and not the front?"

"To express that this is not the usual use for the shovel, but something quite different."

"It was a very short service," I noted.

"Yes, but it is only beginning. For the next week we shall have the *shiva,* the first mourning period. Very good for us, the *shiva.* Friends and associates are encouraged to remember and talk about the departed. It will be a perfect time to question them without appearing to interfere."

With the mourners, we reached what appeared to be the house of mourning. Several people were going in, after washing their hands. The usher with the skullcaps was now holding a washbasin and pitcher, and a towel over his arm. We came forward to speak to him.

"Stop, gentlemen," he said. "I'm afraid this is only for close friends." I'm sure he realized we were not among them, since we were the only men standing in the cemetery without the long, winding prayer shawls.

"I understand," my companion said. "I am Cyrus Barker, and this is my assistant, Thomas Llewelyn. We have been asked by Sir Moses Montefiore to investigate Mr. Pokrzywa's death for the Board of Deputies. I have come to request that I might make a *shiva* call sometime this week. You men, of everyone in London, knew him best. I assure you I will be civil and shall not interfere with your mourning."

The man thought for a moment. "Granted," he said, finally. "Be here tomorrow, late afternoon." Then, with his bowl and his ewer, he went inside. The click of the door, effectively shutting us out, was the end of the service for us. They had politely put up with us for so long. Now they were closing ranks, and the true mourning, the private mourning, would begin.

Like a clockwork figure in a Tyrolean timepiece, Racket's cab came around the corner and stopped in front of us. We climbed in and lounged against the plush seats. I, for one, was exhausted.

"How did I do?" were the first words out of my mouth.

"Passable, lad, passable. At one point you had a vapid grin on your face, but you mastered it."

"I believe you cracked a couple of my ribs back there."

"They'd better get used to it. They won't be the last bones you'll crack in this business."

"I liked the service," I said, changing the subject, "but I missed the flowers and hymns. I might have understood it better in English, of course."

"No doubt. Many of the verses the rabbi spoke were from the Psalms. The same ones I've seen Spurgeon use in his funeral services, in fact."

"It seems strange to find a Baptist such as yourself so well acquainted with Jewish customs," I said.

"Yes, well, knowledge is a good thing. If the Bible says that the Jews are His chosen people, we ought to take it seriously." He banged on the roof overhead with his cane. "Racket! Ho's!"

8

AT THE ENTRANCE TO HO'S, BARKER OPENED the faded door and immediately plunged in, clattering down the steps in the dark.

"Mr. Barker, sir!" I cried. "The lamp!"

"That's for initiates!" he called back. "Twenty-one steps down and the same going up! Thirty paces down the hall, thirty-five with *your* legs. Stay to the left, or you'll stumble into someone coming out!"

Marvelous. When I met the reserved interviewer at 7 Craig's Court half a week ago, I little imagined he would have such a perverse sense of humor. He seemed to rejoice in giving me just enough rope to hang myself with. I plunged in after him and arrived at the other side with nothing worse than a barked shin and toe and a dusty left jacket sleeve.

"Try a thousand-year-old egg," he said, after we were served.

I eyed the appetizer dubiously. The "white" was a dark gray, and the yoke a bilious green. The dish was one of Barker's favorites. I would go very far to please my new boss, but this was one step beyond that. Thanks to Barker, I'd discovered the wonders and subtleties of Chinese cuisine, but I could never bring myself to eat a duck's egg that had been slathered in lime and tea leaves and buried in the ground a hundred days until it was mummified. "I believe I'll stick to the rice," I said.

Soon, the ever helpful waiter was slapping down cups of tea on our roughhewn table, and Barker was reaching for his likeness in meerschaum. I leaned back in the stout Windsor chair, and put my feet against the base of the table, as Barker had done. A full belly and a comfortable chair. What more could any man ask?

"So, how is the investigation going?" I asked.

"Tolerably," he said, between puffs. "It's still early days yet. An investigation is like a drop of water in the cleft of a rock. One must remain fluid and take advantage of every quake and opportunity to get to the bottom of it."

"That sounds like an oriental axiom. You could write a book of them, *The Analects of Barker.*"

He continued to puff, once every thirty seconds or so. "I must learn to guard myself from that scalpel-like humor of yours," he said, finally.

"Sorry, sir. Could you explain how we're to go about the case a little more clearly?"

"Very well. Our purpose is to discover who killed Mr. Pokrzywa and whether there is an attempt afoot to create a pogrom against the Jews in London, correct? Now, somewhere out there are individuals who perpetrated the atrocity and who want to thwart our attempts. Between us, there are dozens of individuals with bits of information that would be helpful to our case. They may be keeping them secret; they may not even know they are important. Our simple task is to find those individuals, out of the three million people presently living in London, and to pry the information out of them, like a pearl out of an oyster."

"You make it sound so easy," I said cynically.

"It's not as difficult as it seems. People are naturally gregarious. And we'll have a wee bit of help. There are a few, let us call them 'watchers,' in the area. We'll parlay with them, next. Let's go brave the tunnel again, shall we? Ho needs the table, and it's hard to investigate with a hatchet in one's back."

Back in the street, which at Ho's insistence shall remain anonymous, Barker and I set out on foot.

"If I may ask a question, sir, what skills should I develop to become a better detective or assistant?"

"Patience, most of all," he said, swinging his stick to match his stride. "Patience is the essential quality of a man. Observation. Doggedness. Imagination. It's all in those books I gave you. Oh, and meditation, or prayer."

"Prayer?" I asked.

"Of course. If you're not connected to the source of all knowledge, you're no better than a telephone when one of these lines is down." He gestured with his stick at the wires over our heads.

We had reached Mile End Road and were heading east. We were near Limehouse, as far as I could tell, and were walking along a blank wooden wall, painted a dull brown, one like a hundred other such walls in London, when he lifted a latch and stepped into a small courtyard with an old pump. Barker did not hesitate but moved to the pump and drew water. He washed his hands with a small piece of glycerin soap and even wiped a little of the grime from his patent leather boots. I'd noted he had a certain catlike cleanliness. He spoke not a word but passed me the soap and renewed the pump. Our ablutions complete, we entered a tall building whose blackened exterior gave no indication of what we would find inside. Barker opened a door and led me into a large room lit only by windows. In the center, four posts were set up and connected with thick ropes to form a makeshift boxing ring. Hanging bags, jumping ropes, and Indian pins gave evidence that this room was used for physical culture. My employer, still silent, led me across the room to a stair at the far end and began to climb.

The upper floor was also in perfect darkness, and I had to follow Barker by sound alone down some hallways. Finally, we came upon a large, gloomy open space which I recognized, by the dim light of a dirty stained-glass skylight, as being some sort of church. Barker passed briskly between the rows of benches, his big hands drumming against the corner of each pew. At the back of the sanctuary, he opened yet another door, then proceeded down a hallway and into a small room. It was dominated by a desk and illuminated by afternoon light from several windows on the west side. Behind the desk was a man of perhaps thirty-five years. He was bald, but that was all I could tell, for while he wrote furiously with his left hand, he held a large piece of beefsteak to his face with the other.

"What a waste of good meat," Barker remarked. The man put down the steak and stared at us. His right eye was swollen and discolored, obviously from a blow, and his misshapen nose and swollen ears plainly showed him to be a pugilist.

"I plan to eat this when my eye is done with it." He smiled, revealing a missing left canine. "Hello, Cyrus. Sportin' another new assistant, I see."

"Thomas Llewelyn, the Reverend Andrew McClain, known at one time to the boxing fancy as 'Handy Andy,' former heavyweight champion of London. Bare knuckle, of course."

"Hello," he said, grasping my hand in a viselike grip. "Don't believe a word he says about that. Never had a day of formal religious training in my life. Just a calling as a missionary to Darkest Mile End Road. Also, regular sparring partner to a certain private detective."

"That's private enquiry agent."

"As you say. What brings you to the mission? No, don't answer that. You seek information. You want me to do your work for you."

Barker leaned against the door frame with his arms

crossed. "I pay for the information. You'd still be prizefighting if it weren't for my contributions to your cash box. But you know I don't discuss money. I have a problem."

McClain leaned back and pressed the meat to his face again. "Enlighten me," he said.

"Not with that cutlet on your eye! Kindly put it down."

The steak made a slapping sound as it hit the plate.

"Thank you. Now, have you heard about this poor Jewish fellow who was killed last week?"

"A man bearing more than a passing resemblance to our Savior Jesus Christ is crucified a mile from here, and you wonder if a missionary has heard of it? Not half!"

"The Jewish community," Barker continued, ignoring the banter, "has requested that I look into it. What I'm wondering is whether his resemblance to Christ might have made him a target, and if the speakers in the area are agitating against the Jews. Not personal remarks, you understand, but actual calls for action against them. Anything that smacks of anti-Semitism, any written materials that might have been translated from the German or Russian—"

"Or the French, or the Dutch," Andrew McClain continued. "I understand. I'll put my ear to the ground. Stay for lunch?" He regarded the steak.

"Thank you, no, we have dined."

"Cheerio, then," he said. "Cash box is on your left as you leave the sanctuary."

Outside, I ventured a remark. "Seems like a good fellow."

Barker nodded. "Salt of the earth. Worth any ten men in London."

"How'd he get the black eye?"

"He has a habit of taking his beliefs to the people directly. Directly, that is, into the pubs on a Saturday night or a Monday afternoon. And since his dramatic conversion a few years back, he's taken to turning the other cheek, at least to a point. Ah, he's got a right hook that'll fair tear your head off. It's a thing of beauty."

"So, he's not officially a member of the clergy."

"No, but that hasn't stopped him from trying to evangelize the entire East End, and he's not doing too bad a job of it. You'd be surprised at how many prostitutes, tramps, and criminals he's helped turn their lives around. It's hard to believe he was once one of the worst drinkers and bruisers in all of London."

We rode an omnibus down Whitechapel Road back to Aldgate. Barker stopped and looked about the Jewish quarter, as if testing which way the wind blew. He dawdled a bit, leading me into one shop or another, chatting with proprietors; some knew him and others did not. Finally, we reached the foot of the Minories, where we found our next destination, the Tower of London.

There were two constables at the entrance to the Tower, and a gatekeeper. The latter was one of the yeoman warders that guarded the Tower. His uniform was not the bright red-and-gold worn on special occasions but the red-trimmed navy uniform known as "blue undress." In his early sixties, he had the bushy white side-whiskers befitting his office. He seemed to know Barker.

"Hello, sir," he said. "Good to see you again. The Chinaman is not with you?"

"No," Barker replied. "Regrettably, he has left my employ. This is my new assistant, Mr. Llewelyn."

"Suh!" The old soldier tugged at the brim of his round hat in greeting.

"I wonder if one of you could give my assistant a tour, while I speak with the yeoman porter. If possible, I'd like us to meet in the old observatory in an hour or so." A sovereign or two passed discreetly from Barker's hand to the warder's.

"Very good, sir." He turned and waved to two others, who came forward. At this point, Barker and I were led our separate ways.

In one hour, the warder brought to life the stories of Shakespeare and the histories I had read. These were the stairs where Richard the Third had crept, this the hall where Henry the Eighth had walked, and here was the tower that William the Conqueror had built on old Roman ruins. So much history was here, and such pathos. I was shown to a cell where the little princes had been confined, and where Lady Jane Grey had spent her final hours. Sir Walter Raleigh, Anne Boleyn, and Elizabeth the First all were imprisoned here at one time or other.

The warder showed me through the armory, where suits of armor and weaponry of all sorts hung by the thousands. I conjectured that this was what had first brought Barker to the Tower. Then I saw the British crown jewels, in their heavily guarded cage, including the infamous Koh-i-noor, all 106 carats of her. Finally, I was led to the northeast corner of the White Tower, which once housed the old observatory.

"Best for last," the warder said, putting his arm out of the window. There was a flapping sound, and when he pulled in his arm, a large black raven was on his wrist. He brought the bird to me. It cocked its eye at me, reminding me of Harm.

"I am the raven master here," the fellow explained. "As you know, legend has it that the Tower and England itself will fall if the ravens ever leave the Tower. We always keep a dozen or so with their wings clipped. Richard here is an exception. He showed up one day with a damaged foot, which we set to rights. He's stayed ever since."

"Why do you call him Richard?" I asked.

"Because he walks with a limp, like Richard the Third. I didn't have the heart to hurt him any further."

Barker and the yeoman porter came in, and the raven took the opportunity to fly out the window. Both men were walking with their hands behind them, like old friends. The porter, master over all the guards in the Tower, was a powerfully built man with salt-and-pepper whiskers cut in a perfect square.

"Ah, Thomas," Barker said. "Excellent. I brought you up to see the view. You can see all of Aldgate from here. There is the High Street and Petticoat Lane. There is where Fenchurch and Leadenhall split, and that large building in the distance is the Bank of England, with Saint Paul's looking over its shoulder."

"It's an incredible view," I agreed. From here the City still looked medieval, with narrow streets and low buildings.

"It's one of my favorite spots in all of the Tower," the porter said. "It makes me feel like we're still watchmen over the City, guardians, as it were."

"You have a great responsibility, sir. This place is so full of history, so much of what made this country what it is," I said. I thanked my guide for giving me a personal tour of the old fortress.

Barker was leaning against the thick stone window frame, contemplating the scene before him. For once, I thought I knew what he was thinking. Somewhere out there were the killers of Louis Pokrzywa.

"Cyrus," the porter prompted.

Barker left the window regretfully. "Thank you for your time, Robert," he said, shaking the porter's hand. "You have my card."

In a few moments, we were walking along the Tower wall to the entrance again.

"That was just wonderful, sir. Words cannot describe it."

"Thought you might like it," he responded.

"Might I take it that the porter was another of your 'watchers'?"

"You heard it from his lips. He takes his responsibilities seriously. See these little flats along the wall? They are called the Casements. The warders live here, in the Tower itself. The old yeomen are an important part of the City community. They may be aging, but they were once the cream of the Royal Army and Marines. They are old hands at intelligence gathering."

"Where to now, sir?"

"Let us go back to our office and check the final post, then step round to the Rising Sun for a light meal. I have an interesting evening planned. And look here! It's John Racket and Juno, right when we need them."

9

BARKER WAS SILENT AFTER WE RETURNED to the office. He sat in his chair, with his fingers intertwined and his elbows on the desk, and did not move for twenty minutes. Whether he was praying, or meditating, or merely thinking, I took the time to go through the final post. At exactly five thirty, Jenkins sprinted out the door on his way to the Rising Sun and his first pint.

"How many men," Barker said aloud, "would it take to start a pogrom in London?"

I considered. "Fifty at least. Perhaps a hundred."

"And how many men in London have such a hatred of the Jews that they would band together to create one?"

"I have no idea."

"It cannot be that many. Oh, there is always that part of society that finds others inferior. We all have our little prejudices. But hatred, enough to form a league bent on destroying them . . ."

He went over to a smoking cabinet among his shelves and took down another carved pipe, a coiled dragon. Then he crossed to an old wooden jar, full of his new tobacco, and charged his pipe.

"There's only one way to gather a group of any size. One

must canvass. Now, if I walked into a pub and said, 'Let's go next door and attack the Jews, beat them, and destroy their businesses,' I don't think I'd get many to go with me. The English are not barbarians. But if I said, 'Those Jews are taking our jobs, our homes, and pretty soon our women; let's teach them a lesson,' I'd probably clear the room. It's how mobs start. Most of the men in pubs are half bored, looking for something to do, and anxious to air their grievances."

"Someone should be watching the pubs, then," I stated.

"I agree."

"That's too tall an order for us. There are hundreds of them."

"We need volunteers watching them."

"The Jews!" I suggested.

"The Sephardim, perhaps. The Ashkenazim would be too obvious. I suppose we're only talking about the East End. Take a letter."

I reached for my notebook.

Sir Moses Montefiore
Saint Swithen Lane
The City

Sir Moses,

I am convinced that any possible pogrom would be pressed from the public houses around the East End. It would be to our advantage to recruit a force of our own to patrol as many of them as possible. Needless to say, these fellows would have to be nondescript. Do you think such an army is feasible?

Your obedient servant,
Cyrus Barker

"What about the Reverend McClain?" I asked. "Didn't you say he frequently went into pubs?"

"Now you're thinking like an enquiry agent, lad! Unfortunately, he is not generally in a position to overhear anything, considering that his face is so well known. He wears the blue ribbon of temperance and is not above busting up a pub with a stout hammer. Also, he wouldn't send any of his own people, for many of them have given up the bottle themselves. It would be too much of a temptation for them."

"Just the letter, then."

"Aye, the one letter will do. We'll drop it in the pillar-box on our way."

I knew he wanted me to ask where we were going, but I decided to keep silent. Barker went down the short hall, into one of the anonymous rooms with the yellow doors, and returned with two disreputable-looking Gladstone bags. He tossed one to me and we left the chambers.

We had sandwiches at the Rising Sun, across from Scotland Yard. The proximity to the Yard rather unnerved me, for I still had the former prisoner's antipathy to policemen. For a moment, I felt the clasp of cold iron around my wrists and ankles again, and the prodding of a truncheon in my kidneys. I had a sense of what would happen next, and I spoke up.

"We're going into 'A' Division, aren't we?"

Barker nodded between bites of ham and cheese. I found the ham almost inedible, but my employer was tucking it away between those square teeth of his.

"I teach a class there most Monday evenings," he explained. "Physical training and antagonistics, adapted to police work. Unarmed defense. You should find it instructive, and you'll get to toss around a few constables for a change."

Reluctantly, I followed my employer across the short street. The Yard looked large and foreboding in the twilight, like a medieval keep. As we walked into the building, I felt as much a prisoner as I did when I wore a convict's broad arrows. *Step by step,* I told myself. *One foot in front of the other.*

We passed a desk by the back entrance and were waved through by an officer. He seemed to know Barker on sight, but then Barker was not easy to forget, once seen. We passed down a congested hall full of constables, regular citizens, and idlers, and through an unmarked door, into a room full of lockers. Following Barker's example, I began to disrobe and hang my clothing in one of the lockers. In the Gladstone I found a thick, cable-knit black jumper and a pair of tight trousers of gray wool, with padding at the knees. The clothing looked comical on me, I thought, and only marginally better on my employer. He wore a pair of canvas shoes with rope soles. I was barefoot.

I was not prepared to walk out into the hallway in this bizarre costume, so I was relieved when Barker opened a side door and led me into a small gymnasium. The room had a wooden floor, with canvas mats here and there, and a wide mirror along one wall. Several men in clothing identical to our own were already in the room. Some were stretching, and others tumbling on the mats. One of them, I noticed, was Inspector Poole. As soon as Barker entered the room, all of the men stopped and moved to the mirror, lining up in a row.

"Good evening, gentlemen," Barker said, giving the men a formal bow. The men returned the bow and mumbled a greeting. "Tonight, I shall be showing you a few 'come-along' tricks that might be helpful to you with reluctant suspects. But first, we must warm up."

We began with various stretching exercises and some push-ups. Barker showed us how to rise swiftly from a seated position on the ground, which we practiced repeatedly. Then my employer taught us some of the "come-alongs" he had spoken of. I will only mention one, which Barker called the "Tokyo come-along," because it is a favorite of the police in that far-off city. As any schoolboy knows, a bully or ruffian often begins his attack by reaching out with the left hand either to seize the lapel in preparation for a blow with the right hand or to inflict a light jab. The defender seizes the attacker's wrist with his left hand and steps back to the left, facing the other direction and pulling the attacker off balance. He snakes his right arm swiftly over and around the extended limb, anchoring his right hand high on his own lapel, or even the bicep of his other arm. Pressing down on the attacker's wrist causes painful overextension of the braced elbow and allows the defender to make the attacker "come along" wherever he wishes, in this case to the local constabulary. It's quite a neat little trick, I thought.

Within an hour we were all quite winded and perspiring, and Barker ended the class. He shook hands with various members of the police force, giving them encouragement and instruction, then we all returned to the locker room and changed back into our street clothes. The late March air, as we left the building, was very bracing compared to the stuffy heat of the gymnasium.

Even at this hour of the evening, there was generally a cab to be found in Whitehall. Barker and I hailed one. How adept I had become in the past four days at entering one, and how complacent over it all! We passed over Waterloo Bridge and took the route I had walked in the rain two days before. The chilling air soon dried me after my exertions in the gymnasium.

Barker had the cabman drop us at the garden gate. He was whistling to himself off-key. I wagered he still had at least one trick up his sleeve for the evening. He led me over the garden bridge and up to the larger of the two outbuildings. I noticed smoke rising from a small chimneypiece. Barker opened the door and motioned me in.

Inside it was stiflingly hot. Barker went over to a barrel, took a gourdful of water from it, and poured it slowly over a brazier of coals, which hissed and sputtered, and filled the small chamber with steam.

"Take off your clothes and hang them there," Barker ordered. "There is a half barrel of water and some Pears soap in the corner, where you may wash."

I did as I was told. Once I was covered in soap, Barker filled a bucket and poured it over my head. I felt like a drowned rat and somewhat embarrassed.

"What is the matter with you, man?" Barker growled. "If you are modest, put this on." He handed me a strip of white cotton fabric with a string at each corner.

"What is it?"

"It's what passes in half the world for undergarments. It's called a *heko.* It ties at each hip. There is a heated bath behind me. Get in."

The bath was perhaps eight foot square and deep enough to go over my head. It looked like it had once been a boiler. There were teak benches submerged on one side. I climbed down into it and soaked, while Barker splashed about in the half barrel. The bath was incredibly hot, almost unbearable. After my exertions, the heat was beginning to make me sleepy. There was a fluttering overhead and the bath suddenly erupted on all sides as Barker's fifteen stone struck the water all at once. I was hurled into one of the underwater benches. Barker eventually surfaced.

"Aah!" he said, his voice echoing in the small room. "Aah! I've been waiting all day for this!" He paddled about, floating on the surface. I noticed that, for modesty's sake, he'd donned one of the little swimming garments. As he reached for a towel to wipe his omnipresent spectacles, I noticed something more. His brawny arms and chest were a mass of scars, burns, brands, and tattoos. Who had seared that circular mark on his shoulder? What had caused the triangular scar on his collarbone, or the three parallel slashes along his ribs? What did the black Arabic-looking lettering on his upper arms mean, or the animal-shaped burns on his forearms? I hazarded a guess that Barker had joined every secret society from here to Kyoto and been in more than his share of battles.

"You're welcome to use this bath any day you like,"

Barker said. "Mac heats the water every evening at seven. This is the Japanese way of bathing. You wash off the daily grime in the foot bath there, then soak the internal impurities away in the bath. I daresay you'll sleep well tonight. How often would you say the average Englishman bathes?"

"I don't know," I answered. "Once a week? Twice a month?"

"And how often does the average Japanese bathe?"

"I'm at a loss. I have no idea."

"Twice a day. A day, mind! Now, which would you rather share an omnibus or cab with, someone who bathes twice a month or twice a day?"

The light dawned. What Barker in his not so subtle manner was trying to say was that I didn't meet his standard of hygiene. I began to take offense. As far as I knew, I bathed as often as everyone else I'd ever met, until now. But then, I'm neither a dog nor a child. A nightly bath wouldn't kill me, if my employer demanded it. Who would suppose a man as large and rough as Barker could be so fastidious?

"Out of the tub now, lad," Barker said briskly. Half asleep, I dried off with a nubby towel. As I sat for a moment on the bare wooden floor, drying my limbs, he suddenly seized my head in his large hands and began twisting it like a cork in a wine bottle until there was a cracking sound in my neck.

"That's better," he said. "It's good to get the kinks out, now and then."

Things got hazy after that. I vaguely remember his pulling back my arms and working his foot along my spine until all the vertebrae popped in a row. Then I have a fuzzy memory of Barker and Maccabee helping me up the stairs to my room. I believe I was singing "Men of Harlech," an old Welsh folk song, a trifle too loudly. After that, oblivion. Sweet oblivion.

10

I AWOKE THE NEXT MORNING FEELING ABSOlutely sensational. Birds twittered in the trees. I could smell the first blooms from the tulips, which had recently burst from the ground. The brook chuckled joyfully in its course, and somewhere, far, far away, as though in another world, I heard the clatter of hooves and the bustle of commerce.

I fairly leaped from my bed and began to dress. Somehow, I noticed, I had acquired a nightshirt. I pictured Barker and Mac trying to stuff my slack limbs into the shirt, and I laughed out loud. Then my thoughts turned to the business at hand. *Trot them in,* I thought to myself. *The whole Anti-Semite League. I'll teach them a thing or two.* I tried a move or two that Barker had shown me the night before. There was a cough behind me. I was posturing in front of the butler.

"I trust you slept well," he said, his voice heavy with irony.

"Never better."

"I've brought you a brioche and some coffee, at Mr. Dummolard's request. I'm not certain what you said to him yesterday, but I believe you've helped settle one of his feuds. Very temperamental, these artistic types."

"It must be hard having to serve up one of Dummolard's

creations when he is in absentia. He leaves you to take the blame."

"Oh, Mr. Barker does not blame me for the cooking, sir. He never shows that he finds the food improper. Nevertheless, I believe he knows the difference. Therefore, I must . . . thank you." It was hard for him to say it, I could see. He'd rather give up a tooth than a word of thanks.

"Not at all," I responded formally. Maccabee nodded and withdrew.

In the hall, I found Harm by the door, waiting to go out into the garden. I felt so good, I chucked the little beast under the chin and let him out. Perhaps he was too surprised to bite. He trotted out and plopped down in a small bed of thyme, rolling over on his back, with his tongue hanging out the side of his mouth.

Barker was there in the garden. He was, well, he was doing *something.* I didn't quite know what to call it. It involved moving about in a kind of slow dance, with elaborate steps and movements. They looked like some of the defense moves he had made in the gymnasium, except that these were very slow and more flowing.

"Internal exercises," Barker said, in answer to my unasked question. He did not break stride, but continued his little movements. "Good for the circulation and general well-being. Do you know what the Asian races think of us? They think we don't eat well, we don't stand well, we don't even breathe well. We never take time to appreciate beauty. We don't value what's important. What do you say to that?"

"I say there's some truth to it, I suppose."

"Did you sleep well?"

"I did, sir, thank you. And you?"

"Me?" he asked, as if I'd made a joke. "I always sleep well." He finished his little dance, took a lungful of air, and slowly blew it out. Then he walked past me. "You coming, lad?"

Racket's cab was not out front this morning, so we hailed a hansom in Elephant and Castle. Our destination, Barker told me, was the Jews' Free School in Spitalfields, just around the corner from the Lane. We had an appointment there for a tour.

"Mr. Pokrzywa has been a cipher for too long," he said. "Today is the day we unmask him."

Sir Moses had paved the way for our entrance, and we were to be given a tour of the place by one of the teachers. I was expecting another stern patriarch to lead us around but was relieved to find the teacher about my own age, not much older than his pupils. His was a comical face, with a shock of thick, black curls, and a profile that was mostly nose and very little chin. He was a thin, scholarly, casual fellow, the kind that has a hard time keeping his clothes in order, and when he wasn't waving his long, sensitive hands in the air like palm fronds, he was stuffing them in his pockets.

"Israel Zangwill, gentlemen," he said to us, shaking our hands in succession. "Welcome to the largest and best school in Europe. I'm so glad you've come. If you hadn't, I would have been forced to endure first-period gymnastics, which is too much like Bethlehem Asylum for my taste. Come this way." He set a brisk pace down the hall.

"The Jews' Free School was founded in 1732. We feel it is one of the most important educational institutions in Europe. Close to a third of all Jewish children in London have come through these doors, myself included. We are bursting at the seams at the moment. We have close to four thousand students."

"Four thousand, you say?" I asked.

"Yes, and sometimes, it feels as if they were all in my class. Of course, many of them arrive here the first day not speaking a word of English, nor do their parents, and they have nothing but the shirts on their backs, which were handed down from their fathers or brothers. To use a Gentile term, we must 'baptize' them into English, immerse them so thoroughly that they are drowning in it. It is no help that they speak not a word of it at home. Normally, however, the children in these families are stair-stepped in age, and within a few years, the children are all speaking English to each other, and so it gets a foothold in their homes. Then they act as translators for the adults. That, coupled with the family's constant need to fill out one government form or another, eventually produces a family that at least somewhat speaks English."

"But that doesn't help you now," Barker stated. I noticed a smile peeking from under his mustache. This fellow amused him.

"Oy, are you telling me! Four thousand children, and none of them the same! We've got Chootes and Latvians, Poles and Spaniards, Estonians and Portuguese. This little fellow was expelled by the tsar a month ago, and Mr. Butter-doesn't-melt-in-my-silver-spoon over there, his family came here from Lisbon in 1652. And we're supposed to stamp 'good Anglo-Jew' on all their foreheads, teach them English and the basics of hygiene, and try to make good little law-abiding Englishmen out of them. And, of course, every one of these little monsters has a mother convinced he is the Messiah, and wouldn't we please give him just a little bit more attention than that other boy, whom we all know is just a bit dull? Ah, here we are. The cafeteria. All kosher prepared, of course."

He led us into a large, sunlit room full of tables. Hebrew children lined each one, elbow to elbow, eating quickly and quietly. Remarkably quietly, considering that there were more than a hundred pupils in the room. The children looked rather thin, as a rule, but none was barefoot, and all seemed very clean. I'd pictured a kind of Dickensian boarding school before I arrived, but I was very wrong. The food, though unrecognizable to me, smelled wholesome, and there was a lot of it. Meat patties of some sort, rolls, cauliflower, and even a cherry tart.

"Why are they eating so early in the day?" I asked. It was just barely nine.

"Your Christ, I believe, performed a miracle by feeding the four thousand. We must perform that miracle every day, and out of just one tiny kitchen. Unfortunately, this is the only meal some of them will have today. Their parents will save the few scraps they can collect for the other children in the family. Small wonder they try to claim their four-year-old is five, in order to get him on the roll. Now, if you will step this way, we will view the gymnasium, the bane of my existence."

We passed down another corridor into the gymnasium. The room appeared to be very organized; three or four classes were going on simultaneously. Students in outfits not unlike sailor suits were tumbling on the mats in one area, tossing a medicine ball around a circle in another, and lined up to use the hanging rings on a third. The teacher, I noticed, looked rather harried.

"Organized chaos, I call it," Zangwill remarked, running a hand through his impossible curls. "Again, I thank you for getting me out of this."

"Have you been told the reason for our visit here today?" Cyrus Barker asked.

"Our headmaster is not very forthcoming, as a rule."

"We are investigating the death of Mr. Pokrzywa. Did you know him?"

"Louis? Of course. Are you gentlemen detectives?"

Barker made a sour face. He did not like the word. "We are enquiry agents, yes. How well did you know him?"

"Rather well. We lived in the same boardinghouse. He hadn't been in the country a great many years, but he was a wonder with languages. He taught Hebrew and Greek."

"What kind of fellow was he?"

"He was quiet. Reserved. He was formal in his English, but

if you spoke Yiddish to him, he'd open up a little. I knew him as well as anyone."

"Did he have any enemies, or was he involved in anything dangerous?"

"Not at all. Far be it from him. I don't know how this could have happened."

"Did you or anyone notice his resemblance to, shall we say, the stereotypical version of Jesus Christ?"

"Oh, certainly, we chaffed him about it. Of course, there were dozens of fellows here in the East End who could pass that description, but he was close enough to receive comments. I've always wondered if he was a little vain about it. His hair was rather long by London standards, and I suspect the headmaster may have wanted him to cut it, aside from the side curls, of course. Louis was very orthodox, otherwise."

"Were there any women in his life?" Barker continued.

"He was a handsome fellow, and there were always intrigues around him. The matchmakers and prospective mothers-in-law were hounding his steps. He was asked to dinner by so many families, he was the best-fed man in the East End. I don't know if he had a sweetheart, but I doubt he led a monk's existence, if you'll forgive the expression, *sholem aleichem.*"

"Aleichem sholem," Barker responded automatically.

"You know your Yiddish, Mr. Barker. Anyway, I believe he was the sort of fellow to keep his private life private, which is generally a good idea, murders notwithstanding."

"Where are his rooms?"

"Number forty-three, Wilkes Street. First floor, back."

"Ah, yes. The *chevra* in Whitechapel. Not the best address."

"You're telling me. I was born in the area. For a Jew, ghettoes are the same everywhere."

"What more can you tell us, Mr. Zangwill? We're trying to understand what sort of fellow he was."

Zangwill took in a deep breath and blew it out, his dark, expressive eyes searching for words. "Serious. He didn't have much of a sense of humor. Mystical. He read the Kabala, and the Talmud, of course. He was a first-rate debater on points of law. He had a passion for Maimonides and quoted him often. He was not really one of the fellows, a bit of a stuffed shirt, if you'll forgive the expression."

"Did he talk about his youth and how he came to England?"

"Not a word. We knew about his impressive escape from the pogroms in Russia, but he didn't like to talk about his personal affairs. He was something of a mystery. His own roommate, Ira Moskowitz, once told me he couldn't make head nor tails of him."

"Tell me more about the *chevra.*"

"We met in a boardinghouse that used to be a private home. It is cheap, and Mrs. Silverman, the landlady, has been so far unsuccessful in killing us with her cooking."

"It is not my intention to sully the reputation of any daughter of Zion," Barker asked, "but could you possibly give me the names of some of the women Louis Pokrzywa knew, or some of the families he visited?"

Zangwill looked a little uncomfortable. "I don't know . . ."

"We merely wish to speak with any young woman who knew Louis, to get a woman's perspective."

"I suppose it wouldn't hurt, but I only know the one," the teacher said, reluctantly. "Her name is Rebecca Mocatta."

"Is she Rabbi Mocatta's daughter?"

"Yes, his younger."

"Capital. We won't take up any more of your time. Thank you for answering our questions."

"Certainly. Come back any day you like, if you have more questions. But be sure it's during first period!"

We came out into the hall just as every door in the place

opened and spewed forth children, all determined to get to their next class immediately, and talking at the top of their lungs in the process. In the midst of the sea of children, like a lone island, Barker stood, rooted to the spot. It was the first time I'd seen him unsettled. His brows must have been a full inch above the top of his spectacles. Discomfort, almost panic, was written on his face. I deduced he was uncomfortable around children. He stood, immobile, as they poured around him on all sides, occasionally buffeting him. Within a few moments they were reduced to a trickle. Barker resettled his jacket and tie and shot his cuffs. He cleared his throat.

"Mmm. Yes, well. Shall we go, Mr. Llewelyn? What are you smiling about?"

"Nothing, sir. I'm ready to go."

The boardinghouse was only a few blocks away. I was beginning to know the area better now. Just north of the school was the cemetery, and two streets east was the Romanian restaurant where we had met the rabbi.

By daylight, Whitechapel looked bedraggled. She was sooty, and the fine rain that was beginning to fall made the red brick look like glowing embers. Windows were boarded up, and conversely, fences were denuded of planks for firewood. I thought of the glory of Whitehall, and the comfortable urban prosperity of Newington. I doubted much money was spent by the mayor of London on repairs in this district.

At the door to the building, Barker put an arm out and began removing his shoes, according to *shiva* custom. It felt strange being out in a public street in one's stockinged feet, but as we stepped in, we set our footwear down at the end of a long line of shoes.

Inside the house, to the left of the front door, was a sitting-room parlor. There was nothing initially to show that this was a boardinghouse for Jewish scholars. The furniture was over-stuffed and dated in a style popular several decades before. In honor of the deceased, all mirrors had been covered, and the room was full of low stools. The students of the yeshiva were all there, sitting on the stools and talking; presumably they had been released from their studies by Jewish custom. Nobody, I noticed, sat in any of the normal chairs.

Barker spoke to the fellow who had supplied our skullcaps and ribbons the day before. He was about thirty, and clean-shaven save for a black square of dense hair from his lips to his chin. He introduced himself.

"I'm Simon Ben Loew, head of this *chevra*. So, you have returned."

"I have. I assume these gentlemen were the closest acquaintances of Louis Pokrzywa."

"We were," one of them spoke up, almost querulously. "Who are you?"

"My name is Barker. I have been retained by Sir Moses and the Board of Deputies to investigate the death of your friend."

"But you are a *goy,*" the fellow protested. "They couldn't find one of our own to investigate?"

"I believe your race has looked down upon the office of 'spy' since they first arrived in Canaan. I have done work for the Board before. They were satisfied with my performance. Perhaps you feel reticent speaking about Mr. Pokrzywa around two Gentiles, but let me say that any information you withhold may be the one clue necessary to finding your fellow teacher's killer."

"But this is *shiva*!" the fellow persisted. "It is unseemly."

"How unseemly?" countered Barker. "Is not the purpose of *shiva* to discuss and remember the deceased?"

"I'm being lectured on Jewish law now by a *goy,*" the student complained.

"Now, with your permission, gentlemen, I would like to ask you a few questions, and I'd prefer that my associate, Mr.

Llewelyn, take notes, so that I can remember everything. Mr. Ben Loew has given us his name. May I have yours as well?"

The first was Arthur Weinberg, a student of about twenty. Levi Rosenthal was next, a very heavyset fellow. Ira Moskowitz, Pokrzywa's roommate, came after him. Then Theodore Ben Judah, the little firebrand who had argued with Barker. Isaiah Birnbaum and Ferd Kosminski were the final two. Most had beards and wore the funereal black. It required all my wits to tell them apart and take everything down accurately.

"What sort of fellow was Louis Pokrzywa?"

"A decent sort," Mr. Kosminski said, and they all agreed. Yes, yes, a very decent sort.

"But was he a scholar, an athlete, a zealot? What were his interests?" Barker had already received some of these answers from Zangwill, but he was keeping that a secret. Or perhaps he was testing the other teacher's answers for their veracity.

"A scholar," Ben Loew responded. "An excellent scholar. Better than any of us." The others agreed, though Ben Judah looked prepared to argue the last point.

"Did he get along well with all of you?" Barker continued. "He was several years older than most."

"No, he didn't always get along with the rest of us. I think he thought we were frivolous at times," Rosenthal responded.

"We made sport of him a little," Birnbaum added. "He could be such a granny. He didn't understand practical jokes, or a fellow's need to relax after a hard day's study. Off he would run to some charity or the other. He was always on some committee or joining a league."

"Did he spend Shabbat here?"

"Yes, he did," Moskowitz, the roommate, answered. "He'd received a box of books from a bookseller in Prague, and he went through them one by one after we got back from the synagogue."

"He took his Sabbath meals with you?"

"He did. As soon as evening came, however, he was off like a shot."

"Where did he go?" Barker asked. He had eased himself down on one of the little stools. I think the young scholars were fascinated by him.

"We don't know," Birnbaum answered.

"He didn't always tell us where he was going," Ben Loew admitted.

"Not that we cared," Ben Judah continued. "I mean, why should it matter to us if he was working for the Jewish Children's Fund tonight or the Sisters of Zion Charity Benefit tomorrow?"

"So, he could have been going anywhere," Barker said.

This put Ben Judah's dander up. "You're twisting our words, Mr. Detective! If Louis said he was going somewhere, that was where he was going."

"I understand he was invited to the homes of several young ladies in the area for dinner. Did he ever talk about any of them when he returned?"

"Oh!" Rosenthal chortled. "He was so funny when he came back from those dinners! The girls would be flashing him little signals, and the mothers simpering in his lap, and the fellow was so solemn and naive he wouldn't know what was going on! He thought one girl had a facial tic, and it turned out she was simply winking at him! Oh, it was funny!"

"But he got along well with women, did he not? I mean, perhaps even better than with men?"

"A number of the committees and charities he was a member of were mostly made up of women," Ben Loew answered. "He got along with them. He once told me they 'got things done.'"

"Were there any particular women he saw more than others? Did he see any of them more than once, or have one as a friend?"

The young fellows looked uncomfortable, as Zangwill had earlier.

"Rabbi Mocatta's daughter spoke with him, sometimes," Kosminski said cautiously. "He went to dinner at their house occasionally. I got the impression that the two of them were merely friends."

"Did any of you see him after the Shabbat was over? On the street, perhaps?"

Nobody had.

"So no one saw him after he 'was off like a shot,' until his body was found. Do you think he had some sort of appointment or rendezvous?"

"If he did," Ben Judah said, "he was certainly very cool about the whole thing."

"And when did you notice he was missing? When did you start to worry about him?"

"I noticed about ten thirty that he was gone overlong," Ira Moskowitz said. "But last year, he directed a Purim play and rehearsals sometimes went on until eleven thirty. By midnight, we certainly began to worry."

"Did you look for him?" Barker asked.

"We couldn't," Birnbaum volunteered. "If we went in search of him in the middle of the night, we would wake Mrs. Silverman. And if she knew Louis was gone after midnight, she might think ill of him and toss him out. We didn't want him to lose his rooms just because he was late. He'd been here for over two years."

"So what did you do?"

"What could we do?" Ben Judah countered. "We went to bed. We didn't believe he could get himself into a real scrape. Certainly, we couldn't predict that something like this would happen to him."

Barker sat for a moment or two without speaking. Then he tried a different tack. "Would you say he was an ambitious fellow?"

"Oh, yes," Moskowitz said. "He was always talking about 'getting on.' I think he wanted to be another prime minister, like Disraeli. He lamented to me once that he was too old to attend Oxford or Cambridge."

"You talk about ambition like it is a bad thing," Ben Judah sputtered. "He was studying to be a rabbi. He would have made a great one, like Maimonides. He had good motives. He was a real *mensch.*"

"I'm not attempting to besmirch Mr. Pokrzywa's memory," Barker said. "I'm trying to get at the truth. Can any of you fellows think of anything Louis Pokrzywa had done recently that seemed out of the ordinary, for him at least?"

"He canceled an appointment last week," Rosenthal said, finally. "He was going to tutor me, but not ten minutes before we were to begin, he came up all apologies and said he couldn't do it, that he had to go somewhere. He didn't say where."

Ben Judah spoke up reluctantly. "I suppose if we're discussing things out of the ordinary, I saw Louis talking with a woman I didn't recognize in Petticoat Lane a couple of weeks ago."

"Could you describe her?"

"Rather pretty, a Choote, I think. That is, a Dutch Jew, by the look of her."

"Did they go off together?"

"How should I know? I saw Pokrzywa every day. I couldn't care less who he spoke to. One minute they were there, then they were gone."

"And this was on market day, you say? Two weeks ago?"

"Yes. Sunday. Midafternoon."

Barker bowed. "Thank you for your time, gentlemen. We'll intrude upon your mourning no longer."

Outside in the hallway, Barker stood a moment, still in his stockinged feet, and pulled on his lower lip in thought.

"What are you thinking?" I asked.

"I'm thinking that, collectively, men are only slightly more observant than mollusks. For insight, we must talk to a woman."

Instead of putting on our shoes, Barker and I padded down the hallway to the landlady's private rooms.

11

IF BARKER WAS THINKING HE'D GET ON BETter with the landlady, he was mistaken. She was a cantankerous-looking woman in her early sixties, wearing the shiny black dress common to matrons and widows. Her hair was pulled back so severely, it would have won approval from the Spanish Inquisition as a method of torture. I could see why, on that fateful night, the gentlemen who were her boarders had decided not to disturb her. When Barker introduced himself, she even had the audacity to demand what I myself had always feared to ask.

"Why are you wearing those glasses indoors? What's wrong with your eyes?"

Barker's more expressive eyebrow, the left one, curled itself into an arch above his spectacles. "An infirmity, madam," he said, "brought on by an injury." His fingers stole to the scar which bisected his right brow. "We'd like to ask you a few questions and to see the late Mr. Pokrzywa's rooms, with your permission."

"Do you have proof that you are who you claim to be?" the woman demanded. In response, Barker presented her with his business card.

"Don't you have a badge or something?"

"We are private enquiry agents, madam, not constables."

Mrs. Silverman gave him a grunt. She weighed no more than a hundred pounds in her full ensemble, but she seemed a formidable match for my employer under the circumstances. Reluctantly, she opened the door and allowed us into her own rooms. The furniture was much like that of the sitting room. The air was so dead and still inside the room, one would have thought it hadn't been aired since Lord Melbourne's day. I was beginning to become a convert to Barker's ideas concerning air circulation and the body, although Mrs. Silverman didn't look like she'd be keeling over dead any time soon.

She sat down on the edge of a chair, and we followed her lead. The padded chair I sat in was so stuffed with horsehair, I might as well have been on the actual horse. She picked up a pair of knitting needles and began to knit.

"You have questions?" she prompted.

"Yes, madam. May I ask what sort of boarder Mr. Pokrzywa had been?"

"He was the best kind. He paid on time. He asked almost nothing of me. He was not wasteful like Mr. Birnbaum, messy like Mr. Moskowitz, gluttonous like Mr. Rosenthal, or constantly complaining like Mr. Ben Judah. My only reservation against him was his large collection of books, which tended to attract cockroaches, and he was able to remedy that by powdering his shelves with boric acid. I do have my doubts about the floorboards under his bookcase, however. Books can be quite heavy, you know."

"Did he keep regular hours?"

"No, he did not. But he peppered me with so many explanations of this charity group and that charity group that I finally gave him leave to go about his business without regaling me. That fellow needed a wife to keep him home nights. That's what got him killed."

"I don't doubt it for a minute," Barker said. I could see he was trying to be conciliatory to Mrs. Silverman, but if I saw it, so did she. Had she been a cat, the fur on her back would have stood on end.

"Had he been regular in his irregularity, then? Out most nights?"

"That boy had a fund of energy like I've never seen. He lived on five hours' sleep. He worked during the day, attended classes in the evening, then was out doing charity work until late. Many is the night I've come upstairs at two in the morning—I'm a restless old woman, and creaks in this old, settling house disturb me—to find light under his door. I warned him reading would undermine his health, and I was right. Tell me I am right!"

We were both quick to agree.

"I suppose he had no time for lady friends."

"Time he could have made, gentlemen," she said, with what passed for a chuckle. "They certainly would have made time for him."

"Did Mr. Pokrzywa ever break an appointment with you, especially in recent months?"

"No, he did not. He was polite to his landlady, unlike the rest here."

"Were there any deviations in his schedule lately?"

"Only that his work seemed to increase. Before he would come home a few nights a week at eight thirty or nine. Now he was out until almost ten at least."

"So, all in all, Louis Pokrzywa was a satisfactory boarder," Barker concluded.

"If that counts for anything," she said. "Mr. Barker, I'm an old widow woman who never had any children. The young men who live here are the closest thing to offspring I will ever have. I know my boys. Some of them go out to the pubs and drink; some attempt to consort with women of easy virtue.

Several of them have the Jew's weakness: gambling. Some have even worse vices. But I tell you the truth, Mr. Barker, a man can get killed just as easily working too hard as he can playing too hard."

"Thank you for the advice, Mrs. Silverman," Barker said. "May we see his room?"

"There are no locks on these doors. The room he shared with Ira Moskowitz was number five, up on the first floor."

We made our adieus and climbed the stairwell. The first floor once held a large ballroom and sitting room, but they had been converted into bachelor flats, requiring added doors in the hall. We came up to number five and walked in.

The room we entered had been split even further. There was an invisible line bisecting it. One side was neat as a pin, and the other such a mass of clothing, papers, sheets, and textbooks as to be merely one large pile. From Mrs. Silverman's description of Ira Moskowitz, I knew which side belonged to the late teacher. On his neat desk was an open box containing the books Pokrzywa had received on the last night of his life. To our left was a wall full of books, but there were too many to look at just now. We concentrated on the box. To a bibliophile, there is but one thing better than a box of new books, and that is a box of old ones.

Barker lifted them out and glanced at each spine before putting them down on the desk in a stack. "Immanuel Kant . . . Schopenhauer . . . Goethe, all in German. Tolstoy's *Anna Karenina* in Russian. Maimonides in Yiddish. A biography of Rabbi Ben Loew in Polish. And, look here! An English-Dutch dictionary."

"Five languages! He was well read," I said.

"He was, indeed. I believe I'll make an offer to the *chevra* on the entire collection."

"Do you have enough room on your shelves?"

"Does a bibliophile ever have enough room on his shelves?

The answer is obvious: get more shelves." He turned to the wall of books. "What have we here? Philosophy; general Jewish studies. Kabala . . ."

"What is this Kabala thing? That's the second time I've heard of it."

Barker looked solemn for a second, and he even put a hand on my shoulder. "Hebrew magic and mysticism. There are some roads even I won't pursue. Look, here's something you don't find on most Jewish shelves: the Holy Bible."

"Yes," I added, "right next to the Koran."

"Don't be cynical, Thomas."

"What else is there?" I asked.

"World literature, Greek classics, some recent books . . ."

"Yes, it looks like Pokrzywa had been studying the Oxford Movement."

"You shall certainly have those if I acquire the collection. I don't read modern literature."

We went through the drawers of the desk, examining the detritus of a man's life, the residue of his hopes, dreams, and aspirations. I thought again of that poor fellow I'd seen on the slab in the morgue, and of how close I had come to the same state. One minute you're a living sentient being, and the next you're but a collection of items in a drawer or, in my case, a pasteboard suitcase.

In the bottom drawer of the desk, Barker found a jumble of filled notebooks. Louis Pokrzywa had kept a journal, of all things. What luck! We began going through them, beginning with the most recent.

"Three months old. Look for his latest."

I searched around the desk and found it under a textbook. We had overlooked it when we searched the first time, thinking it was further study notes. Barker began going through it. He pulled his own notebook from his pocket and took notes in it with a little silver pencil. I wandered about the room, looking for . . . well, looking for anything. And I found it.

"Good Lord!"

"Mr. Llewelyn, please refrain from using the Lord's name in vain. What have you found?"

"It is a picture of Louis Pokrzyra, sir, or rather, of the entire *chevra*. Louis is on the end."

The framed photograph was on the wall on Ira Moskowitz's side of the room. The entire assembly downstairs was here, as well as Israel Zangwill, Louis Pokrzywa, and a few others. Barker hopped onto the mountain of clothes and papers that formed Moskowitz's bed, and snatched the picture off the wall. It was the first time for us to see the man in life, instead of gray and battered and mottled.

He was more handsome than I had expected. His lashes were long and his eyes dark, and his nose was well formed, almost aristocratic. The mustache and beard were fine, and the side-whiskers feathery. He wore a dark suit with a soft-collared shirt and a velvet tie. He looked soulful, like a Pre-Raphaelite version of Christ. He had a dreamy, abstract look in his eye. I could see why every daughter and mother in Whitechapel was courting him, and why most of the men here didn't care much for him.

"I must have this photograph," Barker said. "Llewelyn, go downstairs and ask Mr. Moskowitz if we might borrow it for a day or two."

"Yes, sir," I responded, and clattered down the stairs. I found the group of men downstairs singing some sad, Jewish song, their eyes shut. I couldn't very well barge into the middle of their prayers. I waited an interminable amount of time, all of five minutes. Finally, Ben Loew finished the little service and looked up.

"You needed something?" he asked.

"Just to speak with Mr. Moskowitz."

"Ira, go speak with the fellow."

I got permission to borrow the photograph for a day or so and went back upstairs. Barker was still seated at the desk going over the journals. He was doing that off-key whistling he does sometimes, when he is on to something.

He glanced up at me. "Would you care to try a little detective work of your own?" he asked.

"Alone? Is it too soon? I mean, of course, I'll give it a try. What is it you wish me to do?"

"See if you can pry Moskowitz away, and take him out to the Bucharest. Ask him some questions. Open him up, lad."

"But what do I say? What do I ask?"

"Ask him, 'What was Louis really like?' See if that gets you anywhere. Remember everything. You won't be able to write it down."

"Yes, sir," I said, doubtfully. "I'll do it." I took a step or two toward the door before turning back. "I'm sorry, sir, but shall I use the retainer money? It's all I have."

Barker pulled a large wallet of brown leather from his pocket. He opened it, looked in, hesitated for a moment, then tossed the entire wallet at me. It slapped against my chest and I caught it. I didn't open it in his presence. I wouldn't dare. But even as I shoved it into my own pocket, I could tell that it was stuffed with bills.

So, in a little over five seconds, I had become the wealthy young detective, interviewing a witness on his own. I felt distinctly jaunty, in my elegant new clothes, and I would have sauntered down the stairs like an aristocrat were I not still in my stockinged feet. I reached the bottom and came around the corner, into the sitting room. The prayer session had ended, and the men inside looked rather bored. The *shiva* goes on for days, and one may run out of wonderful things to say about the deceased within hours, possibly within minutes.

"Mr. Moskowitz, may I see you a moment again?" I asked, in a professional manner.

He got up off of his stool almost eagerly. I spoke to him in the hall.

"Needless to say, I'm no expert on Jewish funeral custom," I told him, "but do you think it possible that I might take you down the street to the Bucharest for a bialy and coffee, where we can discuss the case? You must have a wealth of insight into Mr. Pokrzywa's character and history, given your close daily proximity to him."

"Well, I don't know," the fellow said. "One doesn't usually leave during the *shiva.*"

"I understand those who cannot get out of work return when they can," I said.

"That is true."

"Is a man's murder not more important than work?"

"Of course! But, still . . ."

"Have you eaten?"

"No," he said. "Mrs. Silverman will be setting a cold table in an hour or so."

"Let me stand you lunch at the Bucharest Café," I said, figuring that Barker would not mind the expense. "They make a fine moussaka. And their goulash is excellent."

"I've only ever had their coffee and bialies," he admitted. He was not a teacher like Pokrzywa and Zangwill. A glance at his side of the room had told me that not only was he messy, he was also less affluent. Perhaps he attended the school on some sort of scholarship.

"I've also heard good things about their almond torte and strudel," I went on.

"Strudel!" he repeated dreamily.

"Of course, if you can't come, you can't come," I said, twisting the knife. "Some other time, perhaps."

"No, wait!" He laid a hand on my arm. "I'm sure I can get out of it. At least, I hope I can."

He went back into the room while I carefully put on and

laced my new leather pumps. My outfit today included a pair of gray kid leather gaiters with mother-of-pearl buttons. I pulled a handkerchief from my pocket and wiped the road dust from the mirrorlike patent leather, feeling like the Prince of Wales himself.

Ira Moskowitz dashed around the corner. "I can go for an hour," he said, thrusting his feet into a pair of disgraceful sprung elastic boots. I seized my stick, a thin wand of black wood with a maple ball on top which I had liberated from the hall stand that morning, and used it to usher the scholar out the door.

I set a brisk pace as we headed down Wilkes Road. Moskowitz clapped his hands and threw them in the air in total freedom.

"I'm so glad to be out of there!" he cried. He was a funny fellow, an inch or two taller than I, with a doughy body, and kinky, wild hair that defied any comb. He wore spectacles atop a large nose, and his jovial face grew only a scanty beard. If Pokrzywa set the pace for scholarship in the *chevra,* I had a good idea who brought up the rear.

12

WHEN WE HAD EACH ORDERED THE GOU-lash and coffee, I immediately set into him with questions. "So," I asked, "what was Louis Pokrzywa really like?"

"Not to speak ill of the dead, but he was impossible!" Ira Moskowitz said between bites of goulash. "Everything came so easily to him. He could sit down and write an essay in half an hour that would have the rabbis enraptured for months, while the rest of us would cudgel our brains for days and barely make a passing grade. We used all our free time to study our textbooks. He glanced through the text once, read extra books on philosophy and literature for fun, and still had hours in the evenings for good works in the community, or to eat with pretty girls and their families. There's another teacher here, named Zangwill; I've seen him work for hours on his teaching plans, carefully using his skills to bring out the best in his students. But Louis walked into the classroom every morning cold, without notes, and was brilliant. I suspect that there were plans afoot among the Board of Deputies. Certain doors would be opened to him. He could 'write his own ticket.' It just wasn't fair."

"So, you boys used to chaff him a bit," I said, sipping a passable cup of coffee.

"Oh, we did. Who says we didn't?" he conceded, downing his coffee before taking a large bite out of a bialy. "Did you know, he had no sense of humor? None whatsoever! You could tell him the best joke you've ever heard, and he would just stare at you. Either he wouldn't get the joke, in which case you would have to explain it step by step and just why it was funny, or he would say, 'Oh, I see, that was a joke. Very humorous.' We had arguments about him at the *chevra*. Some of us thought he was really otherworldly, and others believed he was just putting on an act. He could be that way, you know. It wasn't just an accident that he looked like Jesus. He cultivated it."

"He was vain, then," I prompted.

"No, no. Not really. A little, I suppose. Not overtly. He didn't stand at the mirror curling his beard or anything. But he knew what effect he had on people. He dressed very carefully. Not as well as you, of course."

For a moment, I was self-conscious of my new suit. Poor Mr. Moskowitz was in the sort of cheap clothing I had been wearing a week before. I told myself never to forget that there were thousands of fellows in London in "reduced circumstances," as I had been.

"How was he around women?" I asked.

"Women!" he exclaimed. "That's a good question. Let's talk about women, by all means. You know how they are. The rabbis' wives had their ears to the door. They had Louis's dance card full very quickly. He gave some of the girls the vapors. One of them even fainted in his presence. I think half the girls in Aldgate set their cap at him. But you know how he was? Indifferent. Completely indifferent! My mouth watered when I heard some of the girls that were trotted out for his inspection. Yet he turned his nose up at all of them."

"Was he the cold, analytical type?"

"No. Actually, I think he was a romantic at heart. I thought to myself, 'Ira, when he falls, he will fall hard.' Do you know what I believe? You'll think me fanciful. I think he was looking for a princess. I think he saw himself as a knight in armor, in search of a damsel to save. Not that I could read his mind, of course. He didn't confide in me. So far as I know, he didn't confide in anyone."

His words put me in mind of my late wife. I had to admit that the desire to play knight-errant was a very powerful motive, indeed.

Moskowitz's fork had reached the bottom of his bowl of goulash. I ordered another cup of coffee and a strudel for him, and more coffee for myself. Then I sent the waiter along with a few shillings, to get us two cigars from a tobacconist down the street. The longer we dawdled, I thought, the more he might reveal. But instead, the conversation reversed itself.

"So, you're a detective," he said. "That must be an exciting sort of life."

"More than you know," I responded, thinking of the last few days.

"Do you have a gun?"

"I do own one, but I'm not armed at the moment."

"Have you ever been shot at?"

"No," I said, "but the last fellow to have this position was killed in the line of duty."

"How terrible!" Moskowitz cried. "Your employer looks most mysterious. What happened to his eyes?"

"An old injury he sustained in the South China Sea," I answered. For all I knew, it was correct.

"The South China Sea! And he sits there, so completely still, staring at you. I felt like a mouse in front of a cobra. I thought he was reading our minds."

"He does have that effect on people."

The strudel arrived, and the poor scholar tucked in. It felt good to buy him lunch. I supposed he ate well only on feast days. I sipped my coffee and lit up the cigar.

"Cyrus Barker. I've seen his advertisements in *The Times.* He must be doing well for himself."

"Quite well. He has a big office hard by Scotland Yard, and a home in Newington with an oriental garden. And a Jewish butler."

"A Jewish butler!" Moskowitz thumped the table and laughed. "I love it! Leave it to Sir Moses to hire the best!"

I handed him the cigar. He held it in his hands like a holy relic. I watched as he drew it slowly under his nose, then brought it to his lips and lit it with a vesta. The Jewish scholar closed his eyes and drew in the smoke.

"Paradise," he said.

"Let's get back to Louis Pokrzywa, if you don't mind. He certainly had a lot of charities."

"He did that. He often tried to talk us into helping with this or that one. Not to give money, of course, but time. He was very free with our time. Much of the responsibility fell on my shoulders or Israel's—that is, the Mr. Zangwill I was telling you about. But we explained to him that we didn't have his gifts. We needed time to study or to prepare lessons. Oh, the face he made! He looked like Jesus after he'd just been kissed by . . . John? Jude? I forget the fellow's name. I'm not up on Christianity."

"Judas," I told him.

"The very man. Anyway, he'd get the long face and mope, and tell us he'd volunteered our help, and how the children would be so disappointed, and well, of course, we'd break down and give him all our study time. Then I'd be vexed by the next Friday when I did poorly on an exam and he received a first."

"Had he done that lately?"

Moskowitz thought. "No, come to think of it, he hadn't. Perhaps he saw that we were beginning to avoid him."

"Was there any change in his behavior over the past month or so?"

"Your employer asked a question similar to that. This is a marvelous cigar, by the way. I don't know. I thought he seemed a bit more . . . reluctant to talk about where he was going. It was always, 'I'm going out, Ira. I shall be late getting back.' Perhaps he had realized that I didn't give a damn what charity he was going to that night."

"Anything else?"

"I wouldn't want to make something of nothing. He seemed a little . . . distracted. When I first met him, his journal was very important to him. I thought he believed that future generations would be reading his collected journals and gaining great insight. Lately, he seemed to lose interest. I doubt he wrote in it more than once a week."

"Fascinating," I said. We'd been gone close to an hour now. "Was there ever anything to suggest that he might be going somewhere or seeing someone clandestinely?"

"Clandestinely? Louis? Doubtful. Why would he do anything clandestine? A scandal might harm his big plans for the future."

"Why, indeed? We should get back. My associate is expecting me." I pulled the large wallet from my jacket pocket and paid the bill. Moskowitz's eyes opened when he saw the size and thickness of the wallet.

"Business must be good," he commented. We walked back, still smoking our cigars.

"Oh, yes, the Barker Agency is the top agency in London," I said. Actually, I had no idea if that was true, but it sounded good.

"I didn't realize that being a detective was so lucrative."

"We in the business prefer to be called 'private enquiry agents.'"

"My apologies, Mr. Private Enquiry Agent."

"Apologies accepted."

As we came down the street, Racket's cab came toward us,

with Barker inside. I shook hands with Ira Moskowitz and hopped aboard, leaving him awestruck at our extravagance. I looked over at Barker, who had a contented look on his face, like a cat that had gotten into the clotted cream. Obviously, his search of the rooms had yielded something.

"Ho's?" I asked.

"Certainly."

Barker sucked the last of his noodles up under that huge brush of a mustache and set the bowl down on the rugged table in front of him. I sat and watched him between half-closed lids. Now he would take a last sip of tea and wipe his mouth before reaching for the pouch he'd been dying to open all morning.

I waited until he'd gotten his traveling pipe stoked. "I presume you discovered something."

Barker shook his head. "You first."

I was to be the opening act, and he the grand finale. I gave him word for word an account of our meal conversation, or as close to one as I could. I'd never had to recount an entire conversation before. I was hoping I hadn't made any mistakes, or left any big questions unasked. Barker sat in stony silence as I gave him my narrative, the only animation being the smoke coming from the bowl of his pipe and the corner of his mouth. As I finished, I was on pins and needles, as they say, hoping for a good word. He puffed on for a moment or two. I wondered if he'd fallen asleep.

"Well done, Mr. Llewelyn," he pronounced, finally. I let out my breath all at once. "Sending the waiter for cigars to prolong the interview was a nice touch."

"Thank you, sir. Had you any reason to suspect that he'd have so many opinions?"

"I did," Barker responded. "First of all, people are always reticent about discussing a fellow's faults after his funeral. It's speaking ill of the dead. But, if you get one fellow alone, you might get your blade in him and pry him open like a razor clam. I chose Mr. Moskowitz because he was Pokrzywa's roommate and would have spoken to him most often, but also because he was messy. Have you ever noticed that a messy person is often the most talkative? I fancy if the situation had been reversed, and you were speaking to Mr. Pokrzywa about the late Mr. Moskowitz, it would have been a lesson in frustration."

I took a sip of the flavorless tea in front of me and glanced about. The room seemed its usual mix of clandestine conspirators. Not only had I become a "regular," but I was now involved in one of those secret conversations that Ho's was famous for, or rather, infamous. Who knows, perhaps some fellow in the room was here for the first time, noticing the small, diffident chap talking to the stone gargoyle in the smoky spectacles.

"So how did you get on with Mr. Pokrzywa's bookcase?" I asked. "Did you make them an offer for the books?"

"I did. They are carefully considering the offer. Louis Pokrzywa was a particularly intelligent and well-ordered man, until recent months. Something set him on his ear. As you said, his personal journal dwindled off after several years of daily entries. The entries were very instructive. Louis really did want to be a prime minister like Disraeli. He hoped to rise to a position in Parliament and convince the government to sponsor a return of the Jews to Palestine. He wanted no restriction against the Jews ever again. In fact, he agreed with Disraeli, who wrote in his political novel, *Sybil,* that the Jews were not genetically inferior, as the eugenicists insist, but actually superior."

"How so?" I asked.

"It's been years since I've read Disraeli's work, but let me see if I can put it plainly. Let's take a nation of people, the Irish, for example. Now, conquer their homeland, and disperse them across every inhabited continent. Scatter them among hundreds of different indigenous peoples. Let them be despised and persecuted, and even periodically slaughtered. Do so for almost two thousand years. Do you suppose, at the end of that time, you would find the average Irishman just as you find him today, with his rusty hair, his brogue, his love of life and good ale, his veneration of the saints, et cetera? Or would he have long ago been subsumed into the general population, leaving the memory of a strange race known as the Hibernians only a footnote in the history books?"

"I see what you mean," I conceded.

"There was a very interesting page I came upon. Just an entry in his journal, among the others. Louis was pondering whether the coming Messiah would know he was the Messiah. He wondered how high he could go, to what heights he could aspire."

"Are you telling me Pokrzywa wondered if *he* was the coming Messiah?" I gasped.

"Not outright, but it was implied."

"And the looking like Jesus Christ?"

"Was all a part of it. I suppose he could not help looking like he did. He didn't grow a beard to look like Christ, only to follow Jewish custom. But looking so much like him affected him in some ways, I believe. It contributed to his grandiose plans."

"Can one be obsessed with Christ and not be a Christian?" I said aloud.

"Well, of course, you saw the New Testament in his room. I even found a book of our own Reverend Spurgeon's sermons. But there were also a half dozen books written by Jewish scholars giving their reasons why Jesus could not have been the Messiah. He was studying them. So, I would have said that, no, he was not a Christian, except for one thing."

Barker reached into his cavernous pockets and pulled out a fold of paper. I took it from his hand. It was a church bulletin from the First Messianic Church of Poplar, dated the ninth of March, not two weeks ago.

"Where did you get this?" I asked.

"It was in the Bible."

"First Messianic Church of Poplar," I said. "It's no denomination I've ever heard of."

"It is a church for Jews that have converted to Christianity."

I sat up in my chair. "Really?"

"Yes, though it was not something he would have spoken about with his friends or rabbis, or put down in journals that didn't have a lock or key."

"Of course! No wonder he stopped the entries! Was he thinking of converting?"

"There may have been more than religion involved. Look at the margins in the back."

I turned the circular over. The service's hymns were printed there. Notes had been scribbled in the margins, in pencil, notes in two different hands.

Can you get away tonight?

I'm not sure.

I'll be at the usual place until nine thirty.

I make no promises. I'm being watched. I'll try to be there.

"An assignation!" I said, and whistled. Barker had not wasted his time.

"Yes, and a feminine hand. Unless I'm entirely mistaken, Pokrzywa had met the princess of whom Moskowitz had spoken."

"I wonder how long it had been going on."

"Three months, I'd say. The journal entries stopped, you see. I think not only did he wish to avoid setting down his feelings about a Christian-convert girl on paper, he also had nothing else to write about. It is not yet proven, but I believe we shall find that Louis Pokrzywa had given up most of his charity work and could generally be found in the girl's neighborhood, mooning under her window. The longer love tarries, the harder it strikes. After twenty-nine years, Louis was deeply smitten."

"Was it the girl Ben Judah mentioned seeing?" I asked. "Was the telegraph pole their 'usual place,' do you think?"

Barker shrugged his thick shoulders. "Who can say, at this point? But it certainly gives us a place to start."

"Where?"

"Why, Poplar, of course."

13

IN CHAPTER SEVEN OF MATTHEW, JESUS says, "Knock and the door shall be opened unto you." That technique did not work at the First Messianic Church of Poplar. No amount of knocking or knob rattling brought anyone forward to open the door. It was not a traditional church. More likely it had been a large shop, converted over for church usage. There was a faded silk banner over the shop's original sign, which bore the name of the church and the message, "If the Lord comes today, will you be ready?" The windows were large, but no amount of pressing my nose to them brought anyone out of the gloom. All I could see were rows of chairs and a makeshift podium. It was not exactly Saint Paul's.

"Do you see anything that says when services are held?" Barker asked, looking in as well.

"Yes, sir. There's a small card stuck to the window here. Sunday mornings at nine thirty, Sunday and Wednesday evenings at six thirty."

"Tomorrow night, then. Very well." He leaned against a lamp post and pulled some notes out of his coat. I think he carried a working office in his breast pocket.

"What have you got there?" I asked.

"These are the lists of anti-Semite speakers and organizations in London, provided by Brother Andy and the chief porter of the Tower. It's probable that one or more of them are members of the Anti-Semite League that murdered Pokrzywa."

I looked over his shoulder at the list.

"Good heavens," I said. "Most of them are pastors of churches."

"That is so. One is not five blocks from here. Shall we go and have a look?"

After ten minutes' walk east, we came upon a modest but venerable church. It was not old by London's standards, mid-seventeenth-century at the earliest. Looking around me at this decayed area east of the City, it was hard to imagine it new a century and a half ago, when this was the edge of town and the church looked out onto acres of empty pasture. Now the façade was crumbling, the stonework blackened with soot, and the board-covered windows were in need of a glazier. Across the entire front were hoardings explaining how the old building was receiving a reprieve:

> **Come hear the VERY REVEREND ALGERNON PAINSLEY preach from his immortal series, "THE WANDERING JEW" or "THE LOST TEN TRIBES OF DIASPORA" every Sunday in April at six P.M. You DARE not miss it!**

From the open doors of the church came the steady pounding of hammer and nail. Work was being done on a new platform for the altar, and I noticed as we stepped inside that the old and musty pews had been augmented with temporary chairs. Attendance must be picking up. I followed Barker down the aisle, as he inquired about the whereabouts of the Reverend Painsley. We found him pounding on the platform, as preachers are wont to do, but not generally with a claw hammer in their hand. He stopped at our approach, rolled down the sleeves of his shirt, and came forward to meet us.

"Good afternoon, gentlemen."

"Sir, we are reporters for the *Daily Dispatch,* and we are investigating the recent unrest among the Jews."

"I'll gladly help in any way I can, sirs," Painsley said. He had a square jaw, blue eyes, and straight, crisp hair the color of straw. A cursory glance told me the fellow was going places and that this crumbling church would not hold him for long. There was high color in his cheeks from his physical exertions, and the strong hand he extended toward me was hard and calloused.

"A terrible tragedy, gentlemen, this crucifixion, but not totally unexpected. The Jews are making things hot for themselves here, flooding in like a Mongol horde from Eastern Europe. I fear the citizenry has grown tired of the steady influx of foreigners, and taken matters into their own hands. It is a mistake, I believe, for our government to leave the drawbridge down for all the refuse of Europe. A worse group of dirty, illiterate communists, anarchists, nihilists, and atheists have never crossed our borders before."

"You have a way with words, if I may say, sir. Are you getting this down, Mr. Llewelyn? Do you believe the Jews have brought this action upon themselves in any way?"

I had never seen Barker play a role before. This pushy, inquisitive reporter was so unlike his normal self, I had to keep from smiling behind my notebook.

"I do," Painsley asserted. "This is a common pattern for the Jews. They move in, as refugees, and there is a general feeling of sympathy for them for a while among the public. Gradually, they prosper and begin to charge higher and higher interest rates, as their natural avarice begins to assert itself. The sympathy fades, eventually to be replaced by disgust. The disgust boils over into anger and violence, and the Jews are driven out. Look at Russia and Eastern Europe. Look at our own history. It shall happen here, again, gentlemen. Mark my works."

"Do you think there will be a pogrom, then, sir?"

"Of course. I mean, I hope not, but I fear it is inevitable."

"So you believe this murder to be the work of citizens justifiably angry at the Jews for usury, or for coming in and stealing jobs?"

"Not necessarily. It is possible the Jews did it themselves."

"Themselves?" Barker almost spat out, letting his mask slip for a moment.

"Yes. Is this the kind of murder an Englishman would commit? Certainly not! A Celt or a Teuton might kill in the heat of anger or a fatal stroke of passion, but remember, it was the Jews who crucified our Lord and Savior."

"Are you keeping up, Mr. Llewelyn? Don't miss a word, now. And why would the Jews crucify one of their own, Reverend Painsley?"

"To gain sympathy, I suppose," the reverend said, breezily. "Or some internal struggle. There are many kinds of Jews, all with their own petty squabbles and hatreds. They carry their feuds for centuries, you know."

"How dastardly." Barker shook his head. "So, if England were to shut its doors to the thousands of Jews arriving from Eastern Europe, where would they go?"

"If the civilized countries were to close their borders, they would have no choice but to return to the oriental countries from whence they came, and through hardship, privation, and war, gradually reduce the seething mass to a more manageable size."

"That would certainly decrease the population," Barker said. "But what of the Jews that have been here for hundreds of years?"

"It was a mistake of Cromwell's to let them return in the

first place. London is the center of Christendom. No doubt the nobility was seduced by the prosperous Jewish merchant families and their millions of pounds. Now they are marrying into English families, even into the aristocracy. I can only hope that succeeding generations shall water down this strain until the dominant Teutonic blood overwhelms it."

"But what of Jesus, sir?" I blurted out. "Wasn't he a Jew?"

The fellow smiled condescendingly. "Not really, Mr., er, Llewelyn, was it? He was the 'New Man.' Can you picture him as a hook-nosed, kinky-haired, furtive little fellow? Of course not! He was a big, bluff carpenter, a robust leader of men, a man's man. He was the perfect specimen of manhood, and in all ways we should aspire to be like him. Gentlemen, I don't like turning away a group of hungry and desperate wretches any more than you. It does not seem Christian, I know. But sometimes, one must do the hard thing, when one knows it to be right."

He sounded so logical, so convincing, that it seemed impossible that he was talking about the deaths by slow starvation and exposure of tens of thousands.

"Bravo!" Barker said, clapping the fellow on the shoulder. "Thank you, sir, for your time and your learned opinions. Look for an article in tomorrow's *Dispatch.*"

"Certainly, gentlemen," the Reverend Painsley said, flashing us a set of perfect teeth. "Thank you."

Barker led me back through the aisles to the entrance. Once outside, he turned immediately to his left and punched the brick three times, until his knuckles were red. The sound was drowned out by the hammering inside. He grimaced, and his teeth looked as ferocious as an angry lion's.

"Such a pathetic mixture of half-truths, twisted logic, and outright lies I have never heard in all my born days. Of all the creatures in the garden, the serpent was the most subtle. Hook-nosed? Kinky-haired? Mongol hordes? Natural avarice? It's a wonder I didn't seize the fellow by the limbs and toss him the length of the sanctuary. I'm going to keep an eye on that man. He wants to make Christ over in his likeness, not the other way round."

"He's not alone there," I noted. "How often have you seen pictures of a flaxen-haired, blue-eyed Christ?"

"More times than I can stomach at the moment. Jesus was a Jew from the line of David. Those paintings make him look like Siegfried from a Wagnerian opera. New Man, indeed! They look upon Christ as the first of a super race, the Aryan race, who must watch over their 'inferiors' and exterminate them, if necessary. Have you ever heard such distorted history? He makes it sound like the Jews sit in their ghettoes, plotting the domination of the world."

"Do you think he actually believes this nonsense?" I asked.

Barker nodded. "You know, I wondered that myself. He got himself appointed to an old church, and now, through preaching vitriol against the Jews, he's revitalized it. He could have a new church in the West End a year from now. He may go far, and I have nothing to fight him with, legally. He's riding a lie to achieve power. And he's just the first on the list. Damn and blast!"

"Who's next?" I asked, hoping to assuage his sudden temper.

"A fellow in Chelsea. That's too far. Here's one in Camden. Ah, yes. Mr. Brunhoff, the Anglo-Israelite. I haven't crossed swords with him for several months. Capital, provided we can find a cab or omnibus to take us there."

We did indeed find an omnibus heading east as fast as a pair of draft horses could pull us. After Racket's fleet vehicle, the pace seemed maddeningly slow, but it allowed us to talk.

"Now, if I've got this right, an Anglo-Israelite is a Jewish person who was born in this country."

"No, lad," Barker corrected, "That's an Anglo-Jew. An

Anglo-Israelite is something utterly different. Are you familiar with your Old Testament?"

"Tolerably, sir," I said. "I've studied the book as a schoolboy."

"You know that God set aside the Jews as a 'peculiar people,' a race chosen to have a special relationship with Him, and with whom He made an eternal blood covenant. The Anglo-Israelites believe that this 'mantle' of being the chosen race has fallen on the shoulders of the Aryan races, notably the British, and to a lesser extent the Germans and Americans."

"Why do they believe that?" I asked. "What makes them think the English and Americans are the new chosen people?"

"Remember the old legend about Joseph of Arimathea coming to England?"

"You mean the 'Stone of Scone' and all that?"

"Correct. The story goes that after Christ's death, Joseph brought the holy relic, the rock upon which old Jacob lay his head, to England, where it now sits under the coronation chair. As proof of the transfer of grace, God sent King Arthur and his Round Table after the Holy Grail, the chalice Jesus drank from at the Last Supper."

"If so," I said, with a smile, "then it never reached the English at all. Arthur was a Welshman at Tintagel. It's the Welsh that are the chosen people, not this Anglo-Saxon lot."

"Ha!" I'd actually made Barker laugh. "Don't be cheeky, lad. Actually, you've shown the problem in microcosm. The entire thing is all about nationalism, and you know how that is sweeping across Europe. Being 'chosen' gives people license to do just about anything they like, from expanding into other countries' territory, to wiping out undesirable people within one's own borders. And the more a country prospers, the more they feel that God is on their side, and the more arrogant they become. In America, they call it 'Manifest Destiny,' this idea that all they do is ordained by God."

"So the Jews are still the chosen people?" I asked, somewhat doubtfully.

"If you are a Christian, you must believe it so, because the Bible never contradicts it. A blood covenant is eternal. God never changes. I know it's more congenial to think we are the chosen people, but one can't build a strong biblical case for it."

"Then how can these Anglo-Israelites go around preaching it?"

"My dear Llewelyn, you have a naive side, if I may say it. People don't read their Bibles. They hire pastors to preach to them. And some pastors will preach total nonsense if it will tickle the congregations' ears enough to open their purses. There are some very rich and very gullible people in the Reverend Mr. Brunhoff's church. And they'll defend the delusions he's indoctrinated in them to the death."

We got off the omnibus and traveled a block or two before coming up to another church. It still seemed strange to me, looking for a group of killers among a church congregation. I would characterize this as a neither-nor church: neither rich nor poor, neither old nor new, neither high church nor low. The name, the Universal Church of the New Jerusalem, was one of those nonconformist titles that make Church of England people uncomfortable, only one can't say exactly why. Barker plunged into the building, going up one hallway and down another, while I bobbed along in his wake. Eventually, he found the church office and the Reverend Brunhoff.

"Not one more step, Mr. Barker!" the preacher thundered, rising from his desk at the first sight of my employer. "Get out of my church!"

"It is good to see you again, Mr. Brunhoff," Barker said politely, as if the man had invited him in for tea. "Have you been doing well since last we spoke?"

"Do you mean, since you last accused me in front of Scotland Yard?" Brunhoff was a stocky bulldog of a fellow, with a Prussian haircut and heavy jowls. He wore a plain black suit with the cleric's badge of office, a white tie.

"We briefly suspected him of being behind the desecration of a synagogue a year ago," Barker said to me, conversationally, as if the threatening preacher were not even there. "That was the first case I handled for the Board of Deputies, of which you heard Sir Moses speak. It turned out to be the work of a Jewish atheist." He turned back to face Brunhoff. "We're investigating the murder and crucifixion of a Jewish teacher not half a mile from here."

"I was innocent of the former charges, and I am innocent of these as well!"

"Prove it, then," Barker said. "Provide me with an alibi for early Sunday morning, and I'll have no reason to darken your door again."

"I will!" the preacher cried. "By the heavens, I will!"

Barker looked about. "I see your little church is about the same," he said. "You know, young Mr. Painsley's is growing mightily. He's adding chairs and building a new platform. I hope he's not taking some of your membership away from you. I'd hate to see you have to shut the place up."

I saw that Barker had struck a nerve. Brunhoff looked ready to choke in his tight collar. "You go to the devil!"

"Thank you, no," my employer answered urbanely. "I'd prefer Abraham's bosom, myself, after seeing this pox on the city's hide shut down forever. Send me an ironclad alibi and I'll let you alone. Come, Llewelyn." We left the preacher near apoplexy.

Outside, John Racket and Juno were sitting patiently at the curb.

"You manhunters need a ride?" he asked laconically.

"Take Thomas back home," Barker called out. "But first, drive me over to the mission in Mile End!" He turned to me. "I'm sparring with Brother Andrew tonight and taking him out to a chophouse he favors. Presumably, the chops will not have been held to someone's eye."

I spoke up, hoping I wouldn't be getting the cook in trouble. "Are you that particular? Mr. Dummolard thinks you have no taste buds."

"Ah, so you've met Etienne. Does he, by Jove? I admit, I'm not much of a gourmand, but I know good food when I taste it. I simply don't rate it as high in importance as he. I've lived on some of the worst food imaginable, aye, and starved as you have in my younger days. I make it a rule never to complain when food is set in front of me. So the answer to your question is no, I am not particular."

We came to a stop in Mile End, and Barker was out and off without a word. Racket's little trap opened up above me, and he looked down at me. "Shall I take you straight to the Elephant, sir, or do you want to stop somewheres first?"

"Home is fine," I said. Presumably Dummolard had returned to normal cooking and had stopped trying to poison us. I might get a decent dinner for a change. Then I realized what I'd said. I'd called Barker's residence "home." My parents still lived in Wales, outside of Newport, but I had long since stopped calling Wales home. Oxford Castle certainly didn't deserve the name, nor did my former rooms in Clerkenwell. But my new room at Barker's residence, was that home? I sat back against the plush cushions of Racket's cab and pondered the question. That is why the bullet that passed through the cab, shattering the window and spraying glass everywhere, didn't pass through my head as well.

14

I WAS STILL SITTING THERE, WIDE-EYED, when the trap opened overhead and Racket's anxious face looked down at me.

"Mr. Llewelyn! Tell me you're not dead!"

"I'm all right!" I called. "I wasn't hit!" There was a sudden violent wrench to the entire hansom and I heard the sound of footsteps. Racket had dismounted and was running somewhere. Juno looked back at me, her eyes white with fear. By the rippling along her withers I could tell she'd been terrified by the shot. I thought for a moment she might bolt, taking me with her, but she'd been trained well. She didn't move a step while her master was away from the cab.

As for myself, I was in shock and covered in glass. I looked to my right, where the small portal was nothing but shards, then looked to my left, where a tiny hole perforated the elegant scarlet padding. I raised a hand to my cheek, and it came away with blood. I'd been cut by a sliver of glass. Suddenly, I wanted to laugh, laugh loud and hard at cheating death, but I mastered myself. If Juno could do it, so could I.

Racket came back, winded from his exertions. He stepped up on the footboard and surveyed the damage.

"Oh, my cab!" he said, almost in tears. "Oh, my beautiful, beautiful cab! What has he done to ye, old girl?"

"Did you see the man who did it?"

"I did. He was a great big fella with a loud suit and a black beard. I think he looked Italian. He put the pistol back in his pocket and light-footed it down the street. Thought I'd catch up with him, but he just disappeared. Crikey! I'll have to patch this up, temporary like. The window's easy to fix, but I'll need all new wood and fabric for this side. One hole and it never looks right, you know. You have to replace the whole panel. He couldn't just break the glass. No, not him! He has to damage the woodwork!"

The fellow was talking about cab repair one minute after I'd just narrowly missed spattering his cab with my brains.

"I'm covered in glass, Mr. Racket," I pointed out. "Is there somewhere nearby I can get cleaned up?"

"My stable ain't more than a mile from here. You sit tight, and I'll have you good as new in fifteen minutes. Then, I'll take you home and send word to your boss. He'll get that blighter. Nobody shoots at Racket's cab and gets away with it."

I sat in a daze, still covered in glass. Through the shattered window, I heard the rubber tires humming along the road. The thought occurred to me that my assailant might have an accomplice waiting to finish me off. I became convinced that I was in imminent danger of a second bullet's tearing through the cab, and that this one wouldn't miss. Like most fears, it was groundless. Without any further mishaps, we arrived.

Racket's stable was in the Minories in Aldgate, not far from the Tower. The cabman opened the large double doors, then led Juno in by the bridle. It was dark and silent inside, and restful on my jangled nerves. Racket crossed to the far end and pushed open another set of doors, allowing light to stream in. Then he came back and helped me out of the hansom.

"We'll have you right as rain in no time, Mr. L.," he said,

taking a brush to my suit. "Wisht I could say the same for my cab."

"This is a nice stable you have here," I said. It was built of old beams and had a high ceiling with a loft. Fresh hay was strewn over the floor, and a couple of stalls had rope, harnesses and tack hanging from hooks. I stepped over to the open back doors. Instead of a mews, there was a drop of twenty feet down to tracks belonging to the underground.

Racket lay a heavy hand on my shoulder, and I jumped, almost precipitating down onto the tracks below.

"Watch your step," he said. "You just missed one killing."

"This is a bit dangerous here, don't you think?" I asked.

"I ain't fallen yet," Racket responded, looking down with me. "It's handy being so close to the rails. I can hoist hay bales into the loft direct from the wagons below, and I've got a hook in front as well and can lift bales from the street. The rent's low, and I can reach the West End in a matter of minutes. Lend me a hand here?"

Between the two of us, we lifted a panel of raw wood from a pile of lumber and eased it into the cab. I held it while Racket hammered it into place with some stout nails. Then I brushed the glass out of the cab while he fed Juno a bucket of oats to soothe her a little.

"We're almost done here. I'll have you home in half an hour. 'Struth. The strain-and-strife will have all kinds of words to say when she sees the state of this here cab."

"Where did you say your wife was?"

"The missus is in Dover, looking after her ailing mum. I been using the time to work extra hours while she's gone. I've even been sleeping here o' nights. Don't hardly seem worth it, going home with her gone."

Racket judged the cab serviceable, and within the prescribed half hour, he deposited me at Barker's front door in Newington.

"What happened?" Maccabee asked at the front door. He was wearing half-moon spectacles perched on his elegant nose. I informed him about the shooting. He took off the spectacles and tapped them on his other wrist for a moment, deep in thought.

"Why don't you sit down in the front room here while I poke about," he said. "I believe we've got a bottle of restorative somewhere on the premises."

He led me into the sitting room and left me in an easy chair. I had glanced into the room once or twice but had never been seated in it before. Most of the furniture was Chinese or Anglo-Indian, lacquer and rattan with lots of pillows and potted palms. The wallpaper looked like it had been stenciled in gilt with peacock feathers.

Mac glided in with an oversized balloon glass containing an opaque liquid the color of café au lait.

"What's this?" I asked, suspiciously.

"Brandy and milk, sir. It will help calm your nerves."

I hazarded a sip. I've never been much of a drinker of spirits, but it seemed to me the mixture was particularly vile. At Mac's insistence, however, I drank it down.

"Wonderful, sir. Are you hungry? No? Perhaps you should go upstairs and rest a while. I must say you are getting on famously. Less than one week! It took Mr. Quong months before his first . . . uh . . . experience."

Usually I would have come back with some retort after such a remark, but it wasn't in me at the moment. Once in my room, I undid my collar and tie, removed my jacket and shoes, and slid my braces from my shoulders. I lay down on the bed and slid into a fitful slumber.

I awoke several hours later. The room was dark, save for a shaft of moonlight coming in from the back window. The silver beam illuminated my employer, who sat in my desk chair by the window, fiddling with some coins in his hands. He was deep in thought, as far as I could tell. What had brought him here? Ah, yes. The shooting. I'd almost forgotten. Was he standing guard? If so, he was a little late.

"What o'clock is it?" I asked.

"Almost ten," he responded. "How do you feel?"

I sat up, and swung my stockinged feet over the side of the bed. "I feel fine, sir," I said. "Why do you ask?"

"You've just been shot at," he growled.

"Yes, but they missed. I'm fine, really."

He sat for a moment, manipulating one of the coins through his fingers like a conjurer. "You're dissembling," he decided. "I'm taking you off the case."

"Why, sir?" I asked. "Have I not given satisfaction?"

"It's too dangerous for an untrained man."

"Begging your pardon, but until today, the only danger I encountered was barking a shin in the tunnel on the way to Ho's. 'Some danger involved in performance of duties' was clearly printed in the advertisement. I didn't enter your employment merely to push papers about."

"You entered my employment because you were desperate. I could see it in your eyes."

"Yes, sir, I was, but you hired me, and I accepted the position. You can't change the rules of the game now."

"It's not a game, Thomas. I came within a hairbreadth of losing an assistant this afternoon."

"Of course, it's your decision, but I don't believe I should be penalized because of the last fellow," I said bitterly.

"You know about Quong, then," he stated.

"Yes, sir, though you've been at some pains to keep it from me."

Barker ran his fingers through his hair. Then he began tapping his pockets for his pouch. He filled and lit his pipe. I watched the smoke drift through the permanently open window. "Quong was a good man, and a good assistant," he said, blowing out his match. "Being Chinese, he couldn't go everywhere, but he had a knack for being unobtrusive and silent. His death three months ago was a blow. I had to tell his father that he had died. I'd rather not have to do that again."

"How did he die?"

"I sent him out on a routine assignment, following a merchant—a merchant of all things! He never came back. His body washed up on the Isle of Dogs two days later. One bullet between the eyes. The merchant knew nothing; he wasn't even aware he'd been followed! The case is still unsolved. I've followed lead after lead. Quong was like a son to me. Don't believe my advertisements, that I solve every case that comes my way."

"You blame yourself for his death."

"Mea culpa."

"Sir, London is a dangerous place, but you didn't send him on a dangerous mission. It was routine work. His getting shot was just . . . random."

"But today was not. You were almost assassinated. I shouldn't have left you alone. You're still new."

"Mr. Barker, I know I'm new, but I'll be all right. I survived eight months in Oxford Prison and I've lived through today so far. I may be as green as Ireland, but I'm a grown man. Heaven knows I've made a grown man's mistakes already. I realize now how serious this work can be and I shall endeavor to be more careful in the future. But you cannot solve this case and be occupied with my safety at the same time. You can't ride one ass to two fairs."

Barker gave another of his wintry smiles. "Where did you pick up that one?"

"It was in one of your Jewish books, sir."

"I still don't like it," Barker said between puffs, but I could see he was wavering.

"Well, I prefer not to be shot at, but I suppose an assistant to a private enquiry agent would be subject to the same dangers as his employer. I accept that, and so should you."

He stood, extended his pipe out the small open space in the window, and knocked the ash from the bowl. Then he carefully wrapped the pipe and tobacco up in the sealskin pouch and returned it to his pocket.

"Agreed," he said, and turned to leave. He was almost out the door, in that way of his, when I made a sound in my throat. He stopped and turned, inquiringly.

"Nothing, sir," I said. "A minor annoyance. I've slept hard these few hours. I shall probably be up all night now."

"Try the library," he suggested.

"We have a library? Where?"

"You're the private enquiry agent's assistant. Find it yourself."

I accepted the challenge. There were only a few doors in the house I hadn't tried. The two on the first floor turned out to be a guest room and a lumber room respectively. That left two on the ground floor. The first, hard by the front door, I took to be Mr. Maccabee's personal domain, which only left the one by the back door, across the hall from the kitchen. My deduction was correct.

The door was ajar, so I stepped in, turned up the gas, and looked about. The room had built-in bookcases on all sides, from floor to ceiling. Two comfortable chairs in studded green leather flanked an Arabian octagonal table, with an oil lamp. There was a fireplace in marble, with a fendered grate, and a faded Persian carpet that dominated the room in an abstract design of red and green. A ladder on rollers navigated most of the shelves, by means of a circular track. It was all a bibliophile could want. I ran a finger along one shelf, and it came away clean. Mac must dust the shelves weekly.

I haven't mentioned the books, of course. Hundreds of

books, thousands, in fact. Any subject, any language; novels, philosophy, classics, language primers, and instructional books on just about everything. There was a shelf full of manuscripts, another of ragged scrolls, and a third fronted with glass to preserve the ancient volumes therein. I settled on Eliot's *Daniel Deronda,* as I thought it might be pertinent to the case, and was just about to sit down when there was a warning growl from behind me. I was about to sit on Harm. I let dozing dogs lie and moved to the other chair.

I was almost immediately engrossed in the book and was coming to the part when Daniel comes into the casino and inadvertently makes Gwendolen lose her money, when the door burst open. It was Mac, in a pajama sleeping suit and robe. He had his shotgun in hand, but all form of menace was gone for he (oh, how priceless) was wearing a silk hair net.

"Oh, it's you," he said, simply.

"Yes. Barker woke me, and I couldn't get back to sleep. I thought I might try reading."

"Of course."

I was aching to mention the net, but I controlled myself. "Thank you for the brandy and milk. It did the trick."

"Not at all, sir." It came to him suddenly. He ripped the net off his head and stuffed it into a pocket of his gown. "I'll leave you to your reading then. *Deronda,* is it? Did the Guv suggest it?"

"No, I chose it on my own. Is it a good book, from your point of view?"

"Oh, yes. Not bad, really, for a Gentile author." He let me alone after that. There are some people one can get along with immediately, and some that one never shall. I began to think Mac might be one of the latter. At first, I had assumed it was because he was Jewish, but I'd gotten along well enough with Zangwill and Moskowitz. No, I decided it was just Mac.

Around midnight the rest and reading had settled my spirit

enough that I was hungry again. Harm and I decided to raid the larder. It proved to be a roomy cupboard in the kitchen with louvered doors and shelves stacked to the ceiling. Dummolard went in for glass-domed servers; there must have been a half dozen. I saw mutton pie, game pie, some sort of quiche covered with rashers of bacon, and a venison stew. The dog and I agreed on the quiche.

Considering how cold and aloof Harm had been to me over the last week or two, I was amazed at the sudden transformation in him. He now wanted to be my best friend. While I searched for a plate and silverware, the Pekingese began making aerial leaps a Chinese acrobat would envy. When I sat down with my slice, he stood beside my knee on his back limbs, waving his paws and gurgling like a baby. What can one do after such a performance? I split the pie with him, then we mutually agreed we needed a second slice. After that, we each had some water and went back to reading. That is, I went back to reading while he dozed in the other chair.

I must confess I thought him useless as a watchdog, snoring in the chair as he was. At less than a stone, he didn't meet my standards in regard to size, though my ankles attested to the sharpness of his teeth. I noticed, however, that at the slightest sound, the settling of the house, perhaps, or a late-night cab passing through the Elephant and Castle Circle outside, he woke from his slumbers and looked about with those goggly eyes of his. The little dog taught me a lesson about Barker, and all the satellites that revolved around him: they may look harmless enough, and perhaps even a trifle ridiculous, but there are hidden abilities behind the outward appearance. Did I dare hope that the same could be said of me?

15

IT WAS NOT A GOOD MORNING. DUMMOLARD made me coffee and an omelet in the kitchen, but neither of us was in a garrulous mood. He moved about, the stump of a cigarette in his teeth, ready to bite off my head at the first comment. I'd had a small disagreement with my employer the night before, had not endeared myself to the butler, and now I was in danger of angering the cook.

Barker came down the stairs, as steady as the eight twenty from Brighton. He greeted me formally and led me outside to the curb. Racket at least had a smile for me, though Juno seemed unimpressed. Perhaps she associated me with the shot last night. The new glass and patch on the woodwork of the cab were as evident as Racket had predicted. Barker and I rode to the office in Craig's Court in relative silence. He asked but one question.

"How's *Deronda* coming along?"

"Fine, sir. How did you know I was reading it?"

"I saw the book on your table just now before I came down," he responded.

"Is it all right for me to borrow it?"

"The library is open to you, lad."

In the office, I felt more like an actor than an agent's assistant. I hadn't sat at my desk more than once or twice, hadn't used any of the materials in the top drawers, and hadn't even opened the bottom ones.

Barker drafted a letter to a *Sûreté* inspector in French. Then we attempted a letter to a retired criminologist in Vienna but bogged down completely. I didn't know a word of German, and when he wrote down a word for me, I couldn't read his horrid scrawl. We agreed to send it in English and hope that the old duffer could find a translator.

Finally, Barker finished his office business, or perhaps he merely took pity on me, and we climbed into another cab. Barker yelled "Chelsea" over our heads, and we were off.

"What is in Chelsea?" I asked.

"Aesthetes," he responded. I had read in *The Times* how that district of the West End was rapidly filling up with artists, poets, authors, and let us not forget the wealthy female patrons who feted them. In drawing rooms there, Mr. Whistler was slinging paint for all he was worth, and the arbiters of taste and fashion walked those gilded streets. I noticed a picturesque fellow in a velveteen suit leaning against a building, looking as if he had barely enough energy to smoke the cigarette that hung limply between his thick lips.

We disembarked in front of a fashionable-looking residence in Cheyne Row, with a brass doorknocker in the form of a sunflower. Our rap brought to the door a Sikh manservant in a suit and a turban of an unrelieved peach color, which in no way diminished his fierce appearance. He took our card and led us through an overdecorated hall, awash in Liberty wallpaper and heavy furniture. He carried our card into a room and emphatically closed the door behind him. After a moment, he opened it again, bowed, and ushered us in. The room was a book-crammed study, filled mostly with classics, less modern and more academic than the outside of the residence would lead one to expect. A white-haired gentleman sat at his desk, scribbling away at his journal. He set down his pen and turned at our approach. I was unprepared for his appearance. It was Walter Rushford, my old tutor from Oxford.

I had read in the newspaper that he was settled now here in London, probably in the same article about the aesthetic movement. A wag therein had called him "Old Nebuchadnezzar," after the Babylonian king from Daniel, for at the pinnacle of his fame and genius, with his books flying out of the bookshops, and with invitations to speak the length and breadth of England, he had suddenly gone quite thoroughly mad. Some called it a brainstorm brought on by overwork, some a natural extension of his genius, and others a punishment for his radical beliefs. No one would say exactly what form this madness took (perhaps he ate grass like his biblical predecessor), but the outcome was swift: he was quietly sent to a sanitarium outside of London. Now that I found myself confronted with him, I was busy worrying that he would recognize me, and wondering what he would say when he did.

"Good morning, gentlemen," he said, graciously. "May I be of service to you?"

"You may, sir, you may," my employer began. "I am Cyrus Barker, and this is my assistant. We'd like a word, if possible."

"Certainly. Won't you be seated?"

We sat. I took a moment to surreptitiously observe my old professor. Though he was only in his late forties, his hair had gone white during his stay in the asylum. All his faculties seemed to be still with him, however, and he appeared hale and hearty for all his recent misfortunes. He turned a curious eye my way, and I could see that he recognized me but couldn't exactly place me. One could see him going through filing cabinets in his mind, looking for my picture. I hoped, for my sake, that the filing room had been overturned enough that one file in particular had been lost forever.

"Mr. Rushford," Barker said. "A few nights ago a young Jew was murdered in Aldgate—crucified, in fact—by a group calling itself the Anti-Semite League. Have you ever heard of such an organization?"

"No, sir, I have not."

"I have been retained to discover the identities of the men responsible for this crime, and I am leaving no stone unturned. You, sir, are one of the stones."

"Me? Surely you're not implying that I had anything to do with the matter?" he asked.

"No, sir, I merely came to solicit your aid in my investigation. It is true, is it not, that you are an exponent of the science of eugenics, that you are in fact its most vocal exponent?"

The scholar got up to pace. "I don't know about that. Sir Francis Galton invented the science, and he still lives. I wholeheartedly believe in it, and I speak my mind when I believe in a cause. I am a philosophical eugenicist; that is to say, I believe some races are genetically inferior to others and must be governed by those more capable. Our superiority is what has made us a world empire. But I would not call for the destruction of other races, not even one little Jew. Certainly I would not be part of an organization that committed such an atrocity."

"Perhaps not, sir," Barker continued, "but in one of your published essays you claimed that were the Jews to be assimilated into the general population, they would produce a race which was 'physically stunted, mentally decayed, and morally corrupt.' What solution do you propose?"

The professor shrugged his shoulders. "None at all. Not for the Jews that are already here. But I think we should shut our borders. I don't object to Jews, and I know many, but I do not wish my country inundated with them. Close to a hundred thousand have arrived here in the past few years. They are uneducated and superstitious, little better than animals. Some are criminal, and some are insane. The East End is already rife with other disasters: the Irish, the Italians, even the Cockneys. It's like some terrible melting pot, producing a noxious brew."

"But, sir," Barker continued, "are you not concerned that your published philosophical musings may encourage your readers to take the crusade into their own hands? We mustn't forget the hysteria in 1291 that resulted in the Jews' being driven out of England. Do you wish that to happen again?"

My old tutor looked at us hard. "I do. I hope it is as bloodless as possible, but I agree with it. We are dealing with issues larger than ourselves: a people, nay, an organism defending itself against contamination. We are seeing one of Darwin's principles at work, that of natural selection. I cannot help you, gentlemen. I cannot interfere."

"Mr. Rushford," Barker continued, "We have not come here today to debate race or religion with you. Names, sir! I need the names of possible members of the Anti-Semite League. I'll concede that to your way of thinking, a pogrom is a naturally occurring phenomenon. But we have a mob of citizens taking a man off the street and crucifying him from a telegraph pole in the middle of the City. That is—"

"Madness?" Rushford drew himself up to his full height and grasped the lapels of his coat, as he once did while pontificating. "I think I am a better judge of madness than you, having so recently escaped it. It is not madness to want the best for one's people. Even now, in Limehouse, the blooms of English womanhood are walking arm in arm with Chinese men. In Soho, they are fawning over Negro minstrel singers from America. It is not madness to wish to safeguard our women and ourselves!"

Barker responded calmly. "We have gotten off track. What of these killers? Will you help us, or will you side with murderers?"

Rushford looked down at the floor for a moment, debating in his head between his beliefs and his disinclination to see blood spilt.

"No, no, no, I cannot help you," he said finally. "If the blood of one Jew may stem the tide of thousands washing in, it has served a purpose. I am not acquainted with anyone whom I believe capable of doing such a deed, and I do not countenance murder, but I will not stop nature from taking its course. Do you know that the Royal Army is complaining that the average recruit is much smaller than a generation ago? Look at this little fellow here." He gestured toward me.

My cheeks burned at the insult. "Sir, I am of a very pure Welsh strain."

Barker gently took my arm. "Llewelyn, it is time for us to leave."

"Llewelyn?" My old tutor pounced on the name. "Thomas Llewelyn, is that you? Of course it is! Well, well, so this is where you finally washed up. I might have known, since no respectable employer would have you. How does it feel to be one of the hounds instead of the fox? I hope your time in jail proved . . . educational."

"More so than Burberry Asylum, apparently, Professor," I retorted. "They let you out too early. You're still as mad as a hatter."

"We were just leaving," Barker rumbled, manhandling me across the room. "Thank you for your time."

I looked over at the tall Sikh, who stood by the door glowering at us. He escorted us out and slammed the door behind us.

"Why the deuce didn't you tell me you knew the fellow?" my employer demanded at the curb.

"If you didn't insist on keeping our every destination as secret as the road to El Dorado, I would have done so. You might have realized the possibility, given that we were both at Oxford. To think I once admired the man! I had signed copies of his essays and poetry. If I had them now, I'd burn them in the dustbin!"

"Thomas, I must ask you to follow my lead," Barker insisted. "You are still untrained and can cause setbacks in my investigations. As it is, I was forced to take you out of there before I had the answers to a few more questions."

"I'm sorry, sir. I'm afraid I had a problem with Rushford. I think I can reasonably state that it won't happen again, unless we suddenly move the investigation to Oxford."

"What do you think of him as a suspect?" Barker asked, nodding in the direction of the house.

"Oh, I think he's an excellent candidate. He despises being out of the limelight, and these new theories of his are controversial enough to get him back in the newspapers and journals. He is still mad; he's just traded obsessions."

"Perhaps you are a trifle prejudiced, but I agree. We cannot rule him out as a suspect."

"He is mad," I insisted. "All these eugenicists are mad."

"No, Thomas, people are like teapots. They need to let out a little steam from time to time. The citizens of London are genuinely worried about the influx of so many aliens; they feel powerless to stop it, so of course, they complain. Complaining is the only civilized form of regress. Crucifixion, on the other hand, is a barbaric form of torture that should have been left in the first century. It is the work not of civilized people but of madmen."

16

FANCY A SPOT OF LUNCH, LAD?" BARKER asked after we returned to the cab. It was nearing noon.

"Ho's?" I asked, glumly. I was beginning to dread the place. Good as it was, I didn't think I could live on a thrice weekly diet of shark's fin soup or the like.

"No, something different," my employer answered, to my relief. He rapped on the trap with his cane. "The Neopolitan, in Marsham Street! Ever eaten Italian food?"

"No. Is it spicy?"

"Well, it's not Etienne's Scottish feast, if that's what you prefer."

We crossed London again. For a Scot, Barker had certainly hugged the town to his bosom. He had a cosmopolitan's knowledge of the whole of the town and thought nothing of crossing it to get to a particular restaurant or public house. We finally found the establishment in Westminster, a respectable-looking building with a façade in dark mahogany and marble. The restaurant's name was in gold letters, flanked by two Italian flags, which, on closer inspection, I could see were actually enameled tin.

Inside, we found checkered floors, white tablecloths, and

dripping candles in old Chianti bottles. The walls were cleverly painted to look like an old piazza in Naples, with red brick showing through crumbling plasterwork. A crack team of Italian waiters stood at the ready in crisp, starched white aprons and waxed mustaches. One of them detached himself from the others and solicitously led us to a table.

Barker ordered for us both: seafood for himself, and some sort of "sampler" fare for me. I had no idea what to expect and I was pleasantly surprised: vermicelli pasta noodles in a flavorful tomato sauce with some sort of white cheese. It was indeed spicy and garlic-laden, but not excessively so. As for Barker, his meal looked like it had been prepared in the galley of Captain Nemo's *Nautilus.* Yawning clamshells, mussels, and octopus tentacles predominated.

"What is this?" I asked, pointing to a breaded item on my plate that looked like fish but was clearly not.

"Aubergine," Barker murmured. "If you will take your face out of the trough for a moment, lad, let's play a little game. I contend that there are three men in this room who are armed, besides myself, of course. Let's see if you can come up with the same three, without appearing to look around."

Honestly, it's a wonder I didn't have a case of permanent dyspepsia. Was every place we went into full of conspirators and thugs? I was beginning to think the world had gone mad. Luckily for me, there were small, mirrored panels around the top of the room, in imitation of the Café Royale. I cleared my throat and brought the napkin up to my mouth.

"The fellow by the staircase," I muttered. He had a foot up on the second rail, and was resting his forearms against the banister, with an air of careless watchfulness.

"Obvious."

"The fellow in the far back by the door, with his chair up on two legs."

"Another guard. And the third?"

I took another bite of aubergine, though it had lost what subtle taste it had, and glanced about again.

"I can't find the third."

"Middle of the room, having a simple bowl of soup and a glass of Chianti. Brilliantined hair, pencil mustache, nicely dressed—"

"Got him. Do you know him?"

"Of course. That's Vittorio, or rather Victor Gigliotti, our host. He's paying for our meal. After we eat, we will pay our respects."

We finished and went to his table. He was a sharp-faced but handsome fellow, immaculately dressed in a dove gray lounge suit. His right hand was a mass of diamond rings and his left hand was bare. Barker and I waited as he addressed the bowl in front of him, and when he was done, he looked up.

"Gentlemen," he said, displaying a mouth of vulpine teeth. "How marvelous that you could come. Did you enjoy your meal?"

"The best in London, as always," Barker bowed.

"That is good, but your friend has a sour face. Perhaps we could get him a bromide."

"That won't be necessary. It is his first time to try Italian cuisine."

"Delicious," I put in. "Very rich."

"And he has not developed that fine sense of mingling pleasure with business. That is for more . . . experienced palates like our own."

"Indeed. But where are my manners? Have a seat, gentlemen. Antony! Bring for the young fellow a small *gelato*. Sometimes chilling the stomach can aid in digestion. Now, Mr. Barker, I am so glad you accepted my invitation. May I ask at this moment whether you are living up to your name?"

"I always live up to my name. Would you expect otherwise?"

"Naturally not. Would you be so kind as to place your weapon here on the extra chair, out of sight under this napkin?"

"I will not. Do you think me so naive as to hand you my pistol when there are four guns in this room able to be pointed at my head within three seconds?"

"Four?" I said, involuntarily. "I thought you said three."

"There is a scattergun under the front desk. Mr. Gigliotti, I promise you that I will not wave my pistol about and frighten the patrons of your excellent establishment unless I am standing in an absolute hail of bullets."

"Fair enough, Mr. Barker. May we get past the preliminaries? I understand from your letter, and I must say that Machiavelli himself could not have written a more subtle missive, that this little fellow here met with a mishap in a hansom cab yesterday, and that a witness tied the crime to one of my associates. A particular associate, in fact. You questioned whether the Italian community has some sort of grudge against the Jews and I will answer truthfully. We do. They come in and offer at a lower cost many of the services we provide. They are taking our work, our livelihood, and our housing. They are like locusts: unstoppable! But let me anticipate your next question. Do we, does the Italian community and any group that claims to protect it have any designs to harm the Jews? No, I don't believe so. Sooner or later we shall have to make an example, as one swats a puppy with a rolled-up newspaper, to teach them what is what, but the Jews are quick. They'll catch on."

"So," Barker said, "the Camorra has no interests in Aldgate."

Gigliotti's eyes grew big and the knuckles of his hand that held the wineglass were suddenly white.

"I don't know where you got that term, Mr. Barker, but I suggest you never use it in my presence again. I don't care how big a fish you are, there are bigger ones than you."

Barker smiled. "I like to swim with the big fish."

"A swim with the fishes in the Thames can be arranged within the hour!"

The men standing guard suddenly grew tense, and I feared there would be gunplay, but Barker gave a sudden shrug.

"Not necessary, sir. I think we understand one another. Forgive my . . . poor choice of words. I am so often among the rough element of my trade that I sometimes lose my tact."

"Apology accepted." The tension, or most of it, eased out of the room. "So, to the best of—"

There was a loud bang at the back of the room, which made everyone jump, and the fellow by the staircase reached inside his jacket. In the back, the other guard's chair had fallen, and a man was helping him up. Or so it appeared. But when the man was upright, it was obvious he wasn't conscious, and the individual who set him up again had just come in through the back door.

"Giorgio!" Gigliotti called and waved him toward us. He flashed those wolfish teeth at us again. "That fellow we were talking about, the one you believe shot at your little friend here—I thought you might like to question him yourself."

Now it was I who stood, ready to fly out of the door or defend myself at a second's notice. This was the man Racket had seen in the street who had attempted to murder me in cold blood. He was a big, stocky fellow, in a loud checked suit the color of Coleman's Mustard. His face was ruddy, and he had short, curly black hair and a beard. There was an air of menace and violence about him as he came toward us. He came right up to Barker, ignoring the rest of the room, and put a hand on his lapel. Barker looked up and regarded him.

"I hear you been looking for me," he said, in a high, reedy voice and, of all things, a Cockney accent.

"Good to see you again, Serafini," Barker said calmly.

"It ain't good seein' your ugly mug, Barker. It ha'n't been

near long enough. Word on the street says you're trying to frame me for something." As he spoke, I saw his thumb wander across my employer's throat and dig into the bundle of arteries and muscle in his neck. I watched the jugular vein stand out prominent and blue.

Barker appeared not to notice for a moment, and then casually, as if swatting at a fly, his hand came up and plucked the hand away. He twisted the hand around, facing its owner, then bore down on the wrist. Serafini frowned at the pain and attempted to turn his hand around again, but Barker had control of it. Serafini stepped back, but the Guv moved in the same direction, anticipating his every move. The Italian had no choice but to fall backward onto the hard tile. Barker stepped by him, still twisting the arm as he went, and rested his boot against the man's chest. Any move on Serafini's part would result in a separation at the shoulder joint.

"Give it up, Giorgio," Gigliotti purred. "You're hopelessly outclassed. You know Mr. Barker's reputation. Our friend here is the most scientific and the dirtiest fighter in England."

Barker didn't talk but hefted Serafini into a chair so violently that it skittered across the tile a foot. The man glared at my employer, and his face was now as red as a side of beef.

"I haven't said you did anything," Barker said. "I'm asking you. Were you paid to shoot at my assistant?"

"I was not," he said, sullenly.

"And did you shoot at him?"

"No, I didn't. I've never even seen this pipsqueak before. If I'm sent to kill someone, I kills 'em. I'm h'on the job every hour, day and night, until it's finished. I heard all about the little muck-up. If I'd missed the first shot, d'you think I'd run? No! I'd drop the cabman and come in and finish the job at my leisure. It don't matter if I'm seen. What can't be bought off can be warned off."

"There you have it, gentlemen," Gigliotti said, "the answer

to your question. You are dealers in logic, and the fact that this little fellow still lives is proof that the great Serafini did not try to kill him."

"Serafini don't *try* anyfing!" the assassin bellowed.

Barker stood. "Very well, gentlemen, you have convinced me. Mr. Serafini, please forgive any pain I may have caused you, emotionally and physically. I suggest ice for your . . . er . . . gun hand. As for you, Mr. Gigliotti, you are, as always, the consummate host. Excellent food, and ah! The fine entertainment. May we use your back door?"

Gigliotti waved a hand toward the rear and bawled over his shoulder, "Antony, forget the *gelato*. Bring Giorgio an espresso and some ice."

We left the restaurant, and I was never so glad to leave a place in my life. On the way out I noticed that the man at the back door was still unconscious. At least, I hoped he was just unconscious.

The alleyway was a simple and ancient lane with a sewer trough in the middle and two rows of anonymous doors. I sensed danger as soon as we stepped outside, and there was a movement in the shadows. I ducked, and just beside me came the sharp sound of metal against the rough brick of the wall. A long, thin dagger clattered at my feet.

"Round the corner, lad, now!" my employer barked. I didn't need a second invitation. There was a small figure approaching in the darkness of the alley. Barker made an abrupt movement, a sudden reaching motion toward it, and a shriek echoed through an alleyway, followed by a volley of curses in a high voice. I reached the street and turned into a shop front, awaiting developments. Barker appeared a moment later, as casually as you please, and began stuffing his pipe, scanning both sides of the street.

"Who was that?" I asked.

"Serafini's wife," came the unlikely response. "Serafini's a pussycat compared to the missus. You don't get one without the other, you know. The woman's practically feral."

"What did you do?"

"Oh, I gave her a lesson in kind. One shouldn't throw knives in public."

"You threw a knife at her?" I asked, incredulously.

"Of course not," he answered, with an air of innocence. "I merely gave her a token of my esteem."

"What is the Camorra?" I asked, remembering the name and its effect upon Gigliotti.

"It, or rather they are one of the crime families of Naples. Like their rivals, the 'Ndrangheta of Calabria and the Mafia of Sicily, they rode into power on the coattails of Garibaldi. They've divided the country into personal city-states, concentrating power like the Medicis."

I shook my head in wonder. "How did you come by the knowledge, if I may ask?"

"It is my duty to know it," he said, once his pipe was lit. "These societies have very long arms, reaching all the way to London, and anywhere else its immigrants go."

"So there's a headquarters of an Italian criminal organization in Westminster, but a stone's throw from Buckingham Palace? I can hardly believe it."

"Yes," Barker said, with one of his rumbling laughs. "London's a right raucous old lass when you get to know her, isn't she?"

17

WE WALKED FOR SEVERAL BLOCKS, WHILE my heart rate slowly returned to normal. Barker appeared to be moving to some purpose, for at one street, he pointed and began moving in another direction. We had reached Belgravia and were heading east, I think. Ornate shopwindows offered chocolates, jewelry, and all of the other baubles of a spoiled society. All was splendor and respectability here. It was hard to imagine that ten minutes ago a madwoman had thrown a dagger at me.

"Did she really mean to kill us?"

"That was no rubber knife she threw, Thomas."

"But if they're telling the truth, and it was some other chap dressed as Serafini, why did she throw the knife at me?"

"She's a vindictive little vixen and dangerous as a king cobra. I just humiliated her husband in there, and she dotes on the fellow."

We walked on for a minute or two, by the pretty shops full of books and millinery. I must admit I'd had some most interesting conversations since I began this case. "What was it you threw at her?" I asked my employer.

He reached into his coat pocket and placed a penny in my

hand. I was perplexed, until I noticed that the edges had been ground down to bladelike sharpness all around. I flipped the heavy coin into the air a time or two, and let it rest in the flat of my palm. "One of my calling cards," he stated.

"Can you hit a target with this?"

"As easily as a bullet. There were rough gangs in Foochow, where I grew up, and any coin or piece of metal that came to hand could become a weapon. We used to make rude targets out of boards and rice sacking and practice for hours."

"It sounds to me as if you had a very interesting childhood."

"Interesting enough, as childhoods go," he said, but I could get nothing further out of him on the subject.

"So where are we going now?"

"Jermyn Street, to look up an old acquaintance."

"Another of your 'watchers'?"

"No, lad, a suspect. Or, at least, I hope he is."

"You . . . hope?"

"I desperately hope. It is Nightwine."

"The explorer? I thought he was dead."

Barker shook his head. "Not Elias Nightwine, but his son, Sebastian. Perhaps you recall that the father, aside from his travels in Asia, wrote several books espousing what he called 'social atheism.' Something like, If there is no God, then to whom are we accountable, and how is society to be restructured in the new century? Anyway, he voiced these ideas up until his unfortunate demise in a hunting accident in Africa two years ago, leaving his son with a valuable estate just in time to pay off Sebastian's list of creditors and some gambling debts."

"Are you suggesting he may have killed his own father?"

"I'm suggesting that he has no respect for human life whatever. Any form of conscience was trained out of him by his father. He's one of the most dangerous men I've ever come across."

"Incredible," I said. "How does this fit in with the Jews?"

"As an avowed atheist, he has a strong aversion to the Bible and its people. More importantly, I've received information that he's consolidating power among the underworld in London, using extortion and other methods. He lives high and goes through money like water. Sooner or later, he'll try to frighten the Jews, who have a strong, conservative money base in the City. A public crucifixion is just the sort of grand display he'd attempt in order to spread fear among them. This is all speculation, of course, and were I to say it in public, I'd be swarming with solicitors in a trice, for he is litigious to a fault. Nevertheless, it rings true, as you shall see in a few minutes."

Jermyn Street is known for its boot makers and its bachelor apartments, and any up-and-coming young men on the Exchange or in the Home Office would be sure to have chambers there. Mr. Nightwine had not contented himself with a mere pied-à-terre, but had taken out an entire residence. His white brick housefront had an air of respectability about it, which was augmented by a solid-looking and phlegmatic butler, to whom Barker presented his card.

"If you gentlemen will wait here in the hall, I shall see if the master is in residence," he said, and left us to cool our heels.

Any air of solidity and British wholesomeness that the butler may have given the house departed with him when he left. The entrance was lined on all sides by graphic evidence of the master's worldwide travels. Glass eyes glared at us from all sides, framed within still forms that had once lived and breathed. Creatures from almost every continent stood in mute attitudes of menace, a silent tribute to the taxidermist's art. It was not the only home in London which bore testament to a fellow's prowess with a rifle, but it was the most singular. All of the animals in this menagerie were white.

Within their niches, polar bears, Siberian tigers, white wolves, and albino lions stood rampant. The heads of

American bison and African rhinoceroses of the same bleached hue stared blankly from the wall. It was unnerving, to say the least. Even Barker looked a trifle uncomfortable.

"Er, I forgot to mention, lad, that he is nominally a big-game hunter, though he makes his money at cards and speculation."

"Remarkable," I said. For a moment, I had the mental picture of their master coming in and, with one word, unleashing all these ungodly creatures to tear us apart. Instead, the butler returned and bowed to us.

"If you gentlemen will please follow me."

He led us down a more prosaic but opulent hall and finally ushered us through glass doors, into a large conservatory. Inside, the heat was oppressive and the lofty palm trees pressing against the panes high overhead gave a tropical jungle feeling to the room. Parrots and other birds, and even a monkey or two, screeched in the trees. A hammock was strung high above us, and a long, white, feline tail as thick as a rope waved lazily in the heat. The butler led us to a circle of cane chairs, where the master of the house was seated.

He was a tall, well-built man of about thirty years of age. I've seldom seen so broad a chest, and I couldn't help but think some rugby team would be glad of his assistance. His skin was bronze from the sun, save for a near snowy whiteness above his eyes and his upper lip, where hair grew. His blond mustache was waxed fashionably and his hair was thick with a tendency to fall forward, which he remedied by occasionally pushing it up with one hand. The most remarkable feature was his eyes, a deep golden color; they regarded you speculatively, as if you were prey. He was quick to smile, but it was a smile that left one cold. His hand rested on a small glass dome, the kind one uses for watches or trinkets. Altogether, it was as if someone had stuffed a tiger into a suit of clothes.

"Mr. Barker, what a pleasant surprise. Forgive me if I do not offer you my hand."

"Not at all. I would not take it," Barker responded.

"You almost missed me. I was just off to the club to play baccarat with the Prince of Wales. What brings you here? No, don't tell me. I have not been a witness to any crime lately, so I can only assume you are here to inform me that I am a suspect. What have I done this time? Stolen the crown jewels, perhaps, or deprived one of the Queen's grandchildren of its rattle?"

"Neither, Mr. Nightwine, though now that you mention them, I'll be sure to see that both are in order. No, I've come about the Jews."

"You mean that crucifixion business? Of course, I should have wondered when you'd get around to me. Was it symbolic, do you think, Mr. Barker? The atheist nails Christianity and Judaism to the cross a final time? Oh, big bad *me.* What a rotter I am. Very well, I confess. I did it. Put on your bracelets or your thumbscrews or whatever, and have me hauled off to Newgate. Another crime solved by the great enquiry agent."

Barker's cheeks were beginning to redden with emotion. He was just keeping his temper in check. "Spare me your attempts at humor. I'm barely worth the effort."

Nightwine's face fell, and there was a snarl on his lips. "I agree. Barker, the last thing I need to do is defeat the Jews. They are already defeated. Tiberius Caesar saw to that. As far as I am concerned, their presence in history has been merely a highly overemphasized footnote, thanks to that stupid little book they created. It's the biggest collection of fables and fairy stories ever written down, and its popularity only shows how anxious the low intellects of the world are to seize upon anything in which to believe. The Jews were an obscure people, and they are still. I would not waste my time on them."

Barker cleared his throat. "I need not mention how many millions of pounds in the Bank of England are in their hands, or what influence they have in this City. You always need money, especially with the little business enterprise you've got going in the East End. Have the Jews proven obstinate to your plan to extort money? Did you need to set an example, perhaps?"

"If I did, I certainly wouldn't sign it with that hackneyed Anti-Jewish League, or whatever they call themselves. There would be no doubt from whence came the threat. Besides, the Jews know their place. One word from me in the proper ears and I could make it quite intolerable for them. But as I said, they do not interest me, and they won't unless your continued persecution causes me to make an example of them."

Just then he took his hand away from the glass dome. Inside was one of those ghastly native trophies, a shrunken head, its eyes and lips sewn shut. Pale hair sprouted from the upper lip and connected to the side-whiskers. It had once been a white man, some poor chap going out to the colonies to seek his fortune.

"Your little girlfriend looks faint," Nightwine said. "I suggest you take her home."

I sat up in my cane chair. I knew he was merely trying to bait me, but it almost worked. My first instinct was to go over to him and wring his neck, but I remembered Barker's instructions and kept my temper in check. It was a good thing, for my chair gave a sudden lurch, as the large albino panther cat came by, rubbing itself along the chair's arm as well as my own. From my vantage point of a foot and a few inches, I saw the gray, ghostlike spots on its ivory back, like sooty footprints. It sauntered over to its master, who scratched it behind the ear. The creature stretched his head up into Nightwine's hand.

"This is Bolivar, gentlemen. He was captured along the Brazil-Venezuelan border a few months ago. He nearly killed a porter. I'm teaching him proper London deportment, and a taste for private detectives."

"A very pretty little pet, Mr. Nightwine, but let us get back to the matter at hand," Barker said. "Can you tell me where you were on the night of the fifteenth?"

"I can tell you to go to the Devil."

"You're making progress, Mr. Nightwine. I thought you didn't believe in deities, Heaven, and Hell."

"I believe in Hell in this instance, Mr. Barker. I will make your life a Hell on earth if you will not stop hounding me in this fashion."

Barker smiled. "You must make allowances, sir. Hounding is what we hounds do. Now, the night of the fifteenth?"

"I have no idea! What day was that?"

"Saturday night, sir."

"Last Saturday night? Let me think. Yes, I was at Lord Ribbondale's estate in Kent for the weekend. Brought down twenty-seven pheasants and a like number of woodcock."

"Stayed there the entire weekend, did you?"

"Yes, damn you."

"You can verify this, can you not? For the evening, I mean?"

"Would you like the name of the peer's wife I spent the evening with? Will that satisfy you?"

"Good heavens," I interjected.

"Well, that would be a start, I suppose."

"Go hang yourself, Barker. I have no need to establish my location that evening. I only humor you because it is entertaining to see you flailing about, trying to find someone upon which to affix the blame. This case must have you flummoxed for you to come in here questioning me. You'd have better luck questioning the prime minister. Presumably, he was in town at the time."

"Thank you for the information," Barker said blandly. "The Prince and the prime minister. You're certainly traveling in exalted circles these days."

"I'm a likable fellow. You know, one of these days, I really must look up whoever is in charge of granting licenses to enquiry agents. It's shocking how just anyone can set out a brass plate these days and place vulgar advertisements in *The Times.*"

Barker gave a slight shake of his head, like a schoolmaster with a troublesome student. "Come, Llewelyn. We wouldn't want to take up any more of his time and keep the Prince waiting."

We caught a hansom outside, and I couldn't help but express my thoughts as I clambered into the cab.

"If if weren't for that cat, I would have wrung his neck," I muttered. "Girlfriend, indeed."

18

WE CLIMBED OUT OF THE HANSOM IN POPlar again. It was our second assault upon the doors of the First Messianic Church. Our luck improved; the knob of the storefront church opened easily in Barker's hand. Inside there were a half dozen people already in attendance, though the service would not begin for an hour. Upon questioning, we were guided down a hall to the office, where we were met by the pastor.

Having spoken to but one rabbi in my life, Pokrzywa's little Russian peasant *rebbe,* I had no idea what to expect, but the leader of the First Messianic still surprised me a little. He put down his sermon and came forward, taking our hands in turn in each of his, as if meeting us had been a delight he had long anticipated.

"Gentlemen, welcome. So good of you to come. I'm Rabbi Mordecai. How may I be of service to you?"

The rabbi looked like Father Christmas in a swallow coat. His long beard was almost pure white, and his hair, parted in the middle and pulled back behind each ear, reminded me of angel wings. Mordecai's eyes were cornflower blue, and his pink skin was as unlined as a baby's, for all his sixty years. He was a gentle, amiable soul.

Barker presented his card and told him our purpose.

"Ah, yes, Louis Pokrzywa," the pastor murmured. "What a tragedy. He had a first-rate mind, you know. I thought he might have made something of himself. I only spoke to him once or twice and was looking forward to getting to know him better."

"Was he a member of your congregation, Rabbi?" my employer asked.

"Alas, no. I do not believe he was a Christian when he died. He was curious, he kept an open mind, but he was not yet convinced that Yeshua was the Messiah."

"Yeshua?" I asked.

"We tend to call people and places from the Bible by their Hebrew names here, Mr. Llewelyn, rather than the Hellenized or Latinized form with which you are more familiar. I assure you, Yeshua never heard the name 'Jesus' in his entire time on earth. We try to present the gospel from a first-century perspective, before the arrival of Gentile scholars who made changes in pronunciation and doctrine."

"I must admit," Barker said, "that this is the first Messianic church I've ever visited. How do you stand regarding the gospel?"

"Very biblically," he said. "We believe it is the duty of all Jews to follow Yeshua, that *that* is the purpose Hashem has always meant for His people."

"Hashem?" I asked.

Rabbi Mordecai patted me on the shoulder. "I'll get you some literature, young fellow. Hashem simply means 'the name.' We never utter the name of our Creator, it being forbidden by our culture, but of course, we must call Him something."

"I see."

"We observe most of the festivals in the Jewish calendar, but we do not believe that their observance leads to salvation, which is a free gift, given through the death and resurrection of the true Messiah, Yeshua Hamashiach. Oh, and since the Apostle Paul said that the gift was given to the 'Jew first, and also to the Greek,' we feel it is our duty to evangelize to both groups. Our doors are open to Jew and Gentile alike. In fact, you are welcome to stay for service."

"We will come back another time, when this case doesn't occupy us so fully," Barker responded, "but I thank you for the invitation. For now, let us please get back to Louis Pokrzywa. When did you first meet him?"

The pastor tapped his lips in thought. "I met him in the street during Chanukah. He was studying at one of the outdoor cafés in Whitechapel, so involved in a book that he didn't notice the cold. I stopped and engaged him in conversation. One could tell before he ever spoke how intelligent and spiritual he was. Wouldn't he have made a great Yeshua in an Easter pageant?"

"Evidently someone thought so," Barker said, soberly.

"Yes, yes. I still cannot believe he is gone. His spirit burned so brightly. Anyway, I challenged him to prove that Yeshua was not the true Messiah, and he readily accepted the challenge. We argued over coffee for half an hour, amiably, of course. He hadn't so much as read the New Testament, or compared it to the Old, so the only arguments he could give were secondhand. His faith was not an obstinate one, you know, merely cautious. I invited him to our church, gave him a spare Bible—I always carry one for emergencies such as this—and offered him the chance for a rematch when he was better prepared. I must admit I was surprised when he actually appeared one Wednesday evening in January."

"How many times did he attend services?"

"Three times, perhaps four. We never had our rematch. And now we never shall."

"Were these Wednesday evenings or Sunday mornings?" Barker asked.

"Both, I believe."

"Tell me, Rabbi, are there many young women of marriageable age in your congregation?"

"A dozen or more. Why do you ask?"

Barker took the program from his pocket and showed it to the pastor, pointing to the notes on it with a stubby finger.

"Louis's handwriting? Hmmm. I see it now. So it wasn't just an old man he was coming to see. Why don't you gentlemen make yourself at home for a few moments, while I ask a few discreet questions. I shall return shortly."

"I like him," I told Barker when we were alone.

"He's likeable enough," Barker agreed. "I encourage you, however, to resist impulsive decisions during an investigation."

"Surely you don't suspect Mordecai of being a member of the league? I should think him the least likely person on the planet."

"It is highly unlikely, I'll admit, but he was an acquaintance of Pokrzywa's and cannot be ruled out yet. This is a nice little office, is it not?"

It was. The rabbi's office was small but cheery, much like its owner. Bookshelves overflowed themselves with volumes standing every which way, along with ancient artifacts, menorahs, prayer shawls, and alms boxes. It was a smaller collection than the one we'd seen in Saint Swithen Lane, but this one was not behind glass. Two clay oil lamps flickered on the desk, by a small marble copy of Michelangelo's Moses, giving a mystical, timeless feeling to the room. Surely, I thought, Barker was just being overcautious.

"A fellow would need to be rather clever to outclass Pokrzywa in an argument," I pointed out.

"He'd need to be even more clever to keep a church like this one going, with opposition from church and synagogue alike. He can't be having an easy time of it. He's neither fish nor fowl, you see."

"'To the Jew first, and also to the Greek,'" I quoted.

"Romans two ten. It's funny how people forget that verse."

The pastor came bustling back, his grin replaced with a sheepish look. "Alas," he said, throwing his arms up. "We are undone. None of the girls will admit to being the coauthor of the notes here, much as it would have pleased them to be her. Also, nobody can recall who sat near Louis during the first Wednesday in March, which is when the program is dated. I will continue to press. If I hear something, I shall send word to you."

"We can ask no more. Tell me, sir, have you noticed any anti-Semitic activity in the neighborhood lately, aside from the crucifixion?"

The pastor nodded gravely. "My congregation has been fearful about getting out at night. A couple of drunken louts gave one of our young men a black eye on the way here last week, and the girl he was with had the comb and veil stolen from her hair. But we're accustomed to persecution here. This is a dangerous area, particularly in the alleyways."

Barker turned to me. "Come, lad. Let's leave the gentleman to his sermon notes. Thank you for your time, sir."

On our way out the door, Barker stopped me with a raised arm. He'd stopped once or twice before during our investigation, for a final look, a remark, or a note to me. I flattered myself that I was beginning to catch on. In this case, there was an offering box by the door. Barker ran a thumb across the side of his index finger, and I reached for the wallet in my pocket. He extracted a ten-pound note and folded it several times before it would fit into the small slot on the top of the wooden box. No doubt they were not accustomed to large denominations in Poplar.

Barker fished the watch from his pocket and popped the case.

"Ten minutes until six. We have just enough time to return home. Have you any plans for tonight, Thomas?"

"None at all, sir." It was a formality, of course. He knew I didn't.

"Excellent. You have no objections, I trust, to accompanying me to the theater? It shall give you an opportunity to try on your evening kit."

My employer had given me the impression that he was not a theatergoer, and it was not in his character to do something so frivolous as to attend an evening's entertainment in the middle of a case. It took me several minutes' silence in the cab before I finally remembered Sir Moses' concern about a production of *The Merchant of Venice.* As he said, Barker was leaving no stone unturned.

Once in the door, the Guv was giving orders to Maccabee, while I went upstairs to change. My evening clothes were my most impressive outfit, and I admit I felt it something of an extravagance, since I would get little or no use out of it. As usual, Barker had prepared for every contingency. I changed my day suit for evening wear and smoothed my unruly hair. I had never been so formally dressed in my life. My shirt front was snowy white, my white silk tie peeped from under the tips of my collar, and my evening jacket was of the latest cut. There was even a pair of kid gloves.

Mac provided himself and me with a cold meal by the door: slices of game pie, a bean salad with vinaigrette, and a carafe of water on a silver platter. I leaned against the wall and ate standing up. Presently, our employer came down as well.

Cyrus Barker in evening dress was a sight to behold. The expanse of white linen across his chest seemed immense. His day spectacles had given way to an evening pair, the round disks inside the tortoiseshell frames as green as jade. Altogether, he looked grand and foreboding, a figure of mystery.

Gloveless, he picked up a slice of game pie in his fingers and consumed half of it in one bite. Mac handed him a goblet of water and began whisking imaginary crumbs from his suit with a small brush. For once, this all seemed rather decadent. Evening wear, cold suppers, and a butler brushing away stray crumbs was a far cry from starving in a garret. London is truly a city of extremes.

"Mr. Llewelyn, I must ask you not to lean on the wall, please. It is indolent. Mac, whisk him."

Mac took the broom to me rather thoroughly. There hadn't been a crumb on me to begin with. Any satisfaction the butler derived was removed by Barker's next question, however.

"Might Llewelyn borrow your silk hat for the evening? I have not had the opportunity to purchase one for him yet, and I did not anticipate he would require one so soon. I fear one of mine would o'erwhelm him."

For a moment, Jacob Maccabee looked as if he'd just been slapped. He glanced at me as if I were a species of vermin that had somehow been carried into the house. Then his professional demeanor took over, he acquiesced, and in a moment or two was adjusting a beautiful silk top hat on my head at just the perfect angle. Somehow I wanted to apologize, though I knew it was not I but Barker who had commanded him. Mac tied a voluminous opera cape around Barker's neck, handed us our sticks, and we were off.

19

ARRIVING AT ONE OF LONDON'S PREMIERE theaters in a top hat and evening kit was a novel experience, but my day had been full of them. In the last twenty-four hours, I had been shot at, had a knife thrown at me, and been nudged by a wild beast. I'd faced down an old tutor and watched a man defeated who may have tried to assassinate me. Still, none of these events had prepared me for a night at the theater, or the sight of my employer in an opera cape.

I suppose I had once aspired to come here and walk among these beautiful, elegant people as one of their own, but that had been long ago, before all my dreams had been dashed like porcelain on paving stones. Now that I was finally here, I felt all the more like a Welsh collier's brat, as if I were still twelve, nose running, and starting to outgrow my brother's cast-offs. I was in the right place at the wrong time. Such was the refrain of my life.

"Cheer up, Thomas, old man," I told myself, looking down at the crowd from one of the immense stairways. I would try to enjoy the evening out for its own sake. Heaven only knew if I would ever be in such a situation again.

The Pavilion was as long in the tooth as an old dowager,

but a fresh coat of paint covered a multitude of sins. The plush was wearing thin on the seatbacks, and plaster showed here and there beneath the gilt of the cherubs and ribbons, but all in all she was still handsome. The marble flooring and stairs had reached that luster of beauty which nothing save time and millions of pairs of shoes could create. Barker and I were admirably situated mid-distance between the orchestra pit and the stalls, close enough to hear all of the dialogue, yet far enough away to have the illusion unspoiled by heavy-handed makeup and garish sets. I must state as well that I am a classicist, and much prefer Shakespeare over the latest patter-operas of Messrs. Gilbert and Sullivan.

The performance was a tragedy in every sense. The actor playing Antonio was stoic and noble, and Bassanio was justly aggrieved at his kinsman's predicament; Portia was just as I imagined her, and in the portrayal of the Jewess Jessica there was nothing of which Sir Moses could disapprove; but in the casting of Shylock the sponsors of the play had made a dreadful mistake. *The Merchant of Venice* is a play which must be done subtly if one is to get the full benefit of the tragedy therein, and the character of Shylock should be portrayed realistically, so that we feel his alienation as a Jew. Instead, the actor, Frederick Rosewood, portrayed him as a cold, calculating villain, whose only desire is to destroy every Gentile he gets in his clutches. Such a performance might have caused little concern to the Board of Deputies had the audience been merely members of the upper class, but the shilling stalls were filled with East Enders who booed and hissed whenever Shylock appeared. They seemed very likely to vent their emotions from the play in the streets afterward.

"No wonder Sir Moses is concerned," Barker murmured, as we gathered our things. "I had the good fortune to attend Irving's interpretation at the Lyceum in 'eighty-one. Now *that* was a performance."

"Rosewood was heavy-handed," I admitted. "He's turned Shakespeare into a cheap melodrama."

Barker and I had fallen in with the crowd making their way out to the staircases, when he turned to me. "There's something I'd like you to do, Thomas. I've got a mind to have a word with Rosewood, and it might be useful if you would mill about and see if you recognize anyone from the investigation."

"Certainly, sir."

"Good, lad. Off with you, then."

I reached the top of the stairwell and leaned against the rail nonchalantly, all the while scanning every face for a connection to the Jews. I did indeed see some faces I recognized, but only from their illustrations in the popular press. The Pavilion may not have been the grandest theater in London, but it still had the ability to bring in the fashionable crowd. One could count the dresses, the suits, and the jewels in the tens of thousands of pounds. I was looking down on this pageant as it passed below me, when I found myself staring into a familiar pair of cool brown eyes.

It was the beautiful young Jewess from Pokrzywa's funeral, moving slowly and gracefully down the stair. She wore a gown in a deep forest green, with a matching mantle over her bare shoulders. She had noticed me again and was giving me the same scrutiny that she had in the cemetery. For some reason, I remembered the scene in Eliot's *Deronda*, when Gwendolen first meets Daniel's gaze. I expected her to look away demurely, but she did not, not immediately, anyway. My heart began fluttering in a way it hadn't in a year; I had thought it cold and dead since my wife's passing. I determined to find out who she was.

She turned her head and spoke to a woman at her side. I wondered if she was speaking of me, but the other woman did not look up. Surely, it must have been some commonplace remark. Her companion was a stern, harsh-looking woman some twenty years her senior, whom I concluded was her mother. I was quite content, therefore, not to be the subject of their conversation. The girl gave me a final glance with those velvety eyes of hers and frowned when I dared offer her a reserved smile. I summoned my pluck and made my way down the staircase after her, but when I reached the lobby, she was gone.

I loitered with intent in the theater as it slowly emptied, but I saw no one else involved in the case. I half expected to see Nightwine or Rushford; this was their type of crowd. Within ten minutes, the time it took Barker to return, the ushers and I had the lobby to ourselves.

"Are you ready, lad?"

"Yes, sir."

"Did you see anyone connected with the case?"

I told him about the girl I'd seen at the funeral. "Have you any idea who she might be?" I asked.

We stepped outside. Barker raised his cane and we hailed a cab. "A Jewess that pretty and still unmarried is rare enough to be remarked upon. I believe she is Rebecca Mocatta, the rabbi's daughter. I've asked her father for a private interview with her, since she was a close friend of Pokrzywa's. So far, the rabbi has not responded. I wish I had been here myself."

"Sorry, sir. I would have gladly stopped her had I known you wanted to speak to her."

"I have no doubt you would, you rascal," he chuckled. "So, the Mocattas went to the theater tonight, did they? I'm sure they enjoyed it about as little as did we. And you saw no one else here tonight you recognized, Jew or Gentile?"

"No, sir. How was your interview?"

My employer snorted. "That egotistical little windbag. To hear him tell it, his fame has been long overdue. He's going to ride this hobbyhorse as far as it will go. He's talking of playing Fagin next in a version of *Oliver Twist.*"

"Is there anything to connect him to the case?"

"I doubt it was his plan to kill Pokrzywa as some sort of publicity stunt for his play. I cannot see Rosewood as some diabolical leader of the Anti-Semite League, not unless he's a much better actor than I give him credit. Frankly, he doesn't seem intelligent enough to orchestrate such an operation."

"Another dead end," I complained.

Barker turned his head my way. "Would you rather I fasten blame on someone without proof or sufficient evidence?"

"No, sir!" I said, realizing he'd taken my remark as a criticism. "I didn't mean it like that."

"Patience, lad. Remember? Every suspect you eliminate brings you closer to a solution. It's still early days yet, and we're coming along. You've discovered something very important."

"What's that, sir?"

"The stunner with the pretty eyes is Rabbi Mocatta's daughter," Barker said, giving me another of his little nudges in the ribs. It galled me to think that he had complained about *my* sense of humor.

20

I WAS AT THE HAMMOND THE NEXT MORNING, typing up all that had occurred so far in our investigation. Barker claimed that a dry listing of facts would be helpful in clearing his mind, but I secretly felt he was giving me busywork. I couldn't think of anyone else to interview, and, I suspected, neither could he. Was this normal, or was my employer floundering out of his depth as Nightwine had suggested? I had no way to judge; the fellow was an enigma to me, and my knowledge of detective work rudimentary at best.

Jenkins came through the room with some papers, moving as slowly and surely as a clockwork automaton. He was always this way in the mornings, half asleep, moving about like a somnambulant and propping himself against door frames for support. As the day progressed, he would become more and more animated, until he was near frantic by five o'clock, trying to get all the duties he had neglected finished.

As for Barker, he, too, was ruminating. He began in the office, pacing from the desk to the window, the window to the bookshelves, and back to the desk. Eventually, he ended up in the little outdoor court, wandering about in the cold. It didn't matter to me how mad he looked, if his thoughts were actually getting him somewhere.

Since joining Barker's employ, I had enjoyed a highly irregular schedule. Some days we ignored the office entirely, our only communication being a telephone call or a message from Jenkins. We had meals at all hours of the day and sometimes went without. Our visit to the theater the night before had been part of our investigation, and since we did not get home to Barker's ritual bath until nearly midnight, I had put in a sixteen-hour day. Not that I'm complaining, you understand. I was fortunate indeed to have an employer who liked a little flexibility in his schedule.

I had picked up *The Times* and was preparing to study it for the day's events. Barker felt a complete reading of the daily was essential in our work. It was nearing noon, and my employer, having completed his circuit, was back by his desk. Jenkins was lazily buzzing around the room, like a trapped bluebottle, lighting here and there. I had finished my report and placed it on Barker's desk, and he was just starting to go over it. I was a bit bored, to tell the truth, and hoped we might go back to the City after lunch, as this inactivity galled me. Those were my thoughts as I picked up the newspaper and noted the date, which was the twentieth of March.

I leapt to my feet, knocking my castered chair across the room. My heart was pumping like a thoroughbred's at Ascot, and though I reached out to the desk to steady myself, I couldn't feel the wood under my fingers.

"Good heavens, man," Barker remonstrated. "What is the matter?" He had that same look on his face his Pekingese got when its dignity was affronted.

"I— I— I—" I began, then tried again. "I have to leave, sir. I require the rest of the day off."

"You what?"

"I have to go, sir. Now! I'm sorry. Oh, hang it!" I ran out of the room. Jenkins was ambulating again, and I got past him just in time. If Barker tried to follow, the clerk had sealed up the doorway for a moment or two. I clattered down the front steps, too upset to even remember my hat and stick. I hurried down Whitehall toward Charing Cross, close to a dead run. I didn't care a pin about what the people who watched me pass by must think. I had more important things on my mind.

I reached Waterloo, and realizing I couldn't keep this pace up, I stopped to catch my breath, while I watched the cold gray water of the Thames pass under the bridge. My mind kept repeating the phrase: *twenty March, twenty March, twenty March.*

It was one year to the day since my wife's death. Her death, her illness had led to my arrest and trial, and my eight months' sentence. How had I not remembered the date until now? What kind of husband was I that I couldn't even remember the first anniversary of my wife's death? While it was true that my time had not been my own since I had been hired, I still felt a crushing weight of guilt on my chest.

I paid the tuppence toll and crossed the bridge, walking aimlessly. Jenny was her name. Memory conjured up her face before me. Her hair was soft and brown, and her large eyes hazel. I had loved the shape of her ears and the way the curls in front of them spiraled. I had loved everything about her. We had been married less than three months. The old loss came back, the loss that had made me howl in my cell, that had taken a young boy of twenty summers and turned him into an old man.

Gradually, having wandered for hours, I felt the enormity of what I had done begin to sink into my troubled brain. I had walked out on my position, after all Barker had done for me, after the expensive clothes, the room, the meals. I was a complete ingrate. I had left him much out of pocket, and now I was back against the wall again, no savings, no position, no prospects. Perhaps I would be swimming in the Thames yet. I recognized the hand of Fate by now, and her cruel little jokes.

Eventually, finding myself with nowhere else to go, I returned home. I passed a curious Mac and made my way upstairs. With a stoical sigh, I reached under the bed and pulled out my old battered suitcase, the one Barker had rescued from the dustbin. It had become my oldest friend. Inside it was the meager suit I had worn to my first interview with Barker. Had it only been a week? Somehow, it seemed longer. I changed into my old clothes again. After wearing some of the finest apparel available in London, I saw that the suit looked shabby indeed, mere refuse for the stalls in Petticoat Lane. A pity. I would have liked to own a nice suit in which to be buried.

There was a knock at the door. I was so deep in thought I didn't notice, until it came again. It startled me. Nobody in this household knocked. Barker bellowed, Maccabee barged right in, and Dummolard never came upstairs. I got up and opened the door. It was Mac.

"Mr. Llewelyn, Mr. Barker requests that you join him in the basement."

"The basement, did you say?"

"Yes, sir." He bowed and left.

So, that was it, then. I was to be dismissed in the basement, unless he intended to shoot me instead. I would have preferred the office, where it all began, but the basement was as good a place to be sacked as any.

I went down the stairs and opened the door. In the middle of the room, Barker was seated at a small deal table of indeterminate age. The table was without benefit of a tablecloth but was covered with plates of bread, cheese, and a cold joint.

"Yes, sir?" I said. "You wanted to see me?"

Barker got up and went through a door leading into the lumber room. "Have a seat. I must say, you had me going," he said, while I heard him rummaging about. "I didn't quite know what to make of it. Then I remembered. Your wife passed away a year ago today, didn't she?"

"Yes, sir. How did you know?"

"I went to Oxford that second day, while you were cramming those first books. Interesting reading. Your files, I mean." He came out again and put two pint glasses on the table. "Why didn't— My word, what are those rags you're wearing?"

I looked down at my suit. He was right. Compared to what I had been wearing the last week, they were rags. "My suit, sir. The one you hired me in."

Barker seemed a bit short-tempered, as I would expect him to be under the circumstances. "I thought I told Mac to burn those. What are you wearing them for?"

"They seemed as good as any to be sacked in, sir."

"Sacked? Who said anything about being sacked? Have I told you that you are sacked?"

"No, sir." I watched him go back into the lumber room again.

"Your records at Oxford were rather vague. The charges were theft and assault, but the full particulars were mislaid. For a city the size of Oxford, I found the constabulary quite bucolic. The sentence seemed very stiff for such a small crime. According to the report, the total worth of the stolen property was exactly one sovereign. Here it is!" He came out with a small barrel, very dusty and cobwebby. "Give me a hand here, lad."

I held the barrel, while he pulled the peg and opened the spigot. A brown liquid filled the glass, producing a tan collar on top. It was porter. He transferred the tan froth to his mustache.

"Eminently drinkable," he pronounced, and poured me a glass.

"What are we doing, sir?"

"That should be obvious. We are getting drunk and hearing the story of your life. Where was I? Yes. You are not the sort to suddenly refuse to do work that is required of you. Something of immense personal import to you made you leave the office suddenly. Obviously, something that happened before your employ, unless, of course, my numerous foibles finally grew to become too great. So, come, lad. Spill it. Confession is good for the soul."

"But, sir," I protested. "I saw you sip at the stout at the pub the other day. It is evident that you dislike it."

"There you go inferring again, without evidence, Llewelyn. What you have taken for dislike is in fact an overfondness. I could pour this stuff down my throat by the gallon, and did, in fact, during my wilder days. But now I must be abstemious, save upon an extraordinary occasion such as this. Tonight we shall drink ourselves into a stupor, and tomorrow morning conduct ourselves once more as sober men, and this occasion need never be discussed again. So tell it, man, and no blubbering. I can take anything but blubbering. Good porter, isn't it?"

"Yes, sir. Excellent."

"Mac makes it himself. Never trust a butler that can't make first-rate spirits."

"I shall remember that." I was trying to put together all the disjointed thoughts in my head and to be coherent. This was a subject I had never spoken of with anyone before. I wanted to get it right.

"Well, sir, I first met my wife—"

"No, no," Barker broke in. "You're making a hash of it already. Go back to the beginning, Thomas. Tell me about your family and your village."

I took another sip of the porter, then a large gulp. I'd never had the luxury of being drunk in my entire life, but this seemed as good a time as any.

21

I WAS BORN IN CWMBRAN, IN GWENT, SIR, the sixth of nine children, and the fourth son. My father was a miner, and my mother took in wash to make ends meet, not that they ever did. We also had a grandfather living with us, my mum's dad, who was retired from the mines after a lifetime underground. He used to take us on long walks around the hills, as a means of coughing up fifty years' worth of coal dust from his lungs. His years in the hole were secondary in his mind, and in that of the town. He was primarily a bard. The townfolk were proud of old Ioan Llewelyn, for he'd won several eisteddfods, storytelling competitions, traveling as far as Cardiff. Granddad used to tell us children stories on our long walks, to entertain us and to keep his skills sharp, and so I grew up on the old tales of Pwyll and Math, and the brave queen, Rhiannon. The stories meant little to my brothers and sisters but were all the world to me. When I was younger, I was sure they were all true, as if they'd just happened. I trembled in terror at the thought of the dark underworld of Annwn more than any glimpse of Hell's fire and brimstone imparted to us children by our Methodist minister. But I was nothing special, just number six of the Llewelyn brood, destined for the coal mines, a family distinct only because my grandfather chose to spell the family name a little differently from the established and royal spelling.

"The first inkling that I was a little different from my family and friends occurred in my fifth year of schooling, when I began to set some of my grandfather's tales down in class for my teacher. Mr. Wynn was something of a hedge bard himself, and he was impressed more by my memory than my syntax. He pushed me to learn English as well as Welsh and drilled me in all the rules of grammar and punctuation. He also undertook to teach me elocution, an hour after school twice a week. In lieu of any payment, I furnished an introduction to my grandfather, and the two gentlemen who were my mentors became fast friends. Mr. Wynn himself set down all my grandfather's tales verbatim, and they were published in Cardiff shortly before Granddad passed away that year. By that time, everyone was convinced that my grandfather's 'gift' had been passed down to me.

"Under my tutor's encouragement, I entered a countywide eisteddfod when I was but twelve. I didn't win, of course, for who would have presented an award to little Number Six, the collier's boy? However, my tale did come to the attention of Lord Glendenning, who was most impressed to have a savant in his district. With Mr. Wynn's encouragement, His Lordship agreed to sponsor my education at a public school in Cardiff. I'll never forget the day I was seen off at our little station by my parents, in the best clothes cobbled together from the family's wardrobe." I paused for a moment. "Could I have a bit of that cheese, there?"

Barker cut a thick slice of Stilton for me and put it on a plate, along with some Huntly biscuits. I poured another glass from the cask. Storytelling is thirsty work.

"In my new school, I kept to myself as much as possible and strove to excel at my schoolwork. I had few friends, for I was a poor lad among all those rich merchants' sons. I did make one friend, though, an English lad named Bryan Pill. It was Pill who introduced me to English literature, which is to say, the modern literary journals: *Blackwood's, Cassall's, Pearson's,* and others. I became as much addicted to them as he. In my naivety, I began to send them odd pieces of prose, poetry, reviews, and the like. In their complete ignorance of the fact that I was but a youth, they accepted one or two.

"I was called into the headmaster's office one morning, during my final year at school, to find myself in the presence of Lord Glendenning himself. He had been watching my progress, his 'investment,' and had even gotten wind of my work in the periodicals, from Mr. Wynn, no doubt. The headmaster was able to offer encouraging words on my academic standing, and the outcome was that His Lordship wished me to sit for the examinations to enter Oxford. If I passed with high marks, he would see fit to finance a frugal year's tuition at Magdalen College. I passed with very high marks indeed."

"Good, lad."

"Thank you, sir, but nothing had prepared me for the enormity that is Oxford. When I was not reading Classics or attending tutorials, I worked at various odd jobs, as well as serving as a batman for an upperclassman, cleaning his rooms and waiting on him, which is a requirement during the first year. The upperclassman, the Honorable Palmister Clay, was a sleek and odious fellow, a peer's son who spent his money on fine clothes and all the rigors of dissipated living. He found occasion to criticize my dress, my speech, my manners, and everything else about me.

"Up to that time, I had lived a Spartan life and, of course, a celibate one. The only females I had known were my own sisters and classmates, and I had been cloistered among boys since I had begun attending public school. Love was something I read in the story cycles of King Arthur and the fairy tales of Hans

Christian Andersen. So I was utterly unprepared when Cupid's arrow finally pointed my way.

"I was on my way to one of my numerous jobs one evening, having come from a bit of tutoring I was doing for a student without much brain but with a wealthy father. I was walking along Holywell Street when I noticed a shape on the ground ahead of me. It was early evening, but it being late October, the day had already grown dark. The gaslights glowed in the midautumn fog, and by their light I saw the shape ahead of me move. I slowed down, realizing the bundle of cloth was human. Even Oxford streets could be dangerous at night. Then my ears detected the sound of abject weeping. Some poor wretch was sobbing piteously, a beggar's child or an old crone decrying her fate. The sound of my shoes on the paving stones must have alerted her, for her face suddenly appeared from under her shawl. I thought then and there that it was the most beautiful face I'd ever seen. Her hair—"

"Spare me the romantic descriptions, lad," Barker interjected. "We'll accept she was pretty. Get on with it."

"Yes, sir. Her eyes were red from crying. She gasped when she saw me.

"'Don't be afraid,' I told her. 'Have you been hurt?'

"'No, sir. I've lost sixpence," she sobbed. She'd been working several hours, taking care of some children for a woman who worked in a factory. She'd been paid sixpence and had accidentally dropped it in the street. She was afraid to go home without it.

"'I shall help you look,' I answered, bending down and beginning to search about. I thought it possible, even more than likely, that she had not dropped any money at all. It is a dodge I have seen done before. But she seemed honest enough and determined to find the coin. Cautiously, I examined every inch of light about us, but the desire to please her was just too great. I palmed sixpence and pretended to find it just outside of the circle of light. I needed the coin myself, but the smile she gave me more than paid for the loss.

"I offered to walk her home, and she settled her hand on my arm as lightly as a dove. Her name was Jenny Ashby. She asked me if I was a student at university, and that was it. We were off on a long conversation, as we walked along Holywell together. Whatever I possessed, and would ever possess, I was willing to throw at her feet by the end of that walk.

"Had I been given the training I have now, sir, I might have noticed her clothing more, but then I'd grown up in cast-off clothing, myself. The building to which she led me was one of the worst tenements in Oxford. I'd grown up in poverty but never in squalor. I could tell she was embarrassed by her surroundings. With a murmured 'good night,' she flew into the doorless opening. I went back to my rooms with my heart and mind in a tumult.

"I took to passing by the old building several times each day, trying to screw up my courage enough to walk into that gaping hole and track her down. Jenny told me she lived with her mother and seven siblings. Her father had taken to drink and run away, but Mrs. Ashby called herself a widow. They made their meager living making paper flowers. Jenny was the eldest. She was sixteen.

"Finally, by the third day, I'd scraped together enough courage to go in. It was even worse than I expected. The halls smelt of decay and unwashed humanity. The fellow whom I asked about the Ashbys was reluctant to tell me, thinking me a creditor. At last, I found her door and knocked. Jenny opened it, and her hands flew to her face at her being discovered there by me. Before we spoke a word, she was elbowed aside by a wan-looking woman whose resemblance to her was coarsened by the ravages of alcohol. It was her mother. She latched onto my arm and drew me into the room. The place was worse than a sty. A broken table was covered with crepe paper, wire, and other detritus of the paper flower trade. Odiferous clothing stood in piles, but whether it was other people's washing or their own, I did not know. Seven half-starved, half-naked children ran about the room or mewled in broken drawers. I asked Mrs. Ashby if I might take her eldest daughter out for a cup of tea and a bun. She seemed ready to protest, but then a cunning look came over her face and she agreed. Looking back on it now, I think she smelled money. Meager as my finances were, they outstripped their own."

"Your mother-in-law was some bit of work," Barker said, pouring me another glass of porter. "I looked up her record by the address on your antecedents. Cora Ashby. She had quite a long sheet. Fraud. Theft. Public drunkenness. Vagrancy, and worse. She was quite a dollymop in her younger days."

I looked up at my employer. "I'm not making a hash of it, am I, sir?"

"No, no. Pray continue."

"The common proprieties of polite society are far different from the economic realities of the English poor. With her mother's subtle conniving, Jenny and I were wed within a month, and I suddenly found myself almost the sole support of a family of nine. No change in our domestic arrangements was possible, and I continued living in my room at Magdalen, while Jenny stayed with her family. I couldn't mention my marriage to my family, my classmates, or the administrators, because it was forbidden to underclassmen. I was a naive nineteen-year-old at the mercy of an older woman with much experience and few scruples. She had me in her clutches. If I'd worked hard before, I did so doubly now.

"Between attending lectures and tutorials, studying, and the odd jobs, I was hard at work eighteen hours a day. I lost weight and began to look sallow. All my money went into Mrs. Ashby's hands. Luckily, the tuition and boarding payments were paid by Lord Glendenning's solicitors directly, and she could not get her hands on them.

"Things can always get worse, and they generally do. That winter, Jenny developed a cough. Her mother treated it with alcohol and morphine-laced patent medicines, but it was not until she coughed up blood one morning that I realized it was more than a cold. With her delicate constitution, she was a natural victim of consumption, and with unheated rooms and scant food, she wouldn't last long. During the few minutes I saw her in and around my work, she was fading like a bouquet of roses.

"At this time, I was still batting for the odious Mr. Clay. If anything, he'd gotten worse. He was complaining constantly now that I was an embarrassment to his rooms. I admit I was looking rather shabby. My clothing was wearing out, and my hair needed a barber's attention. But the worst thing about serving him was the stack of gold sovereigns that sat on the edge of his mantel. They had been won in some sort of wager, and Clay kept them there to rankle his friend who had lost. They meant nothing to him, since his father was one of the richest men in Manchester, but they meant the world to me. With just one of those sovereigns, I could bring a doctor to Jenny's side. I had never stolen in my life, but that stack of coins became an obsession. I was aware of it, no matter what I was doing in the rooms, and no matter who was there.

"One day, I could fight temptation no longer and was just reaching out to touch the top sovereign when Clay and two of his cronies walked in the door unexpectedly. I flinched and dropped the coin, which was as good as admitting my guilt. I saw a look of triumph on the Honorable's face. I tried to get past him, to get out of there and run, but he stepped in my way, seizing me by my thin jacket. My nerves had been at a fever pitch for weeks. He didn't know who he was facing. I clouted him a good one on the chin and he was down. In five seconds I had compounded theft with assault. Clay's friends, two strapping lads, seized me by the arms, while he struggled back onto his feet. Clay was an amateur boxer, but you might have thought him professional for the going-over he gave me. As I sagged, nearly unconscious, bleeding from the nose and mouth, they summoned a constable, who took me into custody.

"I'm sure you've inspected the hearing and trial records, and I'd rather not speak about the uncomfortable interviews with Lord Glendenning and my parents. Clay's father, a merchant turned peer, brought all of his influence to bear on the case, and the result was eight months' hard labor. I was broken to the treadmill, and my hands shredded from picking apart oakum. I endured beatings and surly treatment from the guards and from the other inmates. Worst of all, I was separated from my beloved Jenny. She came to see me twice before my trial and once in prison. After that, she was too ill to leave her bed and come to see me. The tuberculosis was consuming her from the inside. On the twentieth of March, she died in that squalid little flat and was buried in an unmarked grave.

"Directly after my release, I attempted to find Jenny's family, but they had skipped out on the rent, and I never found them again. Eventually, I drifted to London, looking for work, as my name was thoroughly blackened in Oxford forever. What little I possessed, I pawned for food and shelter. Then, one morning at the British Museum Reading Room, I found your advertisement in the 'Situations Vacant' column of *The Times,* and you know the rest."

"I know more than that," Barker said. "You'd skipped out on your rent. The suitcase told me as much. And I suspect that you were considering killing yourself that day. I could see it in your eyes."

"Why did you hire me, sir?" I asked, as Barker replenished my glass yet again.

"I wish you could have seen yourself through *my* eyes, Thomas. I was watching all of you outside from the bow window. You were the most nondescript fellow I'd ever seen. It was as if you were trying to blend in with the brick wall. I almost overlooked you, standing among all the taller men. I was intrigued when you tossed your suitcase into the dustbin, right under my window. Then you came in and presented me with an Oxford education, or at least the beginnings of one. Better still, you had an eight-month tenure at Oxford Prison, which in many ways is more educational than University. You then sailed through every test as if you'd been practicing for weeks, and you kept your temper in check. A man would have had to be an idiot not to hire you on the spot. Whether you know it or not, you're a natural detective's assistant."

"I thought I was fit for nothing."

"You would think that, lad." He patted my sleeve. "You undervalue yourself."

"So, why did you hire Jenkins?" I asked.

I had made Barker chuckle again. "Jenkins came to fill the position temporarily and never went away again. I can sack him any time, and he can quit. He's an odd fellow, but I've grown used to his ways."

I sat up and put my glass down. The beer had thoroughly loosened my lips.

"So, tell me, sir. How did a Scottish boy end up in China?"

Barker put down his porter. He'd been matching me glass for glass, but so far, it hadn't seemed to affect him.

"My father was a missionary from Perth. He followed the tea clippers to Foochow soon after I was born. My parents stayed several years, developing a congregation of Europeans and Chinese as well. They died when I was eleven. Cholera."

"Good Lord!" I said. I could definitely feel the effects of the porter now. I nearly chipped a tooth navigating the glass to my lips. "So, did you go home?"

"That might have happened in England, lad, and possibly in India, but not in China. The right palms were never crossed, so the gist of it was that I was cut loose on my own."

"Cut loose, sir? In China, at eleven? What did you do?"

"Whatever I could to survive. I was just another street urchin. I started out on the docks, scavenging for food, looking for odd work, and learning how to defend myself the hard way. Eventually, I signed on as a cabin boy aboard a broken-down clipper, looking about as thin and desperate as you did that first day I saw you."

I was trying hard to keep up, but the alcohol was swiftly overtaking my brain. If he told me the rest of his story that night, I didn't catch it. After a while, it seemed sensible to rest my hot, throbbing temple against the nice, cool wood of the table. That is the last thing that I remember.

I awoke some hours later. I'd been asleep in my plate, between the bread and the cheese. My head was throbbing and my shoulders ached. Barker was nowhere to be found.

22

THE NEXT MORNING I FELT AS IF MY HEAD had been split open with an axe from the Tower and my tongue slathered in coal tar. What had I been thinking, pouring that noxious stuff down my throat? I suspected Maccabee of having designs on my life. Lifting my head off the pillow required far more energy than my poor powers could muster. How did Jenkins survive this ordeal on a daily basis?

I lay in bed for over an hour, half paralyzed, watching the sunlight slowly illuminate the room. My head throbbed, and even my cheekbones hurt. I decided to forgo any future attempts at self-pickling. I haven't the drinker's constitution.

Barker came bustling in, all health and vigor, shooting his cuffs and adjusting his links. He showed no signs of distress from the night before. My stomach threatened to turn as active as Krakatoa at any moment.

"Morning, lad," he said loudly. "Beautiful day. Time we were about." I was in agony, and Barker, it appeared, was in one of his cheerful, telegraph-message moods.

"I fear I'm too sick to move, sir," I said.

"Nonsense. Get up and walk about. A nice long hike is what you need, and a good soak, to sweat out the impurities, but we don't have the time. Show your body who is master."

"Yes, sir," I answered, and rose to a sitting position. A fireworks demonstration began to go off in my head. I swung my limbs over the side of the bed and waited to see what would happen next. Nothing noteworthy.

"I shall be along, presently, sir," I told my employer, who still stood there, expectantly.

"That's the spirit. Have Etienne make you some eggs and coffee. I'll meet you out front in half an hour."

"Oh, God, please, not eggs," I whimpered after he left. "Anything but eggs."

Dummolard insisted on a concoction of his own, a greenish sludge that looked as if it had been dredged from the sewers. Who knows? Perhaps it had. I managed to keep it down and even swallowed some coffee and toast, but eggs were quite beyond me. Having broken my fast, I dragged myself up the stairs again and traded my old suit for another of my new ones. I was still employed, despite yesterday's little debacle.

"Ready, lad?" Barker asked, as I stepped down into the hall. Mac was helping him into his coat.

"Ready, sir," I responded, far more confidently than I felt. I put on my coat myself. I didn't want Mac near me. I don't approve of hiring poisoners as servants.

I moaned as I climbed into the cab and leaned well forward in case the rocking motion made me ill. John Racket gave me a frown from atop his box. He didn't want anyone ill while in his cab, and I am certain that my complexion was as leaden as the sky overhead. Juno was off, and I held tightly to the leather-covered doors.

We didn't go to the office at all but instead went straight to Tower Bridge. Within half an hour we were seated in the Bucharest Café again. Barker was enjoying strong Romanian tea and a fairly lethal-looking bialy, while I was nursing a bicarbonate of soda.

"Feeling better, lad?"

"Much better, sir," I lied. "What are we doing here this morning?"

"We've been actively pursuing this investigation for several days now, muddying the waters, so to speak. Today, I want us to plumb its depths. We're going to observe the Jews today and the rhythms of their lives. Is there any real evidence of a threat, or is it merely imagined? Was Pokrzywa's death a personal matter or a harbinger of future developments? In a way, we shall be testing the area's temperature."

I thought it more likely that he had run out of leads, and we were to spend the day sitting idly. However, it was politic to agree. After all, I couldn't do much else at the moment but sit and sip soda water.

Despite his plan, Barker was too restive to sit long. After half an hour's time, he announced that he would explore the Lane again. I seconded his decision. His energy was not exactly calming to my stomach. Like a hound let off his lead, Barker shot into the crowd of Brick Lane. Only then did I begin to relax.

The bicarbonate and the absence of my employer began to work their subtle magic on me. In twenty minutes, I ordered a coffee in one of the glass cups, and within another ten, I got up to explore a little bookstall down the street. I bought one of the local Jewish newspapers, in English and Hebrew, more for the novelty than the reading. I also found a book by Maimonides, *A Guide for the Perplexed,* for only a few shillings, and thought I might see why he was such a favorite of Pokrzywa's. The book, as it turned out, was an attempt to reconcile Jewish doctrine with the Hellenistic teachings of Plato and Aristotle and had been written during the Middle Ages.

I returned to the café, ordered a second cup, and even hazarded a bialy, though it was several minutes before I dared the first bite. Begrudgingly, I had to admit that my employer was right. Being up and about was preferable to staying in bed all day, moaning into my pillow. So I sat in the outdoor café, reading the *Jewish Chronicle,* with a bialy, coffee, and a copy of Maimonides, not realizing how Jewish I myself appeared, in my long black coat, curling hair, and bowler hat, until I was interrupted.

A set of knuckles rapped roughly at my table. I looked up over my newspaper at a fellow I'd never seen before, a tall, well-built Jew in his twenties, with a stern face and a long beard. He looked at me intently and said, *"Sholem aleichem."*

"Aleichem sholem," I replied. It was the response Barker had given Zangwill, a few days before, which had impressed the little teacher greatly. The charm worked for me as well, for the fellow nodded once, as if I had given the correct password. He leaned his head to one side and raised his chin, motioning for me to follow him. It was just the sort of break, I realized, that Barker was looking for. I threw down a shilling, gathered my book and paper, and trotted off after the fellow. I only wished I could have had time to write some sort of note to my employer.

I followed him down Brick Lane for several blocks, then he stepped into a warren of doss-houses and ended up on Flower and Dean Street. From there he went into a small court. Where was he taking me, and why all the dodges and turns? After a dozen more yards, I realized we were not alone. There were several silent men moving in our direction. The court was dominated by a set of steps going down in the middle, not unlike an entrance to the underground, save for a large sign at the back that read "Oriental Bazaar."

Down we plunged into semi-darkness. I smelled spices in the air, and incense. The only illumination here was from the opening overhead and dozens of flickering candles. I saw men squatting on the ground, patiently awaiting customers or playing at cards. There were shining copper pots for sale, bags of saffron, rice, and betel nut, and bookstalls in which not one title was in English. For a moment again, I was not in London. I might just as well have been in Cairo or Calcutta. At the foot of the steps, I heard rather than saw my companions turning left and going back alongside the stairway, down a hall full of underground booths. We came up to an open public house, and at the far end, a bar. The proprietor, without a word, lifted the hinged bar with one hand and waved us through. We passed through a green baize curtain behind, into a large room. Even as I crossed the threshold, a young man on a soapbox had begun speaking.

"Greetings to you, gentlemen of Zion. I address you all in English today, for I can see Sephardim and Ashkenazim alike before me. Forgive this sudden summons from your daily activities. There is in London today a grave threat to our well-being. How many of you have known firsthand the deprivations and cruelty inflicted upon us by the *goyim* in Russia and Poland?" There was a sudden murmur. "I thought as much. Do you feel you have arrived at a place of safety? Is your journey over? Louis Pokrzywa thought it was, and look where it got him. Will he be the last Jew in London to give up his life, or is this just one more beginning of anti-Semitic sentiments in a foreign land? Do you not realize that we shall be continually persecuted until we are restored unto our homeland in Palestine? England has been generous in taking in our widows and orphans, but I fear we are no more safe here than we were in Moscow, Kiev, or Odessa.

"But I have not come to speak to you about Zionism. That is in the future. What of now? Sirs, our unknown adversaries are emboldened by our timidity. Our fear gives them courage. Certainly, not all Englishmen wish us ill. I say to you, stand fast! We can go no further west. It is time to turn and fight!

"Do you think Rabbi Ben Loew will build a golem to defend us as he did in Prague three hundred years ago? If so, you are naive. To this day, we do not know where the clay remains are hidden. It is up to us, then, to build our own golem, to patrol our own streets. We cannot be complacent and rely upon the London Metropolitan Police to safeguard our interests. I cannot speak for every one of you; each one of us must weigh his personal needs against the common good. I merely wish to state that there comes a time when one must put aside commercial interests and lift the sword. Those of you who are willing to defend your people in Aldgate, Spitalfields, and Whitechapel, please leave your names and addresses at the door. Your women, your little brothers and sisters, and your old men look to you for support and safety. How shall you young lions of Judah respond?"

The speaker stepped back, and by some prearranged cue, the gaslights were extinguished and the baize curtain raised. I noticed several fellows by the door with clipboards. Men were almost forcing their names on them. As I brushed by, I saw a few stares in my direction. I found myself in an absurd position. I was no Jew, and yet I felt as if I was betraying them by not leaving my name and address. Also, I was already in the employ of a man hired to combat this very evil, yet I could not reveal that fact now. As it was, I lowered my head and slunk from the room, with an inexplicable feeling of guilt.

Back in Flower and Dean Street, I watched the meeting gradually disperse. Reasoning that Barker might have returned and be concerned for my welfare, I began to wend my way back to Brick Lane when I felt a hand on my shoulder. I jumped.

"So, there was a wolf among the sheep, eh?" Israel Zangwill said, an ironic smile on his face. He wore a coat with an Astrakhan collar and a Homburg hat.

"No wolves," I assured him with a laugh. "Merely a Gentile dog, trying to guard the sheep. Somehow I got scooped up in the shearing. Did you sign up?"

"Of course." The little teacher looked at me seriously.

"Without knowing the plans? Or do you know?"

"Not a word. But I trust them all the same. The speaker was Asher Cowen, a good fellow. He's helped organize some soup kitchens in the area and a center for our aged. Asher gets things done. So, how progresses the investigation?"

"To be truthful, I have no idea. This is my first case. I was only hired a couple of weeks ago. Mr. Barker keeps his opinions close to his vest."

Zangwill smiled. I think I had won him over with my candor. "You surprise me, Mr. Llewelyn. Ira Moskowitz has us convinced that you are a master spy and detective. You are his hero, now, I believe."

The idea seemed patently ridiculous. "There is no wretch less worthy of being worshipped than I, Mr. Zangwill."

"Israel, please. I won't disabuse Ira of his fantasy just yet. It has caused him to clean up his room somewhat, though he rather neglects his studies now for the works of Poe and Collins."

"I regret coming between him and his studies."

"He's always looking for an excuse. But come, must you rush off to meet your mysterious boss, or can you stop for a cup of coffee?"

I thought it over for a moment. I didn't know whether Barker was frantic over my disappearance or off somewhere about his business without a care about me. Certainly, I should find out, but it might be helpful to stop and talk with Zangwill. He'd already been involved in much of the case.

"If we could stop by the Bucharest for a moment, I'll check in with Mr. Barker. I'd enjoy a cup of coffee with you."

"Excellent!" the teacher cried. "We'll stop, and then I'll take you to my club." He broke into a grin. With his long nose and wide smile, he looked like Shakespeare's Puck.

"You belong to a club?"

"Of course. Come along, then."

We headed west, one hand in our respective pockets, and the other firm on the brims of our hats, for the north wind was growing blustery.

"So," I said, "what exactly is a golem?"

"He is a large creature made of clay, brought to life by magic, rather like Frankenstein's monster. A famous rabbi brought him to life to defend the Jews of Prague a few centuries ago, if one believes the legend."

"This fellow Cowen surely doesn't intend to build a magical golem of clay, does he?"

"Why not? We've done it before, we can do it again."

"I find a clay man marching around the East End a trifle hard to believe," I confessed.

"Fine. We'll make him out of steel and run him on steam, then. This is the nineteenth century, after all."

Barker was nowhere to be found in Brick Lane. I searched for his familiar form in all directions and even asked the proprietor if any instructions had been left for me. Nothing. Zangwill and I pressed on.

We were walking down Cornhill Street when my companion suddenly tugged me into a narrow and ancient lane. Old entrances to shops and warehouses stood but a few yards from each other, and so close were they that the lanterns at each entrance burned continuously, or the street would have been forever in shadow.

"Where are we?" I asked.

"Use your nose, Mr. Detective. It is Saint Michael's Alley."

I had heard of it before, though I'd never been there. It was the center of the West Indies trade. The air in this cloistered street was redolent of the coffee and tobacco that were stored in the old warehouses and served in the ancient coffeehouses that lined the street. Zangwill stopped in front of a dark-windowed establishment called the Barbados and opened the door. "My club," he murmured, ushering me in.

It was black as pitch inside. The room had a comfortable smell of coffee and Virginia Cavendish. I made out a row of dark wooden pews bracketing tables lit by small candles. We stood until a waiter came up to us out of the gloom and conducted us to a booth.

"Mr. . . . Zangwill, is it not? And you, sir. I don't believe we've seen you before," the waiter, or rather the proprietor, said, looking at me. He was an imperious fellow, about five and fifty, without a hair on his head.

"I'd like to sponsor this fellow for membership," Zangwill declared, placing fourpence on the table. I was mystified at this. Was this yet another secret cabal? Was nothing as it seemed anymore? The proprietor had me fill out a card with my name, address, and date of birth, then he left us. We hadn't even ordered coffee yet.

"'Something is rotten in the state of Denmark,'" I quipped.

"You just wait. You'll see you have joined a select little coterie, at some expense to an impoverished teacher."

The owner returned with a large tray. He handed Zangwill an old clay churchwarden pipe, and gave a fresh white new one to me. Setting down a pen and an inkwell, he had me print "T. Llewelyn" in minute letters on the stem. Then he left us with a wooden bowl full of fresh tobacco and a porcelain striker containing matches. We filled our long pipes and lit up. It felt rather silly, as if we were playing at Drake and Raleigh, but my friend took it rather seriously, and it would have been impolite to laugh at his expense. I had to admit it was convivial sitting there in the booth with a companion, two pipes, and a candle.

"I have a confession to make," my companion admitted. "Your employer makes my flesh creep. He looks like something of a golem himself. I think he rather intimidates me."

"Oh, Barker's all right," I said. "He's treated me dashedly well, bought me a whole new wardrobe and everything. I admit, he can scare the wits out of you at times, and between you and me, he's a walking arsenal, but as an employer he's not bad. He's teaching me the trade."

"Is it a trade?" Zangwill asked, sucking at his long stem.

"Well, not like any trade I've heard of before, but then, I'm no businessman."

"What did you do before Barker hired you?"

"Eight months for theft at Oxford Prison."

Zangwill coughed so hard, he nearly dropped his fragile pipe. At that point, the proprietor came up and my friend, if he was still my friend, ordered for us both. After he left, Zangwill looked me square in the eye.

"Very well, Thomas, confess. How did a bookish little fellow like yourself end up a hardened criminal?"

For the second time in twenty-four hours, I told the story of my life, though a much abbreviated and less personal version this time. Coffee came, and a small dessert which Zangwill jokingly called a "barrister's torte." He seemed fascinated by my story and was not evasive toward me in the least, as I had feared he might be upon hearing my history. We talked and smoked and drank several cups of the strong brew. I hadn't had a real friend since childhood. It felt good to sit here across from a fellow my own age and talk about anything that came into my head.

"A detective and a former convict with a tragic past. Oh, Becky shall eat this up."

"Who is Becky?" I asked, mystified.

"Rebecca Mocatta. Rabbi Mocatta's daughter. You're expected at their house tonight. Hasn't Barker told you?"

"Mr. Barker delights in keeping me in the dark and dancing like a marionette. I always suspect that all of London knows what I am doing before I do. How came you to hear of it?"

"Oh, Barker asked the rabbi, the rabbi informed his family, and Becky told me about it this morning. You're to be the *Shabbes goy* at their house in . . . ," he consulted his watch, "well, in a few hours, I suppose."

I took in the news. "Forgive my ignorance, Israel, but just what is a *Shabbes goy?*"

"You are to keep the lamps and fires lit in their home overnight, since we Jews are forbidden to work on the Sabbath. You'll work from six in the evening tonight until six in the evening tomorrow night. Straight through. I hope you are well rested."

I thought of my few hours of drunken stupor the night before, and my headache suddenly began to return.

"Wonderful," I muttered.

"Well, Mrs. Mocatta is quite a dragon," my friend continued, "and the rabbi is no charmer, but you should get along fine. It's easy work; they generally give it to a child. But I must warn you to be careful around Becky. She's quite vivacious, and they guard her like a treasure. Only two daughters, you know, and she the younger and unmarried. Have a care, Thomas!"

"I'll try to control myself," I assured him, amused at his chiding.

The bill arrived and I pounced on it. The proprietor took possession of our pipes, which he stored with several hundred others in racks overhead. There they would sit, ready for use as long as we would live, Zangwill assured me, and when we passed away, they would be broken in a small but solemn ceremony. Who could ask more of any institution?

"Now you must sponsor someone yourself someday," Zangwill said. "But not just anybody. You must use foresight and discretion. Be selective."

"And where am I going to find a Welsh detective who was formerly a convict? We don't grow on trees, you know."

Zangwill laughed and patted me on the back as we parted company. "You're starting to sound like a Jew now."

Barker was once more seated at our table at the Bucharest. When he saw me approach, he shoved a thumb and finger under his bristly mustache and launched a loud whistle which reverberated off the buildings. There was a clatter of hooves, and Juno and Racket came rattling around the corner.

"Did you have an instructive morning?" he asked.

"I believe I did, yes."

"Climb aboard, and you can tell me all about it."

We climbed into our seats and I gave my employer all the particulars about the secret meeting, from the young man who rapped on my table at the Bucharest to the little ritual at the Barbados. I didn't tell him that Zangwill had revealed my schedule for the evening. It was my trump card.

"I didn't tell too much about our plans to Zangwill, did I? I assume he is a suspect."

"Certainly, he is very close to everything. We cannot rule him out just yet. But you revealed nothing. How is your head, by the way?"

"Not bad."

"Do you think you might be up for something a little out of the ordinary?"

"Of course, sir. Anything."

"I would like you to serve as a *Shabbes goy* for Rabbi Mocatta's family this evening and tomorrow."

"Ah," I said.

"You do know what a *Shabbes goy* is, do you not?"

"Of course." I did now. He looked a little taken aback.

"Excellent. I've told them you were newly hired and that I wanted you to see a typical Jewish home, since we do work for the Board of Deputies, of which Rabbi Mocatta is a member. Actually, of course, your purpose is to speak privately with Miss Mocatta. She was perhaps the only confidante of Louis

Pokrzywa. If anyone would know about his private life, and the girl who wrote the notes at the Poplar Church, it would be her."

"Yes, sir."

"You had a hard night. Are you up to this?"

"I believe I am, sir."

"You should spend the afternoon resting. You'll be up for twenty-four hours in a row, and I want you sharp as a tack. I hear this Mrs. Mocatta is a corker."

"As you wish, sir."

Barker looked a little irritable. Perhaps he was put out at not getting to explain the duties of a *Shabbes goy* to me. "You're deucedly agreeable today. Is there anything I should know?"

"Not a thing, sir."

"Anything you're not telling me?"

"No, sir," I answered, all innocence.

We were at Barker's residence again. I climbed down out of the vehicle. "I'll have Racket here at five thirty, with directions to the rabbi's home."

"Aye, sir."

As I opened the door to our residence, the hansom rattled off in the direction of our offices.

23

DESPITE BARKER'S ADMONITION TO GET some rest, I wasn't really sleepy, having just had several cups of coffee. There was no sign of Mac when I came in, and for a few moments I debated what to do. Should I go upstairs and obey my instructions, or try to read in the library? Perhaps I might have an early soak in the bathhouse.

The hall was so quiet, I could hear the murmuring of the stream in the back yard. I still had my coat on, so I went out to sit in the garden. I am no expert, but the garden appeared well laid out, and Barker's team of Chinese workers took excellent care of the place. Plants of all sorts were already pushing shoots up through the mulch. I peered for a moment through the glass walls of a small greenhouse. Barker certainly knew how to live.

There was a sudden clicking sound and a low curse. I was on my guard instantly. The sounds seemed to be coming from the alleyway behind the garden. I moved forward cautiously. The fence is eight feet high, and there is no way to see out except to open the gate. Carefully, I did so.

Etienne Dummolard was in the alleyway, pitching some sort of metal balls about. I couldn't imagine what he was doing there. It was past noon and he should have been at his restaurant.

"Good afternoon, Etienne."

"Thomas! Come play *boules* with me. I will teach you how. No Englishman is capable of learning the intricacies of the game, but you Welsh are Celts, are you not?"

"Yes," I said, and stepped forward. The game, as it turned out, was rather like lawn bowling: one rolls out the small jack, then tries to get closest to it with the heavy steel spheres. I've no great love for the English historically, knowing what they did to the Welsh, but I did believe them capable of comprehending the simple rules of the game.

"Shouldn't you be at the restaurant, Etienne?" I asked casually.

"Stupid woman," the Frenchman said under his breath.

"Who?"

"Madame Dummolard."

"Your wife?"

"My ruin! Do you know what she wants now? A *saucier.* A *saucier*! As if my sauces are not the greatest to be found outside of France. 'We're too busy, Etienne.' 'Let me get you some help, Etienne.' 'A *saucier* would give you more time, Etienne.' Ha!" He struck the jack.

I hazarded a guess. "So, you're playing *petanque* in frigid weather to teach her a lesson."

"*Oui*! She has the ambition of Napoleon. She will not rest until she has captured all of Soho. I don't know what to do with her."

"That's simple," I quipped. "Open up a restaurant in Waterloo."

The Frenchman's laugh started low in his giant stomach and erupted forcefully. He slapped me hard on the shoulder.

"It's good you are here, Thomas. You bring humor to the place. But now I am ashamed of myself. I have deprived

London of my artistry and left Mireille ringing her hands, no doubt. Not that she does not deserve it. *Saucier*! Bah!" I helped him return the balls to the case lined with faded velvet, and he hurried off. It hadn't been difficult to convince him. I wished this case was as easy to solve as Dummolard's problems with his wife.

I returned to the garden and walked about. Barker could spend hours here, meditating in the peaceful confines, but I'm not Barker. Ten minutes in a garden, and I'm afraid I've exhausted my interest.

There was a yip at my ankle, suddenly. Harm, the sentinel of the garden, was there, with a small rubber ball at his feet. I greeted him and patted his head. He was a bit wary, as I would be if half my head consisted of eyes. I picked up the ball, and he promptly nipped me in the hand.

"Little beast," I said, picking up the ball again, and tossing it along.

"Fetch," I called, pointing to it. The dog did nothing but pant expectantly. "Go on! Get the ball!" He accompanied me across the lawn to see where the ball had gone. I pointed to it. "Pick it up! Come, boy, pick it up!" Perhaps, I reasoned, he only knew Chinese. I bent to pick up the ball, and, of course, he nipped my hand again. It appeared we had been playing at cross-purposes. I was playing "fetch the ball," while he was playing "bite the assistant." That was enough for me. In spite of his insistent barks that I come back and try to pick up the ball again, I went inside. Petulant Frenchmen and heathen dogs. What had I done to deserve such a fate?

I went upstairs to my room and looked through one of the books of Jewish customs that Barker had placed on my desk since the case began. A *Shabbes goy* was to keep all fireplaces, lamps, and candles lit throughout the twenty-four hours of the Sabbath. Lighting a match is considered "working" by Orthodox Jewish standards and is prohibited on Shabbat. I was also to be on hand for the hundreds of other menial tasks that are forbidden the zealous Jew, from opening medicine bottles to cooking. Although Mocatta was keeping a tight restraint on his daughter, I very much wanted to snatch a few moments' speech with her if possible, for Barker's sake if not my own. The success or failure of the case might depend upon it.

Racket was there to take me to Saint John's Wood promptly at five.

"You must be growing as rich as Rothschild by now," I called up to him.

"There's no money I can make that the missus can't spend," he quipped back.

Despite Zangwill's words about the "Jewish ghetto," some Jews had left the confines of the East End for the prosperity and security of the West. Mocatta's home was a small manse set back from the road, a solid three-story, red-brick affair, softened with plenty of climbing ivy. Only the mezuzah on the door betrayed anything out of the ordinary.

I was about to knock, but something—instinct, if enquiry agents have it—prompted me to go around and use the back entrance. I was to be a servant, after all. I was shown into a bustling kitchen which was the headquarters of the Sabbath's day plans. All the servants were Gentiles. The cook, Mrs. Stahl, was everything an English cook should be: a buxom, no-nonsense woman who would die before seeing the joint and peas undercooked. The staff would see to the kitchen fires, while I saw to the rest of the house. Everyone was aware that the Shabbat would begin at 5:47 sharp.

An adenoidal youth who passed for a footman led me solemnly to the woman of the house. Mrs. Mocatta was everything I feared she would be, a hawkish woman with a severe bun and an even more severe expression. I expected her to raise her black shawl like wings, seize me in her talons, and take me up to some remote mountain peak to feed her young.

I understood our relationship at once when she called me over.

"Boy!" she said. "Come here, boy. Let me look at you." She was not yet fifty, and there were only a few silver threads running through her fine black hair, but she could have been a septuagenarian for her temper. "I don't know what Mr. Mocatta was thinking. Do you know what you are about, boy? Do you understand your duties?"

"I believe so, madam."

"I do not expect any fires to go out tonight. Nor, on the other hand, do I expect you to be overliberal with the coal. I abhor waste. After dinner, the dining room fire is to be doused until morning, and the fire in the library when we retire. You may keep the sitting room fire burning for your own warmth, provided you are abstemious with the coal; a boy like yourself shouldn't need more than a shovelful to keep warm. The fires are to be well filled and banked in the bedrooms upstairs, and you are not to enter them after we retire. The tweeny shall attend to them first thing in the morning, and they shall be put into your charge after all are dressed."

"How many fires are lit upstairs, madam?"

"Three. One is for Mr. Mocatta and myself, one for our elder daughter and her husband, and one for our younger daughter."

"Are there any medications I may set out for any of you?" I asked, trying to sound efficient.

"Mr. Mocatta takes pills for his liver, Miss Mocatta has extract of malt every morning, and Mrs. Waldman, our eldest, takes a private medication. She may prefer to take it herself."

"Very good, madam. Which lights are to burn all night?"

"The dining room, sitting room, and hall lights on both floors are to be kept lit, but quite low. The cost of gas is exorbitant these days. Don't just stand there, boy. There is work to be done."

I nodded and tended to the fires. If there is one thing I

know other than storytelling, it's coal. They used a good bituminous Welsh coal here, none of that cheap English coal, but whoever set the fire did not know how to prepare it properly. I filled it well, but not overmuch, knowing that one lump too many would put Mrs. Mocatta's claws into my back. I did the same to the library and sitting room fires. The home was well furnished and prosperous-looking, but every chair was so overstuffed as to be hard as stone. I don't think there was a comfortable place to sit in the entire house.

I went upstairs, greeted Rabbi Mocatta, who was studying at a table with his hand-embroidered prayer shawl about his shoulders, and asked about his medication. I unstopped it for him and built up his fire a little. The Waldmans were not yet arrived, so I set their fire, then moved on to the younger daughter's room. She was also not at home. I went into her room and glanced around swiftly. I felt somewhat guilty going into a girl's private chambers. I passed by her small secretary, where she had begun a letter to a friend. I suppose Barker could have told me if the penmanship was different from the notes in Pokrzywa's Bible, but I wouldn't have had the slightest idea. I moved to the fireplace and began to lay the fire. The room was very feminine, with chintz curtains and toile fabrics on the chairs. I had not spoken to a girl near my own age in almost a year. I had been living in a man's world, with all its harsher realities. This room with its lace and porcelain and gossamer fabrics seemed almost a fairyland.

"Good evening, Mr. Llewelyn."

I stood and turned. Rebecca was standing in the doorway.

"Miss Mocatta," I answered, bowing.

"One doesn't generally find a gentleman in one's private boudoir." There was a touch of playful irony in her tone.

"Not a gentleman, but a humble *Shabbes goy*," I corrected. Though it was rude to stare, I couldn't take my eyes off her. She was a vision. Though she still wore black, it set off her tiny waist and fine figure. There was a comb set in the back of her dark hair, from which hung a veil of black silk.

"I understand I am to set out extract of malt for you," I continued.

"You needn't bother," she said, a smile playing on her pretty lips. "If truth be told, I only pretend to take it for Mama. It tastes quite terrible. And you needn't act like a servant around me. I know exactly why you are here. You wish to speak to me about Louis."

"I admit it. I do," I said, thinking I would willingly speak with her about the price of corn and any other subject under the sun. My conscience smote me then. Was it not only yesterday that I was mourning the anniversary of my wife's passing?

"We cannot speak now," she said. "I shall contrive a time."

"As you wish," I bowed. "I am in your hands."

"A dangerous place," she countered. "I might drop you."

I thought for a moment of how easily she could do just that.

As the family went through the blessings and candle lighting of the traditional Sabbath meal, I sat in a corner and tended the fires, as remote and forgotten as the moon. The members of the dinner party took no notice of me, save for a glance every half hour or so from Rebecca Mocatta. I counted the minutes between every chance meeting of our eyes. It would not do to give any sign, however, for Mrs. Mocatta was in the middle of the room, keeping an eye on me to make sure I was working. For all that Rebecca was there, I found the meal a long affair, full of the rituals which link the modern English Jew to his ancient past. I might have paid more attention had there not been something more distracting in the room.

I hoped for some quiet moment during the evening when I could speak to her again, but it never came. The family went to service, they returned, they played cards, and they talked. They might have been a normal English family on a Friday evening, if one didn't catch the references and Jewish turns of phrase. Finally, the evening party began to wind down, and I was busy replenishing and banking the fires upstairs for the night. Mrs. Mocatta was behind me every moment, fearing perhaps that I would nick the silver. Unhappily, from her point of view, she could find little fault with my work.

Eventually, everyone went to bed, and I was left in charge downstairs. The servants left for the night or retired to their quarters. By eleven, the fire in the sitting room grate, the ticking mantle clock, and I had the place to ourselves. The cook left some food for me, along with a new pot of coffee. I sat in a strange kitchen and ate someone else's bread.

I felt a little brighter after I'd eaten. I got up to look into the library. Perhaps I could find a novel to read. I lit a small lamp. Most of the volumes were in Hebrew, I was sorry to see, but I persevered. On the shelf farthest to the right, I found some English novels; obviously, someone other than the rabbi had chosen these. Most of them I had read, but there was a copy of Hardy's *Far from the Madding Crowd,* which I had not. I took it down and thumbed through it. A cup of coffee and a book seemed a good way to while away the hours. I turned to leave.

I heard a rustle of fabric, and she was there. Rebecca Mocatta, *in her night attire.* True, it covered her as much as her day attire, if not more so. But just the thought that she was uncorseted and ready to retire, and so close, unnerved me.

"Don't look!" she began, a protective hand over the ribbon at her bosom. "You needed to see me, and I wanted to help you find whoever killed Louis. This is the only way, I'm afraid. Mama had her eye on me all night, and no doubt will tomorrow."

"I fear I must look, Miss Mocatta, if only into your eyes. You see, I am trained in knowing if one is telling the truth."

"Very well, if you must."

"I thought to formally ask for a word with you from your father."

"Mama would refuse. She has strong beliefs about propriety, and she does not trust Gentiles. If she catches me here now, I shall be married to someone I don't even know within the fortnight."

"That's fine," I blurted out before thinking. "You don't know me."

Peripherally, I saw her smile. "I don't believe you shall be on Mama's list, you impudent fellow. But come! I want to help you find Louis's killers. What can I do? Ask any question you like, but be quick, I pray." She sat down on the edge of a settee and buried her slippered feet in her voluminous gown.

"I take it you and Mr. Pokrzywa were close. Was there any understanding between you?"

"Between Louis and me? No. Not at all. Louis was a sweet, intelligent fellow, but we had no romantic attachment. We were simply friends. I was tutoring him. He knew little of what passed between the mothers and daughters of his acquaintance, and he asked me candidly if I could help him find a suitable match. But as it turned out, he didn't need any help."

"How so?"

"He fell in love, of course."

I watched her soft hand smooth the fabric of her gown. "With whom?"

"He wouldn't tell me. I called him an ungrateful wretch. Her name is Miriam and she is a Jew, but that was all he would say. There must be a thousand Miriams in the East End. I assume she was low-born, from the neighborhoods farthest east."

"Why do you think that?"

"Had she been of our crowd, he wouldn't have hesitated to announce it. He was in love with a common woman, I fear. Was it my fault, do you think, encouraging him? He once walked halfway across Europe, but for all that he still knew so little of the world."

"One cannot help whom one loves." I believed it, I think, trying not to stare at the jet hair that was down about her shoulders, and the way the light from the lamp caressed her cheek.

"Miriam," I murmured to myself.

"It is all I know, I'm afraid," she said.

"Perhaps not. May I continue?"

"Yes, but hurry!"

"Had Louis Pokrzywa ever mentioned Christianity to you?"

"Yes! He said he'd stopped into a church for Jews who had become Christians. I quite brought him to task. I called him a Marrano and asked if he was thinking of converting to gain political influence, like Mr. Disraeli."

"I don't follow you. What is a Marrano?"

"You don't know your Jewish history, Mr. Llewelyn? They were the Spanish and Portuguese Jews who converted to Christianity, rather than be tortured in your Inquisition."

"It wasn't *my* Inquisition, I assure you. I'm a Welshman, Miss Mocatta, and a nonconformist. I don't believe any of my ancestors were in Spain at the time."

She smiled. "Why, Mr. Llewelyn, that was an attempt at humor. I thought you such a serious fellow."

"What do you know of me?" I asked, but of course the question was rhetorical.

"Only what Mr. Zangwill has told me."

"You've sent your spies before you."

"It's the only power I have," she sighed.

"You have more power than you realize," I responded, unable to hide a smile.

"You shall make me blush. Are all detectives this forward?"

A half dozen remarks teetered on the tip of my tongue, but I swallowed them and returned to the business at hand.

"Did Louis, at any time you knew him, speak as if his life were in danger?"

"No."

"But he was secretive."

"Only near the end, when he spoke of Miriam. Oh, I do hate that—'near the end.' He had no idea he was near the end of his life, you see." She twisted the lace of her gown.

"When did he first mention her?"

"Less than a month before his death."

"Did he ever—" A floorboard overhead creaked. I put out the lamp and flew across the room into the hall, as quietly as I could. I kept to the carpet and got into the sitting room just in time. I was stirring the fire with a poker when her mother came into the room.

She wore a robe so thick it might have been made from carpet, and her jet black hair hung down in a ropelike plait to her waist. Her manner had not changed, however, and she looked at me sternly.

"You're not using too much coal, are you?" she demanded.

"I am trying to be frugal, madam. I will use less, if necessary. Is the fire upstairs satisfactory for Rabbi Mocatta?"

"It is like an oven, but he likes it that way."

"And the fires in your daughters' rooms, are they satisfactory?"

"Yes, yes."

"Is there anything else I might be doing for the household beyond the fires and the lamps?"

"We have servants for that, thank you. There shall be several duties in the morning, but none until then."

"As you wish, madam."

"What is your name again?"

"It is Thomas Llewelyn."

"And Mr. Mocatta says you are some sort of . . . *detective*?"

"Assistant to Cyrus Barker, private enquiry agent. We're

working for the Board of Deputies at the request of Sir Moses Montefiore."

"Mmph," she said. It must have irked her not to find anything to criticize. "Mind you, don't fall asleep and let the rooms grow cold."

"Your cook has left a full pot of coffee in the kitchen, along with some victuals." I was rather enjoying the opportunity to use this servant speech. I don't believe I'd ever actually used the word "victuals" before.

"Very well, then. Good night, Mr. Llewelyn."

"Good night to you, madam. I hope you and your family sleep well."

24

WHEN SHE LEFT, I WAITED A MOMENT AND went into the hallway to look up the staircase. Then I crept into the library again. The room was empty. Rebecca Mocatta must have flitted upstairs while I was talking to her mother. That was close, almost too close, but I was disappointed at not getting to speak with her again. Very disappointed, indeed.

By the time the servants arrived the next morning, I'd become better acquainted with Thomas Hardy, whose heroine, Bathsheba, was a willful, raven-haired beauty, and a danger to all males, coincidentally enough. I helped start the fire in the big iron stove and made myself as useful as possible in the kitchen. I got on well with the staff.

I barely got a glance at Rebecca amidst the flurry of Sabbath morning activity. The rabbi would be reading that day at one of the smaller synagogues in the suburbs. I understood that he made himself available to speak as an interim rabbi wherever he was called upon. At home, he had a distracted air. Perhaps he was thinking about his reading. He seemed to have one foot on this earth and the other in Paradise. His wife was more pragmatic. Both of her feet were firmly on the ground, and had it not been for her, the rabbi might not have made it out the door Saturday mornings.

I carried water to the rooms, acted as a stand-in valet for the rabbi and his son-in-law, a bland and portly fellow with Prince of Wales whiskers, and even added a word or two to Rabbi Mocatta's notes at his request, since he was forbidden to lift a pencil.

With measured precision, the courses were set on the sideboard, and the family broke their fast. I replenished the new dining room fire and removed the ash. Later, I helped the rabbi with his coat, and the family left for service, after which I almost collapsed from exhaustion. I had gotten only four hours sleep out of the last fifty.

The servants cleared the dining room while I went upstairs to clean and rebuild the fires. I trimmed the wicks in the lamps that needed it, while the upstairs maid set every room in order and changed the sheets. It was a lot of work for just one family, and for a moment, I recalled Jacob Maccabee. He performed all of these duties himself, and so smoothly I hadn't noticed he'd done it. Did I think fresh sheets grew like manna, or that Dummolard's meals reheated themselves every night? I reproved myself a little, a very little. It was Mac, after all.

When the breakfast dishes were done, the cook and servants immediately began lunch. The meal would be pheasant consommé, roast beef with mashed potatoes, sprouts, carrots, and trifle, washed down with cabernet and coffee. For some reason, I thought of little Reb Shlomo, Pokrzywa's mystical rabbi. No doubt his repast would be more frugal, but it would also be more exotic: borscht with sour cream, perhaps, or pirozhki, gefilte fish, and homemade rye, washed down with strong tea made in the ever present samovars. The newcomers must think that the Sephardim, so long among the English Gentiles, had lost some of their heritage.

Eventually, the family swept in the door again, flushed from their activities and the brisk air. The cook was kind enough to see that a plate was prepared for me in the kitchen. I had been spoiled by sitting at Barker's table, however. The food tasted like one of Dummolard's experiments. The family did not seem to notice but consumed everything on the table, between the rabbi's blessing on the meal and his benediction.

I came out of the kitchen in time to watch Rebecca Mocatta pass by. She put her head down, but I think there was a smile on her face. The scent of gardenias perfumed the air in her wake. Her black dress swayed like a bell as she passed down the hall, but it was my heart that made the clangor.

The rabbi came down the stairs, dressed in a tattered old sweater, worn thin at the elbows, over his shirt and tie. He came up alongside me and murmured in my ear, "Would you take a turn in the garden with me, Mr. Llewelyn?"

I agreed, of course. He led me not out the front door, but through the kitchen. The back of the Mocatta property was not large, just a simple square of grass returning to life afer the blasts of winter, lined on all sides with shoulder-high walls of red brick. Having clung to life all winter, vegetation began to put forth its first tentative buds. In the center of the lawn, a lone ash tree stood some twenty feet tall, still bare of leaves, but vigorous for all that.

Mocatta stopped me in the little porch outside the back door.

"Mabel does not allow me to indulge in the house, but I am dying for a smoke. Are you as much of a wizard at lighting a pipe as you are at fireplaces, young man?"

I thought of Barker. I'd watched him dozens of times now. "Even better, I think. Have you tobacco?"

He pulled a pipe from his pocket. I expected a Dunhill, or at the very least a Comoy's, but the rabbi's pipe was almost as disreputable as Reb Shlomo's. I took in his sweater and his pipe together. It was obvious that he saved the luxuries of this world for his family.

I packed the pipe with tobacco from a small tin of Arcadia he carried. I filled it, tamped it down with my thumb, and filled it again. When the rabbi had the pipe clenched in his teeth, I struck a match and made those little circles Barker had demonstrated, while Mocatta puffed plumes of smoke, which drifted out and were blasted away by the early spring air. I didn't envy the rabbi his cold smokes, but he didn't seem to notice. He grunted with satisfaction and wandered out into the garden and slowly walked in circles, probably pondering abstract questions from the Torah. From my vantage point on the porch, he reminded me of one of the older inmates at Oxford Prison, the long-termers, taking the air in the small, guarded confines of the prison yard, with only their old pipes to comfort them.

The rabbi wandered over to the tree, and his hand caressed the trunk. "Do you see the stump there?" he asked, pointing to a medallion of wood flush with the lawn. I had not noticed it before. "That was Leah's tree. I planted it the day she was born, and I cut it down a few days before her wedding. We used it, along with the tree her husband's father planted at his birth, to make the *chuppa* under which they were married. Now there is just one tree here, Rebecca's tree. I wonder if it is lonely." He tapped out his pipe, emptying the ash onto its roots. Then he absently patted me on the shoulder and led me inside.

Not even the most virulent invective Madam Mocatta might have come up with could have dashed colder water on my dreams than the gentle words of the rabbi. No one had planted a tree when I was born. We owned no plot in which to grow it. My family had no mansion and had never even heard of a *chuppa*. The water in my father's bath was gray with coal dust when he left it each night, and my mother's faith in Jesus Christ and John Wesley were all that kept her going when times were lean, which was often. I felt just then that I had no more chance of a relationship with Rebecca Mocatta than if she had been a princess among the Venusians. For all the studying and mingling I had done, I felt no closer to this alien race than I had to the crown jewels when I was in the Tower looking through the bars. I am always an outsider.

How had he known? Rebecca and I hadn't exchanged a word in his presence. Was it coincidence, perhaps, or a set speech he made to discourage unworthy suitors? No, he scarce seemed the type. These rabbis seemed rather unworldly to a fellow raised among solid Methodists. I felt they could almost read my mind. And just what *had* Reb Shlomo meant by that remark about trapdoors?

I came into the hall through the kitchen, and the first thing I saw was Rebecca with a look of concern on her face. Did she already know what her father had said to me? Were they all clairvoyant? I wondered. Then she turned her gaze and I saw that it was not her father who caused such anxiety. A tall figure stood in the hallway, black as death against the white entrance door. It was Barker.

I looked into the sitting room at the clock. It was barely four. He was early; I still had almost two hours left. He paid no attention to me but stepped over to the rabbi and spoke to him in low tones. I strained to listen but only caught the words, "Take him." Mocatta nodded his agreement.

"Come, lad," my employer said. "Fetch your hat and coat. We must away."

I collected my things in the kitchen. By the time I came back, the rest of the family had come in, no doubt to look at the spectacle that is Cyrus Barker, agent of enquiry. I couldn't resist one parting shot at Mrs. Mocatta. I spoke up boldly.

"I fear we must leave early, Madam, but it has been a pleasure serving your family. I thank you for inviting me into your beautiful home. Good day."

What could she say after that? She was speechless. She gave a high-pitched squeak as if her pearl necklace was too tight and nodded as I shook her icy hand. Then I turned and put on my bowler hat. I dared look boldly into Rebecca's eyes for just a second, and tilted my hat at enough of an angle to be rakish, before following my employer out the door.

"What was all that about?" Barker muttered as we got into Racket's cab. He missed nothing.

"What do you mean?" I asked.

"Let's not start that again, Thomas. Don't play the innocent with me. I know better. Tell me everything from the moment you walked in the door."

I did so. I had hoped to leave my romancing out, but it was too tied up in everything. The best I could do was to abbreviate. If I hadn't risked that glance and had set my hat on properly, I might have gotten away with it. But I'd forgotten that behind those black lenses Barker sees everything.

"I don't approve of your romancing witnesses," he said, "unless it is on my order. But then, you were in prison for a few months. I suppose you're only human. Just watch yourself, Thomas."

"Yes, sir," I said. I sat back in the cab and looked out ahead of me as Barker did. We were heading northeast, toward the City again.

"You arrived early," I said, with a sudden pricking of my thumbs.

"Yes," Barker responded. "There has been another murder."

25

CYRUS BARKER WAS UPSET. I COULD SEE IT now in the way he sat. He didn't have that calm demeanor I'd come to expect from him. In fact, he was restless, bouncing about in the cab until I could hear the springs underneath protest. I was about to protest, myself.

"I don't like it!" Barker said, smiting his thigh like a petulant child. "Perhaps I am vain, but I like to think that when the criminals hear that I am on a particular case, they blanch in fear, or at least alter their plans. This carrying on as if I were inconsequential is an affront to my abilities. To quote Shylock, 'I shall have my pound of flesh.' "

"Have they crucified another Jew?"

Barker seemed not to hear me, but he finally turned toward me. "What? Oh, I beg pardon, lad. I haven't told you. A body has been found in a quarry wagon on a spur near Aldgate Station. It was buried under rubble. Another message from the Anti-Semite League had been scrawled on the wall by it. It is in a short tunnel of the underground, or it would have been found sooner. I haven't seen it yet. Inspector Poole sent me a message."

"Not crucified, then?" I asked. "How was he killed?"

"Stoned. Another Biblical punishment. But it was not a 'he.' The victim was a woman."

"A woman? They killed a woman? How can anyone kill a woman? This is monstrous!"

"I agree."

The enormity of the whole thing struck me. I pictured a phalanx of angry Englishmen stoning a poor Jewess to death. It made my blood boil. As far as I was concerned, the fair sex was somehow precious, inviolate. Had I not just shared a few brief moments with a daughter of Zion? Somewhere, even now, the poor dead woman's loved ones were wringing their hands, perhaps, wondering what had become of her.

We spent the rest of the journey in silence. Barker was irritable and I did not desire to have his discontent directed toward me. I had an unusual question on my mind, one that had only occasionally occurred to me during the course of the investigation: what if we failed?

What if we failed? We'd taken on a seemingly impossible task, hunting down a pack of murderers, a vigilante group, in a city the size of London, with only a few clues and a good deal of hope. What would happen if the league were successful in hiding their identities? Detective work is not like tailoring; when you engage a tailor, he doesn't have to go out on blind faith, hoping that somewhere in the City there is material of the correct color and yardage sufficient to make a frock coat and trousers. We detectives wander about, making cabmen rich, asking innumerable questions and being tossed out of places, hoping that in the end we don't look like fools with our hats in our hands. What does one say to a client at the end of a month or so? "Sorry, old man, couldn't find the blasted fellow?" A couple of those and it's time to take up your brass plate and see if some barrister in the Middle Temple needs a former detective to clerk and run messages.

Aldgate was the easternmost station of the Metropolitan

Line, serviced by the London, Midland and Scottish line. Once we entered the station and walked down the staircase to the lower level, it was only a matter of following the policemen, who, like so many breadcrumbs, were scattered along the line. Of course, it wasn't as easy as that, because every constable demanded complete particulars. Barker was reasonably pleasant to the first, a little less so to the second, and downright cold to the third. Finally, we came upon a clutch of blue helmets in the tunnel by the tracks, and there in the thick of them was the heavily whiskered face of Inspector Poole, looking somewhat upset himself.

"Have you removed the body?" Barker growled.

"Don't start, Cyrus," Poole said, running a hand through his thinning ginger hair. "We're already in the middle of a jurisdictional nightmare. Scotland Yard maintains that this is part of an ongoing investigation, the city police claim that the murder occurred in Aldgate and belongs to them, and the railway police have announced that the death was on railway property and refuse to give it up. We're waiting for our superiors to arrive and sort it out. The lord mayor himself may be involved by the end of the day. Still, I think I may get you close enough for a look-see."

The body lay beside a row of wagons on a siding near the tunnel wall. It was gloomy here but not dark, for the brief tunnel was lit by gaslight on the station side and by sunlight on the other. Nevertheless, the body was lit by a single lamp which lent a strange and macabre air to the proceedings, rather like limelight from a stage. The woeful form before me was a petite woman of indeterminate age, her face marred by bruising, and her aspect made even more bizarre by her hair's having been shorn close. Poole reached down by her side and lifted what I first took to be a scalp.

"It's a wig," Barker prompted. "Traditionally, married Jewesses cut their hair and wear wigs as proof against vanity. Have we any identification?"

"She had no bag, but there was a pawn ticket in her pocket."

The two detectives discussed the investigation, while I went down on one knee and looked at the victim more closely. Despite the pallor of death and contusions, she had regular features and might once have been attractive. She was not a young woman, perhaps thirty years of age. Her lids were half closed, and the eyes tinged a dark, rusty red. I leaned forward and closed them. They were cool and waxy. I took in her plain, blue dress and stout but serviceable shoes. The last thing I noticed before standing up was the furrow around her ring finger, where a wedding band had once rested.

"Raise the lamp, lad," Barker ordered.

I picked it up and lifted it high.

"How'd she die?" I asked.

"Back of her head's caved in. Someone gave her a good wallop with a rock or something. There may be more, but we're still awaiting the coroner, and I doubt he'll be stripping the body here."

The thought that a coroner would dare subject this poor woman's body to such humiliation I found revolting.

"Over here, lad. Bring the lamp over here," my employer insisted. "I want to see the message!"

"Sorry, sir!" I'd forgotten about the message. I stepped over to the wall and raised the lamp again. Against the soot-encrusted brick of the wall, the white chalk letters stood out in bold relief: "Lev. 20:10 The Anti-Semite League."

"Leviticus twenty ten," I read.

"What say you, Cyrus? Up to the challenge?" Poole asked.

Barker stood for a moment, sifting through chapters and verses in his mind. I've always admired people who would memorize long passages of scripture; a cold challenge to snap off a particular line seemed particularly hard. Finally, Barker spoke.

"And the man that committeth adultery with another man's wife, even he that committeth adultery with his neighbor's wife, the adulterer and the adulteress shall surely be put to death."

We all stood for a moment, taking in the implications of the verse. Then, Poole suddenly let loose a string of curses.

"Anti-Semite League—there's no such thing! It's just one bloke with a grudge. Pokrzywa was sparking the old fellow's lady here, and he set up this whole charade to lead us all on a merry chase after Jew-hating phantoms! We're going to find this woman's name, and then we're going to hang her husband by his thumbs until he confesses. Hundreds of hours wasted patrolling Aldgate, trying to protect the Jews from an attack that will never bloody happen!"

"I think there's more to it than that, Terry," Barker said. "The East End is like a tinderbox, ready for a match to strike, and this fellow is the match. He's still out there, trying to stir up trouble. He shot at Thomas here. I think he's mad at the Jews, perhaps because of a real or imagined relationship between Pokrzywa and this poor woman. He's intelligent and resourceful enough to rattle the Board of Deputies and elude our collective grasp."

"Resourceful or not," Poole said, pulling a notebook from his pocket, "he's just one man. I'm alerting my superiors to issue a manhunt. Hoi! Over here!"

A young constable had come down the line, almost at a run. He pressed a piece of paper into the inspector's hand. Poole glanced at it and thrust it into his pocket with casual indifference.

"I believe we've seen all we need to see here," he suddenly announced, changing tone. "The railway police appear to have everything in hand, and this is not our jurisdiction. We shall leave them with the body. Shall we go, gentlemen?" Poole left, as if he were the living embodiment of the Criminal

Investigation Department of the London Metropolitan Police Force. Barker and I followed behind him more slowly, as if we were merely headed in the same direction. We caught up with him again in the street.

"Her name?" Barker asked, hungry as a dog on the scent.

"Miriam Smith."

"There's your Miriam, Thomas, the one Miss Mocatta spoke of. And the address?"

"Three twenty-seven A Orient Street."

"Poplar. Not far from the church. Have you a vehicle waiting, Terry? No? Then let us take a growler. It appears Racket has picked up another fare."

We took the larger vehicle, Poole promising an extra half crown if we arrived in twenty minutes. As we were leaving, I noticed a few burly police officers in peaked caps arriving at the station cab stand with some speed. Poole had beaten the city and the railway police to the information. He looked pleased with himself.

"So, Mr. Llewelyn, how did you come by the name Miriam?" he demanded.

I looked at my employer.

"That information was obtained while questioning people who knew Pokrzywa," Barker said.

"I suppose asking what you discovered during the course of the investigation is out of the question."

Barker frowned, or seemed to, behind his spectacles. "You know I don't answer questions without the permission of my clients."

"We could compare notes," the inspector said, hopefully.

"The fact that you offer them so readily shows how little you have."

"I could drag you down to the station and sweat it out of you," Poole warned.

"You could try," Barker said.

This went on most of the journey. The two men were obviously friends but rivals when it came to work. Poole backed off several times and came in on a new tack each time, trying to pry information from Barker, but my employer was as impregnable as a clam. He wouldn't even give him information we knew to be useless.

"What about you, young man?" Poole said, turning to me. "We know about your little stretch in Oxford Prison. We may need to question you about recent events, perhaps have you spend the night in 'A' Division at Her Majesty's expense."

It was a good threat, but I was not about to be intimidated. "You know where to find me, sir."

"That I do!" Poole chuckled. "I could throw a sandwich from my window in Scotland Yard, and it would land on your office roof!"

The inspector alternately wheedled for information and crowed over his small triumphs. Barker balked like a stubborn bull, and I leaned against the cold window and thought of the poor thing that had until recently been called Miriam Smith. To think that days ago, the woman had been pretty enough to have a young scholar in love with her, a man who could have his pick of young women in the City. I pictured her brutal husband murdering her with some blunt instrument, destroying the skull of the woman he had promised to shelter and protect all his days. Who was this fellow? I had seen two bodies now, dead as a result of this man's hand. Obviously, the wretch thought himself justified in murdering for their betrayal.

When we reached Orient Street, Poole was out of the cab before the vehicle even stopped. Perhaps he hoped to catch the killer at home. The street was respectable, if a little down-at-heel. Number 327A proved to be a residence turned into flats. Our knocking at Smith's door brought many of the residents out into the hall.

"Has anyone seen Miriam Smith recently?" Poole demanded with authority.

"She gone to see her muvver days ago, now," a stout woman spoke up.

"You saw her leave?" Poole asked.

"No. Her old man told me Tuesday. What you want wiv her?"

"Mrs. Smith was found this morning, dead at Aldgate Station!" Poole said. He seemed to enjoy causing a sensation. "What is Mr. Smith's first name?"

"John!" the chorus called out.

"Not a very original alias," Barker growled in my ear. "You'll find in the East End that people change names as often as we change suits. It is possible that Mrs. Smith was not even his legal wife at all. We are on the fringe of Anglo-Jewish society here, where Jewish-Gentile couples live, and the few fallen Jewish women ply their trade."

"When did any of you last see John Smith?"

There was a buzz of conversation, and an old fellow obviously in failing health spoke up. "Three days ago, near abouts."

"What was Mr. Smith's occupation?" Poole demanded.

Another murmur arose, accompanied by the shrugging of many shoulders. No words were forthcoming.

"Well?"

"Dunno, sir," the old man answered. "'E told me 'e were in the sugar-making trade like, sir, but Jasper 'ere says Smith claimed to be an 'ostler. Reckon 'e changed jobs reg'lar, as people do, 'ereabouts."

"What were the Smiths like?" Barker asked.

"Kept to themselves," the plump woman said. "Bit high and mighty, if you ask me. I fink they was Jews, or at least she was. Been havin' rows lately. Shoutin' several times at night. Reckoned she'd packed up and gone home to mum. Looks like he done her in, he has."

"Does anyone else live in this flat along with the Smiths?" Poole continued.

"No, sir."

"And they haven't been here in three days?"

They all agreed neither had been there.

"Then I declare this flat abandoned. Is the landlord here?"

"Not 'im," the old man cackled. "'E's absentee, every day but rent day."

"Very well!" Poole called. Turning, he raised his foot and brought it forward against the lock with great force. Barker had trained him well. Part of the door frame splintered, and the door swung open with a crash against the wall. The inspector stepped inside, we followed, and the residents of number 327A Orient crowded around the door and peered in.

It was a spare little working-class flat, though opulent by the standards I had once lived under. There were antimacassars on the backs of faded stuffed chairs and framed pictures pulled from magazines on the walls. Miriam Smith had worked hard to make the shabby apartment habitable. Everything was spartan but clean. The flat seemed unnaturally still, however, and I had to agree with Inspector Poole's assertion that it had been abandoned.

The room was divided by a screen and a blanket hanging from the ceiling. We moved into the back portion of the room.

"No blood," Barker noted, looking about. "She wasn't murdered here, unless Smith cleaned up afterwards."

"Search the drawers," Poole suggested, and we immediately began going through everything. Most of the dead woman's personal effects were still here, worn but carefully repaired. The suspect's clothing was gone, as was anything referring to him, save for a certificate of marriage on the wall, from a church in Brighton. There were no photographs and no evidence of where Smith might have gone.

"Scampered," Poole pronounced. "I'll have my men take

this place apart board by board in the morning, but we're losing valuable time now." He turned to the crowd. "Can anyone describe John Smith?"

The crowd pushed forward a hesitant-looking Jewish fellow with long side locks and a cap he was twisting in his hand.

"Sir," he said gravely to the inspector, wringing his hat until it resembled a challah. "Sir, I am a street artist. If I could just go get my charcoal and some paper, I could sketch him in just a few minutes."

"Get your things, by all means," Poole agreed. The fellow ran downstairs and returned with a piece of butcher's paper and a charcoal pencil. We sat him down in one of the worn dining chairs and left him to reconstruct the man from memory, while we combed the flat for more clues. All we found of interest was Miriam Smith's Bible. It had no bulletin from the Poplar church, but her handwritten name on the dedication page was in the same handwriting as the notes we had, or so Barker pronounced. Miriam Smith was definitely the woman with whom Louis Pokrzywa had been passing messages.

"I've got it," the street artist called in triumph. The three of us crowded around him and looked into the face of our possible murderer for the first time. It was a square, clean-shaven face, a man of perhaps forty years with a birthmark on his chin. He had typically British features and gave the appearance of a stern, no-nonsense sort of person. It was an intelligent face, and not one I would associate with violent behavior. Most of all, though I did not recognize his face, I somehow felt I had seen him recently, if only I could place just where.

"He matches the description of the man in the park who Da Silva said was speaking against the Jew," Barker said, turning to Poole. "I believe this has answered your question, Terry. Whether the deaths were personally motivated or not, this fellow obviously has an agenda against the Jews. I still think he will attempt to force a pogrom if he can."

When we came out of the building, it was nearing six. Poole was anxious to take the sketch to Scotland Yard, and Barker and I were hungry, neither of us having eaten since breakfast. We parted company, and the Guv and I walked back to the station, where we were able to catch a hansom dropping a fare. I fell asleep in the cab and knew nothing until Barker shook me roughly to say we were at the Elephant and Castle. We were a couple of tired and hungry men as we passed down the lane behind Barker's home and reached for the latch of the back gate. All my thoughts were of a filling dinner and a warm bed. The last thing I expected was for us to be set upon in our own alleyway.

26

AT LEAST A DOZEN MEN CAME AT US OUT OF the gloom of the alley, their hands filled with staves, axe handles, and other makeshift weapons. I recognized none of them. Was this it, I wondered? Were we finally being set upon by the Anti-Semite League? Roughly, Barker thrust me through the gate and followed behind. With a ham-sized fist, he smacked a small brass gong which hung near the entrance. The sound reverberated around the small enclosure. At the far end of the garden there was a horrid screech. It was Harm giving the alarm. Without slowing his cacophony, he flew across the lawn, charging the first intruder. Pekingese, I have discovered, have absolutely no fear when it comes to protecting their property from invasion.

Harm sunk his razorlike teeth into the ankle of the first man, bringing a cry of pain to his lips. Before he could do any further damage, however, a second fellow caught the little dog full in the ribs, a savage kick that brought a yelp of pain from the poor animal, and sent him flying several feet into the bushes.

That tore it, as far as I was concerned. I saw red. Just who did these blighters think they were, coming onto our property and kicking our dog? There the big blackguard stood, his foot still in the air. Is it any wonder I seized the offending foot in my hands and planted my own full in the fellow's stomach?

Another scoundrel seized my lapel and raised a club, ready to strike me down. It was just like an exercise in Barker's class. I trapped his hand with my own, stepped back, and raised my other arm up hard, striking him in the elbow joint. I felt rather than heard the break, and the fellow went down holding his arm. At that moment, I was struck two different blows by men armed with staves, and I tried another trick that Barker had demonstrated in class: run when you are momentarily outnumbered.

As I passed him, Barker appeared in little trouble. He was mowing men down as if they were skittles. I saw him pick up one fellow like a doll and toss him into two more. Then he seized one of the others by the wrist, and flipped him so fast, he caught another in the jaw with the man's foot. My employer might have been out for a little light evening's entertainment, but I had a ringing head and a sore shoulder and was in need of a good wall to put my back against.

I was running toward the house when our back door opened and Maccabee jumped out. He braced his back against the door and brought his shotgun to bear. I had just enough time to throw myself on the ground before both barrels went off, peppering the crowd with buckshot. There were oaths and cries aplenty after that.

I sat up and turned around, in time to see Barker shoot out of the crowd, running toward us. His hands were in the pockets of his overcoat, and just before he reached me, he stopped and turned back. His hands came out and suddenly the air was filled with pennies, dozens of copper pence, glittering in the light from the kitchen window. They flew across the enclosure, and wherever they landed, they stuck, whether in wood or plant or human flesh. The advance stopped as men reached for an injured limb or a cut forehead. One poor blighter was spinning around, trying to remove the coin from between his shoulder blades. It was too much for the visiting team, who, one by one, began to break and run. Barker inflicted more punishment on the retreating figures, while I rushed to shut the gate after them. In a moment, the latch clicked after the last of them, and we heard the men running away down the lane. It was over as quickly as it had begun.

"Are you hurt, lad?" Barker asked. We were both a little winded and still leaning against the gate.

"No, sir," I said, and it was true. I'd been thumped twice and would have bruises, but I felt rather good.

"Gave as well as got?"

"Broke one fellow's arm, sir," I said, as if it were something to take pride in. "And kicked another in the stomach."

"Mac?" he called. The butler had his shotgun broken open and was removing the shells. By his coolness one would think this was the standard Saturday night's fare.

"I am well, sir."

"Harm?" Barker called. "Harm?"

It was the first time I'd seen my employer actually look frightened. He stepped away from the gate, still calling the little dog's name. I'd felt it was silly at first, this big, rough fellow so fond of his little lapdog, but now I had to admit I was worried myself. I hadn't seen the little creature since he'd received the boot in the ribs. I feared the worst might have happened.

"In the bushes, there, sir," I said, pointing to the left. We both converged on the spot, and Barker pushed back the leaves. Harm was lying there, not moving, but his head was up and he was panting.

"Oh, Harm, what have they done to you?" Barker asked.

"He may have a broken rib or two," I hazarded. "That was quite some kick he received."

"Mac! Bring a large pillow!"

The butler nodded and glided into the house.

"Are you hurt, boy?" Barker asked, patting the little fellow on the head. The dog gave a feeble bark, almost like a cough. When Mac returned, we gently transferred him to the pillow. Despite our efforts to be careful, he gave a yip of pain. I knew nothing of dog anatomy, but I worried that a broken rib might have punctured a lung. I'm sure Barker was thinking much the same. We got him safely onto the pillow and Mac took him into the house.

Barker turned his head and seized my shoulder.

"What is it, sir?"

"I heard something."

The thought that they might return in greater numbers hadn't occurred to me. We would be overrun in that case. We listened closely to the gurgle of the stream and horses clopping in the streets. Then I heard it: a moan.

"Someone's still here!" I cried.

"Over there, behind the bath house. Hop it, lad!"

I ran over to the far side of the outbuilding, hands raised, ready to defend myself again if necessary. There was a man lying on the ground, moaning softly. My nose told me that he had been ill. Barker joined me, looking over my shoulder.

"Mac!" he called. "Bring a lamp!"

The butler came out into the garden again, an oil lamp in his hand, as placid-looking as if he were bringing the morning *Times*. If he didn't hurry up with the lamp, I thought, I was going to run up and take it out of his hand. He finally arrived and held the lamp high. The man lying against the side of the building looked like a day laborer, in an old suit, a cloth cap, and worn boots. I say man, but he couldn't have been much more than my own age, perhaps two and twenty. It wasn't until he turned his head and blinked into the light that I recognized him.

"It's the one that kicked Harm, sir," I stated. "The one I got in the stomach."

"By the looks of him, Thomas, I'd say you missed his stomach by a good margin." He reached forward and pulled the fellow up by the lapels of his flimsy jacket. "So, you're the fellow that kicks poor, defenseless little dogs. Who sent you?"

"Sod off, mate," the young man summoned the courage to say.

I saw Barker reach back his fist, ready to strike the man down, there and then, but he suddenly changed his mind.

"Mac, Thomas, take this fellow down to the cellar, and tie him up in a chair. We'll let him cool his heels awhile. Then afterwards, Mac, I want you to prepare a light supper. Is the bath ready?"

"Yes, sir."

"Splendid. Then there is no need to alter our routine. We shall question this fellow at our leisure. But now, I must make a telephone call. Several, in fact. Take him, gentlemen."

Maccabee and I did as Barker asked. I used the approved Tokyo come-along hold. The man we carried down the stairs outweighed us each by three stone, but he was not in much shape to protest. Mac brought a spindle chair and some rope from the lumber room, and between the two of us we trussed him up rather snugly. Then we left him, as Barker had ordered. For his sake, I hoped the police arrived soon. He looked the very picture of misery.

Barker was still on the telephone by the front door when we came up into the hall. He was speaking rapidly in Chinese. Obviously, it wasn't the Yard he was speaking with. Finally, he set the earpiece back in its cradle.

"They shall be here within the hour," he said.

"Scotland Yard?"

"No, the gardening crew. My garden is a disaster! It shall take months to get it back the way it was. And someone shall be coming to take Harm away. I want you to handle that. They shall arrive in a black carriage. Carry him out on the pillow."

"Yes, sir," I said. "When will Scotland Yard come for the fellow in the basement?"

"I haven't called Scotland Yard just yet," Barker replied. "I wanted to question him myself first."

There was something in Barker's look that I didn't like. If he had been stone-faced before, he now looked like solid granite.

"But, sir, isn't it unlawful to detain a man against his will?"

"Mr. Llewelyn," Barker said, "I'm not sure of your meaning. The fellow is our guest."

It was several hours before we got back to our "guest." We ate a cold supper of French sausages, cheese, and hard-boiled eggs, then Barker had his bath, as if it were any other night. I sat in the front room, with Harm on his pillow, waiting for the carriage to arrive.

Almost an hour after Barker's phone call, as he'd predicted, a closed carriage arrived at the front door. No one got out to ring the bell. I opened the door and carried the pillow and Harm out to the vehicle. The driver got down from his box and opened the door; I got a glimpse of a female figure all in black, with a heavy veil. She took the dog, pillow and all, into her lap. The driver closed the door before I could speak, and they drove off without a word. I hoped Barker knew what he was doing, trusting Harm's health to these mysterious persons.

By the time I reached the back garden to tell Barker, the garden crew had arrived. They carried paper lanterns on long poles. There must have been twenty workers at least. They swarmed all over the garden, sweeping, clipping, digging and replanting, while Barker moved about in shirtsleeves, inspecting everything. I helped by picking up pence. They were in the path, on the lawn, and buried in the back wall. I only found about a dozen. Presumably, the rest went home with our attackers as souvenirs.

I gave Barker his pence and told him that the carriage had taken Harm away. He nodded without speaking, rolling up his sleeves. I noticed that the marks on his arms made the Chinese nervous. Perhaps there was some emblem there that had meaning to them. My employer was not pleased with the way one fellow was raking the stones, and he took the rake himself, working until he was satisfied with his own efforts.

Finally, close to midnight, the gardeners finished their work and loaded their tools into an ox-driven cart. By the time they left, the garden had returned to its general appearance, or so it seemed to a layman such as myself. Barker washed his hands at a delicate pump by the windmill and struggled back into his suit jacket, clean as ever.

"Let us go speak to our guest," my employer said. "He should be well primed by now."

Our "guest" was wide awake and wary as we came down into the cellar. He looked frightened, and well he might. Sitting alone for hours, not sure of his fate, must have terrified him. I noticed his wrists were chafed from struggling to get free. Barker took another chair, spun it around, and straddled it.

"So," he said conversationally, "what am I going to do with you?"

"I ain't peachin' on my mates," the poor man spoke up, bravely. "That's a promise."

"Oh, you'll sing like a nightingale before I'm done with you. I'm no Scotland Yard inspector, you know. I don't have to play by any rules. I could keep you here indefinitely. Your mates, as you call them, are long gone. They've probably written you off as a loss. For all they know, this place is crawling with constables. I could keep you down here for days. Weeks even. No one's coming to save you. This could very well be the night you disappear from the face of the earth."

The poor soul went to work, struggling against his bonds again and grunting for all he was worth. It was a helpless ordeal. Barker sat there and watched him. The man finally gave up and almost swooned from fatigue.

"What is your name?" my employer asked.

"Jim Brown."

Barker brought his foot up, kicking the bottom of the man's seat. The fellow jumped and grimaced. After the kick I had recently given him, he must have been sore.

"What is your real name?"

"McElroy, sir," he responded. "Albert McElroy."

"Very well, Albert. Now we're going to play a little game. I'm going to ask you some questions, and you're going to answer them if you wish. Strictly voluntarily, of course. What do you say?"

"Do your worst, peeler. You can't scare me."

Barker's foot came up again, and this time McElroy and the chair went with it. All four legs lifted off the floor, and the chair smashed into the padded wall, breaking apart like a matchstick. Our guest fell hard on the mat, and pieces of wood rained down all around him.

"Mr. Barker!" I protested.

"Mr. Llewelyn, our guest seems to have had an accident. Would you pull up another chair for him? I don't think you shall have to tie him up again. He'll be much more cooperative now, won't you, Mr. McElroy?"

The man groaned as I helped him into another chair. I was very concerned now. Mr. Barker was cutting it quite rough. Just how angry was he about Harm? I feared he might go too far. In fact, I believed he'd done so already.

"Now," Barker continued. "We were about to begin our game. Any objections, Albert? No? Excellent. Question one: Do you belong to any organizations?"

"Yes, sir."

"To what organizations do you belong?"

"Do I have to answer, sir? Didn't you just say they were voluntary-like?"

"They are."

"Then I'd rather not say."

Barker reached into his pocket and McElroy flinched, no doubt expecting a gun or some knuckle-dusters. Instead, he produced his pipe and filled it with tobacco from his sealskin pouch.

"Very well. Let me rephrase the question. Are you involved in any organizations that aren't for the benefit and support of the Irish people?"

"No, sir, I am not."

"So, you don't belong to any organization whose purpose is to harm or remove the Jews from London."

"No, sir."

"Have you ever heard of a group called the Anti-Semite League?"

"No, sir. Can't recollect any group like that."

"What do you do for a living, McElroy?"

"I'm a carpenter as was, sir, afore the Jews moved in and took over all the work."

"And might I assume that you now spend your days with some of your fellows, bending an arm and talking about general conditions in what one might call a social club?"

"Social club! That's a good'un, sir. Aye, we philosophize most afternoons, down at the Crook and Harp."

"Oh, the good old Crooked Harp. I know it well. Excellent. Now, Albert, I'm not going to ask you to name any of your mates. I'm not after the little fish, only the big one. Did someone come in and get you fellows all stirred up, someone blaming all your present troubles on the Jews? Not one of the regulars, mind, but someone new? Someone extra?"

"Aye, sir, he did. Said there was no end to 'em and that they'd run us out of England. Said he knew how hard we worked to start a new life after bein' forced out of Ireland. Said they needed to be taught a lesson. A good hard lesson, if you get my meanin', sir."

"You're being wonderfully cooperative, Mr. McElroy. My, but this is thirsty work. I believe we still have some good home-made porter in the lumber room. Mr. Llewelyn, would you be so good as to get our new friend a drink?"

In a moment or so, I had the Irishman seated at the table with a glass in his hands. McElroy was obviously relieved, but he kept flicking his eyes Barker's way, in case his mercurial temper suddenly rose again.

"Thank ye, sir," he said.

"Not at all. Pray continue. What did your fellows say when he made this proposal?"

"Oh, they was all for it. They've been spoilin' to smash a few heads for months, only didn't know how to go about it. The bloke said he had a cart outside, ready to take any fellow man enough to teach them Jew-boys a lesson, and to get the fellow responsible for takin' our positions."

"And that was . . . ?"

"You, sir."

"As I thought," Barker said, and made that *harumph* in his throat that was meant for a chuckle. "It might interest you to know neither of us are Jewish."

"He didn't mention that, sir, nor did he say that you kick like a Skibbereen mule."

"What did he look like, Albert, this fellow that talked you into coming here with your mates?"

"Middlin' sort o' fellow, sir. Midthirties. Clean shaven. Claret mark on his chin. Dressed well, not flashy. But he weren't no toff, spoke like one of us."

Barker turned to me. "John Smith."

"So it would appear, sir."

"Did this fellow intimate that there might be more 'action' than just tonight's little bit of fun, that there might be an attempt to teach all the Jews a lesson?" he asked the Irishman.

"Aye, he did, sir. I can't remember all he said, on account of my havin' had a pint or three. But I got the impression he was goin' from pub to pub lookin' for any blokes with a grievance against the Jews. Tomorrow mornin' it's to be, sir, in Petticoat Lane."

"Thank you, Mr. McElroy. You've been a fount of information. I regret the incident with the chair."

"No hard feelin's, sir. Sorry I kicked your little dog. Me blood was up. Hope the little chap's all right."

"Llewelyn, see if you can get a cab at this late hour for Albert."

Racket was at his post across the street when I looked outside. He rattled over and tapped his top hat with his crop. McElroy looked all in from the action, and I helped him into his seat. The cabman took me aside.

"Bit of a to-do here tonight?" Racket asked, stroking his thick beard. "If you need any help, I'm your man."

"It was nothing we couldn't handle," I answered smugly. "A group of men were stupid enough to attack Barker in his own garden."

"Sorry I missed all the fun. Old Push is a real corker, ain't he?"

I thought of Barker working his way through a bunch of armed ruffians, as easily as if he'd been in his exercise class. "That he is."

Racket flicked the reins and Juno tossed her head and began to move. The last I saw of Albert McElroy that night was his waving hand as the cab rattled down the street.

I went back inside. Barker was just coming into the hall.

"Get some sleep, lad, but stay in your clothes. I might need you. We'll have a very early start in the morning."

27

TOO SOON, BARKER'S HAND WAS ON MY shoulder, shaking me awake.

"Get up and ready," he said. "Take your revolver this time. I want us in the Lane within the hour."

I rose quickly, and loaded my Webley. Then I met Barker in the hall. Mac brought out coffee and croissants with gooseberry jam. There was no telling when we would eat again.

"You think McElroy was telling the truth, that there shall be further trouble this morning?" I asked.

"Last night was just a preliminary skirmish. There will be a larger conflict today, you can count upon it. One doesn't collect an army of troops and just let them sit on their hands, not if one is a competent general."

"Do you think the 'general' was among the men last night? I didn't see anyone I knew."

"Nor I, but I believe he would be recognizable to us, should he show his face. Therefore, he shall hide it. This is one leader who shall not be at the head of his army."

"You know who he is?"

"I have an idea."

"Have you alerted the Jews?"

"I sent a message to Sir Moses an hour ago. All ready, then? Let us be off."

It was dark when I stepped outside, and too early for Juno and Racket to be about. I wondered just how early it was.

"What o'clock do you have?" I asked.

"Shortly after five. It is imperative that we reach Petticoat Lane before it opens. We should find a cab in the Elephant and Castle. Speaking of time, remind me to purchase a pocket watch for you. We can't have you constantly asking the time from everyone. It makes the agency look incompetent."

Middlesex Street was nearly deserted when we arrived, but a few vendors were wheeling in handcarts, overflowing with old clothes. It must have been even more empty the night the Anti-Semite League had arrived, with its sad cargo. Would there really be an attempt at a pogrom here today? At the moment, it seemed unlikely. I'd have called it a rumor, a fantasy, were it not for the events of the night before.

The sun began to rise lazily. Street hawkers filed in and started setting up their booths. Jewesses hung used but freshly washed and ironed clothing on lines and makeshift racks. Food vendors roasted potatoes and boiled milk for cocoa. An enterprising fellow set out a samovar of tea and began a brisk trade immediately, Barker and myself being early in the queue. I began to have doubts about my employer's plan. Business seemed very much as usual in the Lane. Perhaps the affair had spent itself the night before.

They came west from Whitechapel when they finally arrived, from the warren of doss-houses, public houses, and gin shops. They were close to a hundred strong, the offscourings of the district: rampsmen, bruisers and brawlers, sodden with Saturday night liquor and brimming with hate and violence in their yellow, piggish eyes. Like the group in our garden, they were armed with anything that came to hand, from a board pried from a fence in passing, to a spanner for tapping railway wheels. It was an ugly mob, a twin in every way to the ones that had murdered men, raped women, and terrorized children in Eastern Europe, except for one difference: these fellows were English, a race which prided itself around the world for its decency and common sense.

A wail broke from the lips of the vendors when they realized what was about to happen. I even heard a Russian Jew near me mutter the word "Cossack." The inchoate mob collected at the foot of Aldgate High Street, then surged forward with bloodlust in their eyes. They tore apart the first stall they reached. From where I stood, it seemed to explode. Wood and clothes flew up into the air. There was a rending of cloth and the sound of axes. The vendor himself went down, streaming blood, after being knocked on the head with a sailor's belaying pin. His fat wife ran up the Lane screaming in Yiddish. The next three stalls followed in succession. Skulls were being thumped like melons, and Jew and Gentile alike were wrestling in the dirty and rubbish-strewn street.

"I thought you called Sir Moses," I shouted. "Where are the police?"

"No police, lad. The Jews are handling this themselves," Barker replied in my ear. "Keep your wits about you. Remember what I've taught you. Don't use your pistol unless your life is in dire distress."

A fellow leaped by me from behind, knocking against my shoulder. He was a young Jewish fellow with what appeared to be a length of wood in his hand. He ran up to the first rank of leaguers and gave one fellow a good clout on the noggin. Eager hands clutched him, and suddenly he was lifted overhead, amidst a sea of rough hands and angry faces; he was punched and pummeled for his bravery. But he was not the lone brave Jew. More came running, no longer willing to wait passively to be expelled from another country, ready to fight for themselves and their people and a permanent home here. Men were running from all directions, shouting, and suddenly the tide of antagonists crashed over my head, and I was engulfed in the very thick of it.

Soft spots. That was the key for someone as unskilled as myself, Barker said. Only an idiot would try to attack a larger fellow by hitting him in the stomach or the head. But what of the throat? I ducked as a six-footer swung a cricket bat at my head, then gave him a good, solid punch to the neck, right above the collar. The man went down satisfactorily, clutching his throat for air. A second seized my lapels roughly and pulled me off my feet. I clapped my hands hard against his ears, as I'd been taught. The sudden pressure would burst the eardrum and cause a loss of balance. He reeled away and looked disinclined to fight anymore. A third swung back a fence post, intent on cracking my skull, but I ignored the Queensberry Rules and kicked him on the side of the knee. He went down among his brothers, clutching his injured limb.

Just then I got a good wallop on the back of the head. I was down for a moment or two myself, but I shook it off and climbed back into the fray, fists raised. As I stood up again, I saw none other than Brother Andrew McClain standing close by with a fellow in each hand, shaking them as a ratter does two rats before knocking their heads together.

"Hallo, there, Tommy, my boy!" he roared with evident pleasure. "Grand day for a scrap, isn't it?" He laid hands on another fellow, but I knew that there would be no healing involved. When last I saw him, he was singing a hymn as he knocked combatants about.

I'd lost sight of Barker. I stepped up on the lip of a gas lamp and looked across a sea of men beating the tar out of each other for no good reason. It was like a war, only with poor ammunition. Bottles flew, boards cracked, and elbows separated people from their teeth, but there were no fatalities. I couldn't tell if one side was prevailing over the other, and I couldn't find my employer anywhere.

Just then, a strong-looking chap seized my leg and pulled me off the gas lamp, intent on mischief. As I fell into him, I reached for his nose, and slid a thumb into his eye socket. Barker says that the eye is the most sensitive organ of all. This fellow obviously agreed, or would have if he weren't busy holding his face and cursing. My luck went dry then. I met my match with the next man. He was more cautious, and he had a good right cross. We took turns beating on each other and posturing, waving our fists in the air, when there was a sudden, awful din.

At first, I thought it was elephants, an entire herd of them coming our way. That would certainly put to rout the members of the league, along with everyone else. Elephants are undiscriminating as a species. My opponent and I broke off in mid-blow and craned our necks to see what the next thing to come along would be. It felt like the end of the world. As I watched, something large and gray began to loom over the crowd, but it was not an elephant. The creature looked human. My mind turned to the legend of the golem that Israel had told me about. Had he somehow come to life? He had, but not in the way I expected. He was painted on a banner with a menacing attitude, a very tall banner, held aloft on a long pole. The crowd began to part at the far end of Middlesex, and a phalanx of Jewish men came marching along, four across and ten deep, clad in their voluminous black coats and fedoras. The men in front were holding shofars to their lips, the curling ram's-horn instruments of Old Israel. The sound was unearthly. It jangled on the nerves like a clarion cry, calling everyone to attention. The crowd, Jew and Gentile alike, stopped in their tracks, jaws hanging open in astonishment at these resolute young men in their side curls and beards, as if to say, "What's next?" One Whitechapel wag tried to make some snickering remark, but it died in the sudden hush. I recognized some of the men in the ranks from that strange assembly a few days before. One was the impassioned zealot Asher Cowen, who spoke so eloquently to us all. This was the Golem Squad.

The young orator spoke loudly in his own tongue, and every man came to an abrupt halt. He spoke again, and they all answered in unison, like a crack regiment. He spoke in English next, perhaps for the benefit of the crowd.

"A sword for the Lord!" he cried, and they answered in kind. Then each man reached into his coat and pulled out an actual sword, twenty-four inches of newly minted steel, glinting magnificently in the morning sun. On the blade, in swirling Hebrew characters, were the symbols I had seen on the banner at the meeting, the script that formed the word "golem." So, this was their defense against the pogrom. These men were prepared to defend their home here to the death. The shofars blasted again, and I felt a holy chill go down my spine. The blasts rattled the casements of the windows. Could these old city buildings withstand what had brought Jericho to its knees?

With a savage cry, the new army charged into the fray, their swords waving in the air. As they ran by, and just before my opponent resumed our fight with a clout to the jaw that rang bells in my ears, I saw a face I recognized. It was distorted by war cries and resolution, but I recognized it nonetheless. It was my new friend, Israel Zangwill, in his coat and hat, a sword in his hand, leaping into the melee. And you will think me fanciful, but I'd swear I caught a glimpse of Jacob Maccabee behind him.

Well, that was it. I wasn't going to be outdone by a spindle-shanked teacher and a fastidious butler. I bent down, retrieved the fallen cricket bat from the street, and caught my adversary one that would have gone over the wall at Lords. He raised a hand, either to admit the touch or to raise some objection, then he retired from the field or, rather, fell onto it.

A hand plucked at my shoulder, and I brandished the bat, but it was only Racket, in his long coat and cabman's topper.

"Don't crown me, Mr. L!" he said, raising his hands. "I'm on your side. Old Push is in hot pursuit after the ringleader. He wants me to take you to where he's got him pinned down."

Racket and I dodged our way through the crowd. Swords flashed in the sun, and there were cries and curses in the air in several languages. As one sword came down on a big fellow's shoulder, I noticed something: the swords were not sharpened. They were mostly being used to frighten and confuse the attackers. My mind went back to the old Bible story of Gideon and how he had used torches, clay pots, swords, and shofars to put to flight an army much larger than his own. As I watched men in twos and threes fleeing back to Whitechapel to bind their bleeding heads and fix their broken bones, I saw the old trick was winning again. This pogrom, unlike the others in Europe, would not succeed. You should never fight a creature when its back is to the wall.

Racket and I were soon around the corner and clambering aboard the hansom. What a day! My head was bleeding, my ears were ringing, most of my knuckles were barked, and I had never felt better in my entire life.

Racket cracked his lash over Juno's head, and her ironclad hooves dug into the grime-covered road. We rattled at a fast clip down Aldgate High Street. Barker had done fast work, slipping off like that and going after the real leader. I was a little put out with him for not including me in his plans, but I'd had a great time at the little to-do the league had set up for us. Now all we had to do was catch the slippery beast that had instigated this whole show, and we could go collect our fee. I didn't know who it was, but I hoped at least Barker did.

Abruptly, a loop of rope fell around my neck. I jumped and looked up. The trap was open, but Racket's familiar whiskers were nowhere to be found. I seized the rope and tried to pull, more annoyed than alarmed, but it was suddenly drawn tight. Very tight. The hemp bit into the flesh of my throat.

Slowly, I was hauled up out of my seat, as someone heaved upon the rope. My shoulders came in contact with the edges of the trap, but my head was pulled through. For a second or two, I found myself looking out over the top of the cab. I wanted to turn around and see my attacker, but I couldn't breathe, and my fingers couldn't loosen the rope enough for me to catch my breath. I wanted to cough, to gasp, to drag oxygen into my tortured lungs, but I couldn't. Spots began to appear in front of my eyes, as if someone were spattering India ink on me. The last thing I remembered before I passed out was the voice of Pokrzywa's funny little mystical rebbe, Reb Shlomo, saying, "Look out for trapdoors!"

28

THE PAIN THAT CAUSED ME TO PASS OUT WAS as nothing compared to the pain that awakened me again. My head throbbed, my muscles burned, and my heart was hammering in my chest. Searing pain radiated out in waves to my toes and fingertips and back. It felt as if I had been in pain for hours, perhaps forever.

I willed my eyes to open, to move beyond the pain, but what I saw made no sense. I was disoriented. Perhaps I was having a nightmare. I was in some sort of large, dark room, my head close to the ceiling. My eyes refused to focus. Something flitted in front of me, causing my head to move back and strike a post behind me. More pain. The post and I began swaying. Where was I? Flit, there it was again. Limbs. I think it was a man's limbs I saw, but they were upside down. No, it was *I* who was upside down. I was tied to a post and suspended from the ceiling somehow. I lifted my head, slowly, and focused on my body. I was near naked and lashed to the post, only it wasn't a post. It was a cross.

Finally, I was able to focus my eyes on the ropes that bound my wrists and ankles. They that bore my entire weight. My chest was on fire, and breathing was difficult. Every joint felt dislocated. What I had first taken for the ceiling was in fact the floor under my head. The cross, suspended from a rope going up into the darkness, was affixed to a pulley in the top of the building.

"Awake, already, are you?" a familiar voice came out of the darkness.

The limbs appeared again, and my eyes saw something red above me. It was John Racket's rusty beard.

"Racket," I croaked, licking lips, which were parched. "Racket, cut me down."

"When I went to all this trouble to truss you up? Not half. Try calling on your precious Mr. Barker to come cut you down."

"Why?" I gasped.

"I'm glad you asked that," Racket said. "I've been studying the Good Book a lot lately, searching for some really spectacular way to kill you. That bullet I put through my cab was just to put Barker off for a while. I thought of hanging you from your hair like Absalom, but yours was too short, or of gutting you like Abraham almost did to Isaac, but I didn't think anyone would get the idea. I about gave up when I remembered Peter being crucified upside down. Now that, my friend, is the dramatic moment. Truly artistic, and not above my poor powers. I'm just going to leave you hanging here until Barker finds you, though at this rate that might just be sometime in the next century. Of course, by then, all the blood will have run to your brain and burst your vessels. Poor Barker will have to find a new assistant all over again."

"Why are you doing this?" I spat out, before my chest convulsed in a paroxysm of pain. My ears were ringing with the thunder of my own labored heartbeat.

"I'm just throwing our little bloodhound off his scent," Racket continued. "You see, the Jew was stealing my girl, after we'd been married for five years. I didn't mind that she was a Jewess, since she had converted to Christianity, but for her to take up with another of her kind, after all I'd done for her, after I'd made her respectable, that was too much. I knew Barker would be hired to take the case, him being all friendly with the Jews and all. So, I began early. I preached against the Jews in Hyde Park days before I killed him, just to throw your boss off the track. I got Miriam's sweetheart in an alleyway not far from their church in Poplar. It was incredible, a real feeling of power. I smacked him about for a couple of minutes, then I got him with the knife. One blow, right to the heart, and he was a goner. I bundled him into the cab and brought him here. Saw the resemblance to Christ, though I'm a trade unionist and an unbeliever. In a trice, I'd stripped him down and nailed him to a stall plank. I thought, *Why not hang him high in Petticoat Lane for all the Jews to see? That'd keep 'em all away from my Miriam.* Then I had a stroke of genius. I took a piece of chalk and wrote 'The Anti-Semite League' on it, along with a verse I culled from Miriam's Bible. Told her I was thinking of going to church. I tossed him in the cab, board and all, covered in an old blanket, and found plenty of rope. Nobody saw a thing in the heavy fog, or if they did, they were too terrified to squeal. The Lane was quiet as the tomb. Juno didn't care for it when I used her to haul the Jew up the telegraph pole, but she's a good ol' gal. From sticking him to hanging him didn't take more than an hour or two.

"I tell you, it was a real pleasure watching your Guv'nor chase all over town looking for a group of Jew-haters that didn't exist. When I wasn't looking over your shoulders, I was in the pubs, agitating against the Jews, blaming them for stealing jobs and running up prices. It's amazing what one bloke can do."

I moaned as my body was wracked by another spasm. I could no longer feel my legs. They were ice cold, while my chest was on fire. I couldn't take much more before I passed out, and death would inevitably follow. While Racket went on, boasting of his evil accomplishments, I prayed and prepared myself to meet my Maker.

"Miriam was a good wife for a while, before she cuckolded me. I had to tell her what I done, and how I knew about both of them. If she'd been smart, she'd have kept her gob shut and chalked it up to a hard lesson. But she started yammering, and it was obvious she was gonna peach on me. I took her down, right here, with a rubber-headed mallet. Bashed her head in one stroke. I tossed her out the back loading door, down onto the tracks below, then dragged her down the tunnel and chalked another note. Your boss was too stupid to get it without a little hint. Did you like the shooting? Nobody'd suspect a cabbie of putting holes in his own cab. I wrapped the pistol in a scarf to keep the powder burns off the side, but Barker didn't even check.

"Later, I piled some fellows from the Crook and Harp pub into a cart and drove 'em all down to your place. Shoulda bloody well known they'd get their heads bashed. But young McElroy got left behind, and you know what he did? He turned Judas on me. He told you everything he knew, didn't he? Of course, you remember what happened to Judas, don't you?"

Racket took an arm of my cross and turned me around slowly. There was a pair of slack limbs dangling behind me. I didn't have to look up into the bloated face to know that the body was once Albert McElroy.

"Stupid sod. If he'd had half a brain, he would've looked to see who his cabman was, but then you weren't much smarter with your educated ways, were you? I even brought you here to the stable, overlooking the tracks.

"So, here we are again. I'm going to set you up proper here, like old Peter, and see how Barker likes losing his new assistant. But you don't look much like Peter, I must say. Here." He raised a hand to his ear and pulled the false whiskers from his face. Underneath them was the man we'd been looking for,

with the birthmark on his chin. He stepped forward and s
them over my own ears.

"Very nice," he decided. "Artistic-like. You didn't know yo
was sending Albert to his doom last night, did you, boy? Barke
should get a kick out of this. I'm afraid he turned out to be
disappointment, not much better than the peelers. I was jus
making things up as I went along. Old Push never suspected a
thing."

I was starting to lose consciousness. My whole body had gone cold, and breathing had become almost impossible. I was beginning to hallucinate. I thought I heard my employer's voice.

"I wouldn't say that, Mr. Racket. I've had my eye on you for some time."

The cross spun in a circle, and when it stopped, a pistol was clapped to my head. It was my own revolver. I recognized the filed-down sight. I closed my eyes and felt surprisingly at ease. I was ready to die now. I gave it all over. At that point, I would have preferred a bullet to slow death. There was a short scream in my ear, and I opened my eyes in time for them to be sprayed with blood. One of Barker's copper pennies was imbedded in the back of Racket's hand. Racket dropped the gun and slammed into me, sending my makeshift cross spinning in wide circles. New paroxysms of pain began, as the centrifugal force pulled my entire body away from the post.

Abruptly, I was dragged aloft, into the darkness above. There were stairs, and I saw the second level and the hayloft. A gun went off almost in my ear, and my cross began plummeting, plummeting to earth. I came to an abrupt stop, and strong arms grasped my chest. I felt flesh rip and sinews snap.

"I've got you, lad," Cyrus Barker said. Then I heard no more.

I opened my eyes dully. Terence Poole was lifting me up and putting a flask of brandy between my lips. I was off the cross.

Who knew how long I'd been out? I began to sputter, and with the kind assistance of the inspector, who thumped me soundly between the shoulder blades several times, progressed to a full-blown cough.

"Thank you, Inspector," I finally managed to squeak out.

"Don't mention it, young fellow. Looks as though you had a close call here."

"Where's Mr. Barker?" I asked, for I couldn't see him for the swarm of blues. There must have been a dozen constables combing the stable.

"He's out front, helping with Racket's body."

"What happened?"

Poole's bucolic face broke into a grin. "I'm still figuring that out, myself. Barker spat it at me so fast, I couldn't make head nor tail of it. Something about Racket jumping out the upper granary door on a rope attached to your cross. He went down, and you went up. He would have escaped, leaving Barker behind to save you, only Barker was too clever for him. He parted the rope with one shot. You and the cross fell into his waiting arms, while Racket fell and dashed his brains out. Very messy way to die. But I can't say I feel sorry for the blighter, considering all the pains he put the Yard to."

Barker and a further handful of constables brought the body of our former cabman in, wrapped in a blanket. It was probably the one he had used to conceal the body of Louis Pokrzywa. I could see part of the head under the bloodied blanket. As Poole said, it was a very messy way to die.

My employer came over and looked down at me.

"Alive, are you, Thomas?"

"I'll pull through, I reckon, sir," I rasped.

"Don't try to talk. You have a bad rope burn on your throat. I believe you'll be spending some time in hospital."

"No, sir!" I have no love of hospitals any more than any other public institution. "Could I not recuperate at home?"

"What did I tell you, Terry?" he said, turning toward the inspector.

"You've got a corking little terrier here, Cyrus," he responded. Terrier, indeed!

"He's in no condition for questioning. I'll stop by your office in the morning with a prepared statement. You can question him in a day or so, if that is agreeable."

"Be at my office tomorrow for questioning," Poole countered, "and I think we can wait until he can talk again."

"Done. Let's get him home."

Racket's corpse was to remain for the coroner, Vandeleur, to issue a death certificate. A constable was assigned the task of taking Barker and me back to Newington in that fateful hansom which had twice brought me so close to dying. Death had no sting for me at the moment. After Barker gingerly lifted me into the cab, still clad in blankets, I lay back in a corner and drifted into a sound, dreamless sleep.

29

I FLOATED ON OPIUM CLOUDS FOR SEVERAL days. Barker's physician, a dried apple core of a fellow named Allcroft, kept me on a steady diet of morphine and little else. I had endured a severe trauma not only to my body but to my brain as well. Dr. Allcroft feared brain fever, and with good reason. Due to the heavy tissue damage, I ran a high fever. Any weight I may have gained due to Dummolard's cooking and the nice restaurants in which we had dined, melted off my frame quickly. I must have looked quite the apple core myself, I suppose.

Barker decided that the logistics of the situation called for turning the infrequently used sitting room into a convalescing room. He and Mac carried my bed and mattress down the stairs and consigned much of the sitting room furniture to the lumber room upstairs. Nurses were hired round the clock. Apparently, things were rather touch and go one night. I had an irregular heartbeat, and Allcroft feared there might have been damage to the muscle itself. Somehow I pulled through. Later, Barker asked me how it was to walk through the valley of the shadow of death. I recalled intensely vivid dreams, constantly changing like a child's kaleidoscope, but the events in these dreams slipped through my fingers when I finally woke.

A woman's face came into view, a careworn but friendly enough face it was, with a healthy dusting of freckles.

"Who are you?" I croaked. My throat was raw.

"So you're awake, are you?" she said. "That's a mercy. How do you feel?"

"Like I've been crucified." My throat was afire.

"You just take it easy-like, young gentleman. I'm your nurse. We'll fetch the doctor in. You've had a lot of people here concerned about your health."

"May I have some water, please?"

She sat me up a little, to pour a tumbler of water down my parched throat. It was the first time I realized I was in the sitting room. I tried to raise my arms but found myself almost incapable of movement. My shoulders and back had received a great strain, and only time and the Great Physician Himself would ever heal them again.

"What o'clock is it?" I asked.

"'Tis three in the afternoon, if you must know," the nurse said. "Did you have an appointment you must be off to?"

"And the day?"

"It's Thursday."

"Thursday," I repeated to myself. Four days. My mind was on the case. Was it over? What had Barker been doing without me these last hundred hours? I tried sitting up, to get out of bed. I've made many mistakes in my life, and that was definitely one of them.

"Now you've gone and done it, young man," the nurse chided me as I lay, my teeth gritted, and every muscle in my body screamed at once. "You stay there and don't you move, or so help me, I'll have straps brought in and we'll lash you to this bed. I'm calling in Dr. Allcroft directly."

The doctor came within the hour. He looked in my throat and under my eyelids, he took my pulse, he prodded me in a thousand places, then asked me a thousand times if that hurt.

Finally, he pronounced me on the mend, though not completely out of danger, and reduced me to only partial doses of morphine. Had I been able to move, I would have tossed him down the front step. As it was, I just lay there, while the tide of dreams washed over me again.

"Lad." I opened my eyes.

"Hello, sir," I answered weakly.

"Back among the living, are we?"

"So it would seem. How's the case?"

"Spoken like a true assistant. It's all but over. I've just been tying up the loose ends. All that remains is the presentation of the bill, and I won't do that until you are up and about."

"Tell me about the case. How did you—"

"Another time, Thomas. Allcroft is a capital fellow. He'll soon set you to rights. You just get some rest. Plenty of time to discuss the investigation later."

I relaxed and the spectacles faded away into nothingness.

It was morning, presumably Friday morning, although I couldn't be sure. Mac was opening the curtains.

"Good morning, Mr. Llewelyn," he said. "I trust you've slept well." He came round and fluffed my pillows. "The nurses have all been dismissed, more's the pity."

"Sorry I missed them," I rasped.

"Are you hungry?"

"Starved," I admitted.

"Guv'nor's spread the word to Cook that he's to fatten you up a bit. I saw Dummolard bringing in a goose liver pie a half hour ago. I'll tell them you're awake."

He glided out, and I closed my eyes. I was in a rather enviable position if one forgot for the moment that I couldn't raise my arms. I had nothing to do but lie in bed and wonder what a first class chef was preparing for my breakfast. It turned out to be crepes with heavy cream and strawberries. The strawberries had been preserved in kirsch brandy. The meal came with a tisane, hot honey and lemon with a bit of single malt.

"I suppose you can't raise your arms."

"Not an inch."

Mac grumbled under his breath and cut the first crepe into quarters. I opened my mouth just in time, before he would have plastered cream all over my face. It was very rich. It wouldn't take much of this to put the weight back on me.

"Drink!" I said, almost gagging on the clotted cream in my throat.

"This will wear thin rather quickly, I think," Maccabee complained, bringing the cup to my lips.

"I'll remind you, I was injured trying to save your people," I told him, when I could breathe again.

"We are forever in your debt," he said archly, cramming another bite in my mouth. The combination of preserves and cream was delicious, but I wasn't much up to swallowing yet.

The meal was mercifully short. Mac replaced the empty plate and cup on the silver tray. He turned back at the door.

"Actually, you have a visitor waiting."

Was it Rebecca, perhaps, or Zangwill? Possibly it was Ira Moskowitz. I had made more friends in the last two weeks than during my entire previous time in London.

Mac opened the door, and a streak of black fur shot across the room. Harm leapt onto the bed and walked up onto my chest. The little dog looked back to his old self again. He cocked his head to the side and regarded me quizzically for a minute, then walked past my head and curled up on the edge of the pillow behind me.

"All right, dog," Maccabee said. "None of that. Come on." Harm gave him a low growl. "Mangy cur! After I announced you and everything! Very well, stay if you like, but I'm booting you out the door at the earliest opportunity."

"Were you referring to the dog or me?" I asked.

"Don't tempt me," he responded, and left with the tray.

Harm and I settled back on the pillows and soon drifted off to sleep together.

Shortly after noon, Inspector Poole and a constable arrived to take down my statement. Poole wanted to be sure that Barker and I had not compared notes, and I could honestly say that we hadn't spoken more than a few sentences to each other since that day. The case, according to Scotland Yard, was officially closed, although they wanted the names of the sword-wielding Jews. Strange, but my memory was rather hazy about the specifics. As for the press, the papers spoke of little else for weeks, but the Golem Squad had disappeared without a trace.

After a slice of goose liver pie, which Mac fed me successfully, Dr. Allcroft stopped in for a short visit and pronounced that I was healing rapidly. Before leaving, he traded the morphine injections for a green, laudanum-based syrup that was particularly vile. Licorice is a flavor best left in the nursery. With the doctor out of the way, Barker and Mac brought in a little oriental fellow, who gave me an all-over massage. It was torture during the actual process, but when he was done, I felt a little better than before. He left me his own Chinese tonic in a blue bottle beside the laudanum. I had no intention of taking that, either.

It was shortly after six when Barker and Mac appeared with my dinner tray. Barker settled a napkin on my chest and prepared to feed me. I had never seen him looking so domestic. Mac returned to his duties.

"I think you dismissed the nurses too quickly, sir," I told him.

"It was necessary," he said, cutting up some roast beef on my nightstand. "A few more nights and there would have been an understanding between Mac and one of the nurses. Two, if he was persistent. Open."

I opened. It was beef in some sort of wine sauce. No doubt it had a fancy French name. Dummolard had outdone himself, but there were more pressing matters.

"Can we talk about the case now?"

"Of course," he said. "What did you want to know?"

"Only everything."

He loaded my mouth again. "Everything, is it? That's a tall order. You'll have to be a wee bit more specific."

"Very well," I said, after I swallowed. "When did you first suspect Racket?"

"I noted him at the beginning. I've had him as a cabman once or twice in the past, but only randomly. His sudden attentiveness, coinciding with the start of a new investigation, put me on my guard. However, he was only one of several leads at the time. I gave him more serious attention after the shooting. Later, he gave us information that proved to be suspect. I knew that Serafini didn't fire on you, and to believe that there was another assassin out there matching his description stretched my credulity.

"He was my key suspect after that, but I couldn't be certain he was working alone until we found poor Miriam Smith's body. That scripture he quoted made me certain of his sole guilt. He wanted me to know, I believe. Were the case to remain unsolved, no one would ever know how clever he had been."

"How far behind me were you when I was in the cab alone with Racket?"

"I saw you getting in the cab, but there were two dozen men trying to spill each other's blood between us. I also hazard some of the bigger fellows had been ordered by Racket to attack me personally. It took me a moment or two to get through the crowd. By then, the cab was halfway down the street and going at a fast pace. I had to run like the dickens to keep it in sight, all of five or six blocks. Of course, I had no idea he was choking you as he went along. I'm sorry about that, lad."

I smiled.

"What?" Barker demanded, frowning. I was getting better at reading his expressions behind those huge spectacles of his.

" 'Some danger involved,' " I quoted. "Is it often this dangerous?"

"Not often, no," my employer said. "Sometimes it is. I won't lie to you. I'm very sorry that you were hurt, that I was unable to stop Racket from almost killing you. I cannot control every situation. I can understand if you wish to leave my employ. I shall pay you handsomely for your services and give a sterling reference."

I actually thought about it for a moment. Perhaps I could find a more normal position, something unthreatening, a quiet job clerking for a solicitor. But could I stand being locked in an office every day, dotting i's and crossing t's, after this? Could I live in a lodging house, wondering what Barker was doing just then or whether Dummolard had taken offense, and never seeing Mac in a hair net? Would I be able to sleep without Harm snoring at the foot of my bed? Most of all, could I live my life knowing that someone else was using my room, sleeping in my bed, and using my desk, because I had disappointed Cyrus Barker by turning him down?

"No, sir," I found myself saying. "I'd like the position permanently, if you'll have me."

Barker patted my shoulder and smiled. "That's grand, lad. Just grand."

"But have I given satisfaction, sir? I feel as if I've failed miserably."

"You did well," Barker answered. "Your survival in such a dangerous case is an achievement in itself. I threw you in, untrained, and you adapted yourself and worked very hard under threat of your life. I have no possible cause for complaint."

I have to admit, the words felt good.

"So, what happened in Racket's stable?" I asked, picking up our earlier conversation. "Was I already tied up when you arrived?"

"Yes," Barker continued. "He must have planned it all beforehand, because he had the cross already prepared for you. He hoisted you up on pulleys and tied the other end of the rope to the bale hook that overlooks the street. Racket must have been desperate, to use his own stable like that. Perhaps he planned to escape to the Continent. Some details we shall never know."

"I remember his taunting me. He said he enjoyed watching us take all those wrong turns in the investigation."

"As I said before, an enquiry agent must cultivate patience. One must be thorough, investigating every lead. There is no way to know which one will lead to the proper conclusion."

"You heard him, then?"

"Of course. I can't tell you what a pathetic sight you were, suspended upside down like Peter. I thought you were lost to me, as Quong was. But you're a plucky fellow, and a tough one, too, to have survived all you've been through."

"So what happened then?" I asked. "I must admit it was all a jumble after you struck Racket with one of those coins of yours. By the way, that was an incredible throw."

Barker shrugged. "As I told you, I've had a lot of training. After he dropped the gun, he shoved the cross, sending it spinning, and ran to the stairs leading to the loft, making sure you were between us the entire time, for I had drawn my gun. I ran to you, and actually had my hand on the crossbeam, when you suddenly shot out of my hands. Racket had seized the hook and swung out, you see, hoping to escape. As he plummeted down, you spiraled upward."

"And then?" I asked, still perplexed.

"I shot the rope in the middle, which brought you down into my outstretched arms, and by the way, lad, I could swear you'd put on a pound or two, despite my instructions. Racket came down in the street a little faster than he'd anticipated. I hadn't expected to kill him, just to slow him down enough to catch up to him, but I don't believe I'll lose any sleep over his death. Like yourself, I'll remember the pathetic figures of Louis Pokrzywa and Miriam Smith."

I shook my head. "Incredible. An inch either way, and the outcome might have been entirely different."

He shrugged, as if his marksmanship were nothing out of the ordinary.

"This is some profession, Mr. Barker," I mused.

"It's the only profession, as far as I am concerned."

"Perhaps I'm dim, sir, but what caused you to suspect Racket instead of Painsley or any of the other suspects? Why didn't you think the league was real?"

"There were different reasons for each suspect. Give me a name."

"Painsley, then."

Barker set aside the tray. We had both forgotten about the food, and I wasn't really hungry. "I do not believe he could have derived any benefit from killing Pokrzywa. Should an attack have been made upon the Jews, it would have aroused sympathy toward them and emptied out his church on Sunday mornings. Painsley very much needed the Jews to continue pouring in from Europe because the public anxiety about them was keeping his coffers full. Also, he would have run a very big risk, were he seen at the head of a mob. But as I said, I'm going to keep a watch on that fellow."

"And Brunhoff, the Anglo-Israelite?"

Barker gave a snort. "Brunhoff couldn't gather a handful of supporters to a free meal in Bethnal Green. He's got all the warmth and charisma of a wounded badger. To think that he could gather a band of followers loyal enough to risk jail or injury is preposterous. By the way, he never sent me his alibi. I suppose we'll have to let him alone . . . for now."

My employer got that look again, and his hand brushed his pocket.

"Smoke, by all means," I encouraged. "And what about my old tutor, Rushford?"

Barker reached in his pocket.

"Of all the suspects, I would have thought him most likely. He was a eugenicist and a recent inmate of Burberry Asylum. However, I thought him too fastidious to actually go into the pubs of Whitechapel, recruiting men, and the men too unlikely to follow him unless it was for pay. I suspect Rushford is rather hard up at the moment, with his position gone and little revenue from his books coming in. If he recruited anyone, it would be his acolytes in Chelsea, and I can't picture those dandies forming an angry mob, unless the Grosvenor Gallery hangs one of Mr. Whistler's paintings upside down."

"Drat," I said. "So, there's no way we could tar him with it?"

"Sorry, lad." Barker knew I was joking, of course.

"What about your choice, Mr. Nightwine?"

Barker blew out his vesta and set his pipe between his teeth.

"Ah, yes, Nightwine. I toyed with the idea for quite a while. Crucifying a Jew in Petticoat Lane is just the sort of ruthless message he would send the Board of Deputies to cow them, if possible, and he could raise a mob as soon as he opened his pocketbook. I wondered if he might be trying to corner the gold and diamond markets in London, extorting money from them or the pawnbrokers, who, though they may appear more humble, have a lucrative business nonetheless. I thought Nightwine the only man in London dangerous enough to threaten the Jews in such a fashion. Obviously, I was mistaken on that point."

"So what made you discount him?"

"There was nothing to tie Pokrzywa into all of this. Nightwine would have chosen a jeweler or pawnbroker to string up, not a poor little teacher. I think Nightwine bears no personal animosity toward the Jews, beyond their founding of two religions he despises. As he said, he believes them a defeated race."

I was running out of suspects. "Gigliotti? Serafini?"

"Nothing the Jews had done to the Italians warranted crucifixion, even as an example. The Camorra has an established way of doing things. There would have been a private meeting with someone like Sir Moses, airing their grievances. Then they would have busted a few kneecaps to get their point across. But no good Catholic would dare crucify a Jew, and in their own twisted logic, they're all good Catholic boys."

"Not Serafini," I pointed out. "He's an assassin."

"So he is, but Serafini saves the bullets for more 'deserving' targets: politicians, diplomats, and kings. In a way, he has his own principles. He wouldn't shoot a working lad."

I was scraping the bottom of my memory now. "The Irish, then. Why not suspect them? McElroy was an Irishman."

"All their efforts at the moment are directed toward Home Rule. After the bombing of the Tower Bridge last November, their leader, Parnell, has made sure they keep their noses clean."

I made one final, desperate try. "Perhaps I'm obtuse, but how did you know that it wasn't someone we hadn't heard from, someone laying very low?"

Barker puffed on his pipe. He was sitting back in the chair with his hands laced across his stomach and his feet on my bed.

"I trust my contacts," he said, simply. "You see, I try to throw a web over London and sit like a spider in the midst of it all, my fingers on the strands, ready for any subtle vibration. When we're riding in a cab and I'm scanning the street ahead of me, hundreds of impressions are crowding in on me. I recognize criminals and friends and see who is in town. I note changes of class and nationality within an area. I watch new businesses open up and old ones shut their doors. I find the city endlessly fascinating."

I'd run out of arguments, but I still had some questions.

"What about Pokrzywa, sir? Why did he have a relationship with Miriam Smith in the first place? She seemed an unlikely choice with beauties like Miss Mocatta about."

"I can only speculate. They were of an age, and if you

recall, she was a Choote, a Dutch Jew. We know he spent some time in Amsterdam before coming to London. I think he knew her there. Years later, he ran into her in Petticoat Lane, married to Racket, or rather, Smith. It can't have been a successful marriage. She needed help. Remember Mr. Moskowitz's remark about Louis being a knight searching for a damsel in distress? In Miriam Smith, he found her. He threw his not inconsiderable energies into trying to love and protect her and got himself killed in the process. Poor fellow. Even the wisest man can be made a fool by love."

I wondered if Barker was making a veiled reference to my own emotional upheavals during the case, but I decided not to mention them.

"One more question, sir. Who was he originally, John Racket or John Smith?"

"Neither, I suspect. Scotland Yard has no record of the first and too many records of the other. All we have is the marriage certificate and his cabman's license, and I suspect he lied on both. What I do know is that John Smith is the most common name taken by former criminals."

"I can't believe we were taken in by a false beard," I complained.

"The most important thing is that we caught the killer and averted the pogrom, which was our objective."

"I must admit, sir," I confessed, "that I doubted you a little. I didn't see how anyone in London could find Pokrzywa's killer—one man in the midst of three million people. But you did it. You were a complete success."

Barker put the chair back and turned to leave.

"I don't believe Albert McElroy's parents would say so, Thomas. I should have asked you if the cabman who picked him up was Racket, but I was tired and preoccupied," he said sadly. It gave me something to ponder after he left.

30

AFTER A WEEK, I WAS FINALLY ABLE TO move back into my old room again. Despite the great pains Mac and Barker had gone to in order to make the ground floor habitable during my convalescence, I far preferred to be in my own room, simple and spartan as it was. I shaved slowly and donned my last new suit of clothes, which included a single-breasted frock coat in light blue-gray, striped trousers of matching shades, and a tie of red silk. The effect was marred, however, by slings of black grosgrain on both arms, made for me by Mac at our employer's insistence. The tie proved a problem; my fingers fumbled helplessly with the ends, and my arms refused to reach high enough for more than a few seconds. I gave up and went downstairs, hoping someone could help me.

The duty fell to Dummolard, who tied it over my shoulder, our image reflected in the bottom of one of his copper pots. Half of the ash from his cigarette went down the back of my collar. The cook seemed to be in one of his moods, and my suspicions were confirmed when he set my breakfast plate down in front of me.

"A two-egg omelet for monsieur," he said coolly.

"Not three?"

"Non."

"No *champignons?"*

"Non."

"No *fromage?"*

"Non."

"Not even toast and jam?"

"Non."

I turned the matter over in my mind. "Has Barker said anything about my weight?"

"He has not."

"Have I done something to offend you, then?"

"Non."

"And you're not going to tell me what this is about?"

"Non."

"Very well, then," I said, the aggrieved party. I played my trump card. I cut the pathetic little omelet in half, folded it over, and ate it in two quick bites. Then I washed it down with coffee and patted my mouth with a napkin. Dummolard's eyes grew large, and the corners of his mouth quivered at the insult. For a moment, I hoped he would drop his cigarette entirely, but somehow, it stayed in the corner of his mouth. I rose, bowed to the fellow, and took myself off with as much dignity as my spare Welsh frame could carry.

"You cut a splendid figure today, Mr. Llewelyn," my employer said. He was standing in the entranceway, putting on his gloves.

"I can't wear gloves, I'm afraid," I said, holding up my slings. "Or at least, I can't put them on."

"Don't. I need you to strike a pathetic note. We have our hardest battle ahead of us today. We are going to attempt a reckoning of accounts with Lord Rothschild, and he drives a very hard bargain, indeed."

Outside, it felt strange to see a different cab at our curb and a perfect stranger atop it. Even now, I found it hard to believe that Racket was the murderer, and that I was almost his last victim. I half expected to look up and see his long, fiery beard through the trap and hear him give me a brisk greeting.

"What's to become of Juno and the cab?" I asked Barker.

"I made an offer on both, contingent on whether any relative of Racket is found. Juno's been boarded in another stable, and the cab is locked up at the murder scene."

"A private cab, eh?"

"I thought I might advertise on the side. Something small, but tasteful. The name of the agency in discreet gold letters, perhaps."

"The name of the agency . . . You mean your name, don't you?" I said.

"Well, it is a name to be reckoned with."

"That it is. Wouldn't it be easier just to paint a target, instead?"

"Spare me your humor this morning, Thomas."

Sir Moses was glad to see us again. He was serene and joyful, shaking hands with Barker, clucking over my injuries, and congratulating us both. Not so his nephew, Lord Rothschild, a small, bald man with a spade beard.

"Tempest in a teapot," he said, sourly. "A total false alarm. They were a bunch of drunken cowards, who turned and ran at the first sign of a real fight. There was no real danger at all."

"Tell that to the dozen or so who went to hospital, or to my assistant here," Barker replied to the baron. "He has been shot at, barely missed by a dagger, physically beaten, strangled, and nearly crucified."

Lord Rothschild gave me a look, as if to say, "He looks all right to me."

"Of course, we are so glad of your assistance," Sir Moses said, trying to keep the peace. "I don't know what would have happened had you not been there. A 'Golem Squad!' What an incredible idea."

I turned to my employer. "Your idea, sir?"

"You'll recall the letter I wrote, suggesting the Jews have some of their young men watching the public houses? After a little thought, I wondered if they might be able to do a bit more. But it was they who formed the Golem Squad and forged the swords."

"I shall ring for tea," Sir Moses continued.

"No, sir," Barker insisted. "We are businessmen here, are we not? Pray, let us get down to business."

"Spoken like a businessman, indeed, sir," Rothschild said, rubbing his hands together briskly. "Now, I understand that there was no actual fee proposed."

"That is so," Barker stated. "Would you like to make an estimate for my services?"

"We would rather you gave us an evaluation of your time and expenses."

"Certainly," my employer continued. He flashed one of his rare smiles. The devil was enjoying this. "Before I start, I wish two things be understood. The first is that our investigation has helped avert what could have been a major crisis among the Jews in London."

"I contest that!" his lordship said. "That cannot be proven."

"The second factor was the injury to my assistant, which included a week under a doctor's care and round-the-clock nursing. He nearly died in the performance of his duties."

Rothschild began to speak again, but checked himself. Was he going to somehow refute the fact that I had nearly been crucified trying to protect his people? I looked straight into the eye of one of the most powerful men in England and did not blink.

"I'll concede that he was injured during the course of the investigation," His Lordship said, finally.

Barker cleared his throat. "I am now prepared to offer a fee for my services. My fee is . . . one hundred pounds . . ."

Both men raised an eyebrow.

"For each of us."

"A hundred pounds? One hundred pounds, did you say?" Sir Moses asked. Rothschild smiled into his beard. I myself couldn't believe the lowness of the offer. It barely covered the two weeks' expenses, with cab rides and meals, and the nursing. "Are you sure?"

"Yes, sir, with one stipulation."

"Name it," Rothschild stated.

"That the money be kept with Your Lordship's own accounts, to invest and reinvest along with your own business accounts for a period of one year."

"Now, wait a minute—" Rothschild began.

"And that a tenth of the interest from the account be given over at the end of that year for the benefit of the Jews' Free School in memory of Louis Pokrzywa. If that is agreeable to Mr. Llewelyn."

"Absolutely, sir," I said.

"See here!" Lord Rothschild blustered. "Of all the—"

"Done!" the old patriarch decided, slapping his hand on the table.

"Sir Moses!" his nephew remonstrated.

"Now, Nathan, he's done us a remarkable service and shall do so in the future again, I am certain."

"Very well," he conceded, with ill grace. "But only as a favor to you, Uncle."

Barker pulled two contracts from his coat pocket. The crafty fellow had typed them himself, in the presence of his solicitor. For one who made such a public display of shunning finances, he proved himself shrewd enough when necessary.

The contract concluded, Lord Rothschild nodded to us all and left the room, no doubt to return to the bank with his copy, to begin looking for loopholes.

As for Sir Moses, he was inclined to linger and talk. Tea and biscuits were brought in, and we discussed the school, our agency, my health, and the future of Anglo-Jewry. It was an hour before we got away again. The old man shook my injured hand gently.

Finally, we took our leave. Outside, Barker looked quite pleased with himself. His sitting in the cab with a smile on his face was like any other man's doing a jig in the street.

"You assume the investments shall pay out," I said.

"Rothschild's got the Midas touch. Mark my words. That two hundred shall be at least two thousand a year hence."

"I don't believe I can wait that long, myself, being unsalaried."

The cab pulled out of Saint Swithen Lane.

"I understand," Barker said. "You are hired on a permanent basis. The pay for the position is five pounds per month."

I could hardly believe it. That was a great deal of money, along with the free room and meals.

"Thank you, sir," I said. "That's very generous."

"Not at all. You've more than earned it. Now, let's go celebrate."

"At Ho's?" I asked. I was getting a bit hungry. It was nearly eleven already, and the two-egg omelet had been a rather meager start to the day.

"No. Someplace special. Cabbie, Soho!"

Our destination was none other than Dummolard's Le Tondre d'Or. It was an elegant little restaurant, with bistro chairs and tables in front that gave it a Gallic air. As we entered, we were met by Dummolard's vivacious and incredibly beautiful wife. She was a French blonde of almost Amazonian proportions, and she took a liking to me the minute she laid eyes on me. She put us at the best table, and had a half dozen waiters hovering around, bringing us the best that Etienne could frantically prepare. Now I saw why he had fed me so sparingly at breakfast. He was preparing to fete us for lunch. I'm no expert at French cuisine, but what can you do when a beautiful woman is cutting up your meal and feeding it to you, except to eat without complaining?

"Thank you, Madame Dummolard. Everything is delicious."

"Call me Mireille, *mon petite chou.* But this veal! It is like shoe leather! Etienne!"

She took the plate back to the kitchen, and suddenly a fight broke out behind the door. She screamed. Dummolard bellowed. There was a slap. Crockery crashed. I heard curses in two languages. Then, serenely, Mireille Dummolard returned, a new plate of veal in her hand. No one seemed to notice the melee. Presumably, it was an hourly occurrence.

The restaurant door opened, and a trio of young men entered off the street. The first was Israel Zangwill, who smiled and waved. The second was Ira Moskowitz, and the third . . . the third, I was interested to see, was Jacob Maccabee.

"We heard there was a party here," Mac said, as they all pulled up chairs and helped themselves to the incredible buffet of food and wine, selecting, of course, only those items lawful to them as Jews.

"Hallo, Thomas!" Zangwill said. "You don't look to be doing too poorly."

"No!" the scholar, Ira, put in. "It would be worth all the pain to be situated where you are now."

I couldn't disagree, partly because Madame Dummolard was pouring champagne down my throat. Had she been any closer, one of us would have been in the other's lap.

"By the way," Zangwill said. "Perhaps this is not the time to mention it, but I have a message for you. A certain person understands that her father was somewhat curt with you and hopes you didn't take offense. She'd like to speak with you again, under different circumstances, and sends best wishes for your full and swift recovery."

"Thank you," I said, as Mireille dabbed at my mouth with a

napkin. "Tell her I hope to see her again, and if you mention *this* to her, well, just remember, I won't be this helpless forever, and I know where you live."

"A toast!" Ira Moskowitz said, raising his champagne flute. "To the best detective in London . . . Damn! Where is the fellow?"

I looked about. My employer was missing. I couldn't recall the last time I'd seen him.

"Mr. Barker has gone," Mac informed us. "I just spoke to him before he left. He had an appointment in Saint James to see a certain widow."

"A widow? You mean a new case?" I asked.

"No, sir. He is meeting her for lunch. I believe the relationship has been a long-standing one."

We all looked at each other. A widow? Barker was seeing a widow?

Hours later, after all the food had been eaten and the good-byes said, and I had enjoyed a long afternoon nap in my now permanent room, I heard Barker's tread upon the stair. I gave him half an hour before I went up to speak with him.

"Ah, Llewelyn," he said, as I reached the top of the stair. He was seated in his chair by the fire, in a glossy silk robe, feeding Harm green tea from his saucer. He was smoking a new pipe, I noticed, as white as a bone. It was a bearded head that looked rather like Moses. Around him were boxes full of books, which I recognized at once as having belonged to Louis Pokrzywa. Obviously, his bid had been successful.

"It was a grand celebration, sir," I stated. "Pity you had to leave early."

He refused to rise to the bait.

"Madame Dummolard was quite attentive."

"Yes, I would watch that, lad. She likes to make Etienne jealous. I'd hate to be your second in Hyde Park, one cold winter morning."

"He's good with a sword and pistol, then?"

"Yes, and with his feet. *La boxe française*. Don't let his girth fool you."

"You have some formidable associates," I said. "Mac with his shotgun. Brother Andrew with his fists. Ho with his cleaver. You yourself with your pistols and . . . pocket change. I'm afraid I have no such ability."

"You acquitted yourself admirably in the Lane with a cricket bat. I'll train you myself, and when the time is right, you'll discover your own weapon of choice."

"I don't know," I conceded. "I wish I had your confidence in me. When you listed the attacks upon my person to Sir Moses and Lord Rothschild, I felt like a complete fool. In fact, I have a mind to return the hundred pounds you so generously gave me as part of the fee."

"Now you really are being foolish," Barker said. "You followed my lead, and did all that I asked of you. What more could I wish? If anything, it was I who failed you. Had I been but a few minutes earlier, you would not have come so close to dying."

"I disagree," I protested. "You saved my life."

"It took both of us to solve the case. I couldn't have done it without you," Barker said. Having finished his tea, Harm belched and went to sleep by his master's side.

I mused for a moment. "We did it, didn't we? We actually solved a case. Well, you did, anyway. Racket tried to throw us off the scent, but you saw through it all. There's just one thing that puzzles me."

"What is that?" he asked.

"Who's this widow you haven't mentioned before?"

He didn't say anything, but I knew I'd struck a nerve. His pipe went out.

Author's Note

For several years, I was a book reviewer for various organizations, as well as a speaker on Victorian crime fiction. Many recent Victorian mysteries have been written by women, and could be classified as "cozies." I wondered what it would be like to create a more dangerous detective, a shamus, a gumshoe, and to set him down in this world of Queen Victoria and Jack the Ripper. As a longtime student of nineteenth-century fighting arts, both Asian and European, I wanted to present my own view of those times, in which a walking stick was a weapon and London was a perilous place. I also decided early that my detective would not be the narrator. Instead, I gave him a much-beleaguered assistant, a Watson who is constantly out of his depth, but with a cheeky attitude.

Somehow, from this mélange Cyrus Barker and Thomas Llewelyn began to live and move and have their being, as if without my help. Enquiry Agent Barker proved to be an enigmatic evangelical with a past in China, while young Thomas was overcoming a tragic, George Gissing–like past. Barker's world began to fill quickly with his own entourage, all with their own quirks and habits. Then one day I came upon a book by Chaim Bermant called *London's East End: Point of Arrival,* about the Jews pouring into England after pogroms in Eastern

Europe, and the germ that became *Some Danger Involved* was born.

I had never attempted to write a novel before, but gradually, over a five-year period, it coalesced. All the while, Llewelyn was jabbering in my ear, demanding I tell his story. What could I do but to take it all down?

Acknowledgments

Unlike Thomas Llewelyn, I am awash in a sea of women, an enviable position, as any man will tell you. I'd like to thank my wife, Julia, who worked even harder than I to see that this novel was set before the public; my daughters, Caitlin and Heather, who encouraged me and listened to some scenes several times. Thank you, ladies.

To Maria Carvainis, my agent, who boldly took a chance upon a complete unknown; Moira Sullivan, who first thought this book had merit; and Amanda Patten, my editor, who helped to fan the flames, a tip of the hat to each of you.

To Ann, Tracy, and Jennifer, and my other cheerleaders at the Tulsa City-County Library, thanks for being there.

To my family, who always knew I had this in me, thank you. Here it is.